DEATH LIGHTS
A CANDLE

PHOEBE ATWOOD TAYLOR

DEATH LIGHTS A CANDLE

An Asey Mayo Cape Cod Mystery

A Foul Play Press Book

THE COUNTRYMAN PRESS
Woodstock, Vermont

Copyright © 1932, 1960 by Phoebe Atwood Taylor

This edition published in 1989 by Foul Play Press, an imprint
of The Countryman Press, Inc., Woodstock, Vermont 05091.

ISBN 0-88150-145-X

Printed in the United States of America

For
A. T. A.

*All of the characters in this book, with
the single exception of Ginger the
cat, are entirely fictitious*

CONTENTS

DEATH LIGHTS
A CANDLE

Death Lights a Candle

CHAPTER ONE

MISS WHITSBY GOES VISITING

I STARTED out that Tuesday morning with no other purpose in mind than to buy a spool of orange silk at Jordan Marsh's.

I can not emphasize that fact too highly. I didn't expect to meet Rowena Fible. I didn't know that John Kent was phoning the house at five-minute intervals, vainly trying to get hold of me. I had absolutely no intention of ending up, as I eventually did, at Cape Cod on a house-party during the course of which two people lost their lives and I myself was very nearly killed.

All I wanted, and all I set out to get, was a spool of orange silk to mend the sleeve of my niece's mandarin coat.

It was just as I was turning the corner of Temple Place and Tremont Street that Rowena Fible grabbed me by the arm.

"Prue! Prudence Whitsby! I've been dashing after you ever since you started across the Common. Prue, I have an idea!"

I was not surprised. Rowena Fible and I have been friends since we were babes in swaddling clothes a good fifty-one years ago, and during that period she has seldom been without an idea of one sort or another. And she has usually dashed around with them, too. This combination of ideas and energy has landed her in the head-lines as frequently as it landed her father, the late Governor. Rowena's friends have become quite resigned to the flaring captions of "Boston Spinster Joins Caterpillar Club" or "Miss Fible Parades for Light Wines and Beer."

"What is it now?" I asked. "And where've you been lately?"

"That's just it. Why I have the idea, I mean. You see, I've been in Chicago modeling a fountain for that gangster. Don't shudder, Prue. It wasn't so bad and I made a lot of money. The only drawback was that he made me use his nasty children as models for the cherubs. That's what's laid me low. I've simply got to do something to get them out of my mind, and just as I got off the train this morning I remembered the Wellfleet house. Prue, I want you to come down to the Cape with me and spend a week or so and help me forget those Mantinis."

"You want me to go to Cape Cod in March? Are you crazy? We'd freeze."

"Cape Cod in March," Rowena observed with a shiver, "is no whit colder than Tremont Street in March. It couldn't be any colder than this corner, anyway. And I've decided to paint the house. Cream with wagon-blue blinds, and you know how you love to paint. And the Whitings are in Orleans and they'll come down for bridge."

"I shouldn't go." I spoke without much determination. Boston had been dull with my niece away. "Really, I shouldn't. There's a tea at the Lamsons' this afternoon and a dinner to-morrow night———"

"Let 'em go." Rowena waved a casual hand. "You need a change. I've already wired Phrone to have the house opened, and the roadster's being greased and groomed right this minute. We can start off within an hour."

"But I've got to pack."

"Olga's packing for you. I stopped at the house to see where you were, told her what I wanted you to do and she thought it was a fine idea. She said you'd been losing your appetite and that the Cape always brought it back. She said she'd look after Ginger, too. Or you could bring him with you."

"I think," I said, "that we'd better take him along. He has a wicker traveling case, you know. It's pretty dull for him, having only the roof to run around in, and it would do him good to get out in the open. He's been craving to catch a field-mouse for weeks. I've seen it in his eye. D'you mind cats?"

"You know I love them. I'll do a figure of him for you, too. I've always meant to. Well, that's all settled. Suppose we walk back to the house. I left my bags there and they'll bring the car around when it's ready."

"But what about my orange silk?"

"Was that what you were after? Olga told me but I couldn't for the life of me make out what she said. Do you really want it? I mean, we can get orange silk in Wellfleet just as well and we want to get started while it's still warmish."

"Let it go," I said resignedly. "I've been trying to mend the sleeve of Betsey's mandarin coat for six months and a few weeks more won't hurt."

So we turned and made our way across the Common back to my house.

Olga met us at the door.

"Miss Whitsby, a man he call up every five minutes since you go."

"Who was it? What did he want? What was the matter?"

Olga shrugged. "Mr. Kent, he called an' called an' ask where you are. He say nothing is the matter, he yust want to ask you something. I tell him you are at Yordan's for a spool of silk, but he don't understand."

"If it's John Kent," Rowena said, "he probably wanted to know who your great-great-grandfather married and what the names of his stepson's children by his second wife were. That's the only sort of thing he ever wants to know. When he got out that second book of the Kent family he called me up from London to ask me some such fool question."

I nodded. "I had dinner with him last week, and he found out that Uncle Theophilus Whitsby was a Sturgis and he talked of nothing else. I shan't bother with him. Olga, if he calls again, you tell him you can't understand him and that you don't know where I am. And now, put Ginger in his basket. Your car's come, Rowena. Olga, you can stay here, or lock up and go to your cousin's. Only see that my mail gets forwarded and have the furnace man keep the fire. I'll be back in a week or so. I'll let you know just when. You packed my heavy clothes? Good. And if anything goes wrong, telegraph me."

And by three that afternoon we were climbing the rutted lane to Rowena's Wellfleet house.

At the fork she stopped the roadster. "I've been thinking of those pine-covered hills and the blue stretch of bay and the white clouds and the fresh salt air ever since I began Vittorio Mantini's vulgar face. He had the most evil leer—and, good lord above, Prue, where did that come from?"

On the next hill, beyond her little house, was a magnificent Colonial mansion, sparklingly new.

"I'm sure I don't know," I said helplessly. "I don't remember seeing anything like it before I went home from here in September."

"It wasn't there when I left in August. How amazing! But there's smoke coming from my chimney and that means Phrone has come. She'll know all about it."

I smiled. Sophronia Knowles was Rowena's house-keeper and maid of all work in Wellfleet. She baked and sewed and cleaned and scrubbed and managed to pick up most of the local news at the same time. Not that Phrone was a gossip. "If a body's put on to this world," I've heard her say, "a body might just as well take a little interest in his fellow men." Phrone took a very generous interest.

She stood on the millstone which served as the front door-step.

"Glad to see you back, Miss Rena. And Miss Whitsby! Well, well. Didn't expect to see you. How's your niece an' Bill Porter?"

"They're honeymooning in Majorca," I said, shaking hands. "From what I hear, they're very happy."

"I guess Bill Porter can afford to have a good long honeymoon. What's that you got in that wicker basket? Your cat? Ginger? Well, I declare. Shall I let him out?"

She opened the basket and Ginger jumped out. He sniffed the air, shook himself and, to prove that the winter had not incapacitated him in the least, ran up to the top of one of Rena's apple trees, and descended as quickly as he had gone up.

"Some cat," Phrone observed. "Well, I only got your telegram an hour ago. I got the Smalley boy to bring me up an' he turned on the water an' the 'lectricity. I'd done some bakin' this mornin' an' there's plenty of canned stuff. You want some lunch now?"

Rena nodded. "And tell us, Phrone, what's that mansion over yonder?"

Phrone chuckled. "That's Adelbert Stires's new house. That's whose it is."

Rowena howled. "Adelbert Stires? Prue, did you hear that? Adelbert Stires!"

"You know him?" Phrone asked interestedly. "What's he like? I guess I'm the only one in town that ain't seen him."

"Know him?" I said. "Phrone, she even knocked out his front teeth once! She did!"

"That," said Rowena with dignity, "is not worthy of you, Prue. Yes, I knocked out his front teeth, Phrone, but it was purely an accident, even though he told the newspapers it wasn't. The horrid things he said about me! I was glad afterward that I'd done it."

"How'd you come to knock 'em out in the first place?"

"It was years ago when we were suffragettes. I threw a brick at his factory—he'd fired some women because they were suffragettes, you see—anyway, we all threw bricks and it happened to be mine that sailed through a window and knocked out his teeth. I've never laid eyes on him from that day to this, but the horrid things he's said about me make up for any meetings we may have missed."

"He know you live here?"

Rowena shook her head. "I doubt it. The Holloways had the house last fall and he probably thought it belonged to them. We've never been what you might call neighborly—and isn't it going to be a blow when he discovers I live next door!"

"He's comin' down to-day," Phrone announced. "He's havin' a house-warmin'. Lot of servants an' all are already there, an' two big cars come just before you did."

"When did he build?" I asked. "And I thought he had a house up the Cape."

"He did, but he got mad at something and come down here. They started to build last fall an' thirty or forty men been workin' on it every good day this winter. Done a few weeks ago, 'twas. It all runs by 'lectricity. Ice-chests an' stoves an' I don't know what all. Got twenty-six rooms, they say. Is he—Stires—is he the sort they say he is?"

"Well," Rowena told her blandly, "he's short and fat and red-faced. He's got eyes—well, like blueberries in skimmed milk. He hates women and me in particular. He's vain and fussy and he'd build a house like this and lay off men in his factories—he makes shingles, you know—and personally I'd believe anything any one said about him that was horrid. Of course," she added pleasantly, "he may be a fine business man and it's possible that he has a heart of gold, but I doubt it."

Phrone laughed, and I laughed with her.

"That's about what I heard," she said. "Only, Miss Rena, there's a woman that come a while ago. She had red hair."

"A red-haired woman came to Bert Stires's? Impossible."

"Yessir. I been watchin' with that old telescope of your grandfather's. Red-headed, she was. She come in a big sedan with a shover. You can see fine out of the west window. Look. There's another car comin' now." She picked up the telescope and fixed it to her eye. "Nope, he's comin' here. Hey, the wind blew the feller's hat off. He's bald."

"One of Bert's guests," Rena commented.

"He's comin' here. He's got out an' got his hat an' he's comin' right up." Phrone put down the glass. "I'll go and see what he wants."

Rowena turned to me. "Prue, have you been making dates with bald-headed men behind my back?"

"Nary a date. I don't know any bald men anyway."

In a few minutes the great iron knocker on the front door banged. We heard Phrone's voice. "Yup. She's here. This is Miss Fible's house."

"Sounds like John Kent," I muttered.

"But he isn't bald, is he?" Rena whispered back.

"I've always suspected that he wore a toupee, but I never was certain. His wig probably blew off with his hat, Rena!" We snickered as John Kent entered.

"Phrone said a bald man was paying us a visit," I began, but stopped as I noticed his look of irritation.

"Hullo, you two. Prue, I've been hunting you for hours. Didn't that brass image of a cook of yours tell you I wanted you? I had to track her into the wilds of Melrose and even then I had a job trying to find out where you were. I wanted to ask a favor."

Rowena got up. "You'll stay for a late-lunch-early-tea?"

"Thank you, but I've eaten." He took off his polo coat and slung it over a chair. "Don't leave, Rena. This is nothing private."

He lighted a cigarette and sat down in a big armchair.

"What's the favor?" I asked.

"Well." He blew out a cloud of smoke. "Well, it's hard to begin. D'you remember Bert Stires's half-sister, Lucia Hammond?"

I nodded. "We went to the same china-painting school on Berkeley Street one winter and covered otherwise excellent china with pansies and goldenrod."

"Well, she ran off with the youngest Allerton boy, Cass. Remember that? And she died in Rome during the war, and Cass drank himself to death. He finished the job about a month ago. Their daughter arrived in Boston this morning to make her home with her guardian, who happens to be Adelbert Stires."

Rowena and I made no attempt to restrain our laughter.

"What's she like?"

"Young, about twenty. She has red hair"—
Rowena and I looked at each other; the red-haired
woman was explained—"and her finger-nails match her
clothes and she has violet eyes."

"How is Bert bearing up?" Rowena asked.

"Well, you can imagine. He'd been planning this
house-warming—a bunch of us come down every
year—and he didn't dare leave the girl alone in Boston,
so he had to have her come along. It went against his
principles to have a young girl alone with a lot of men,
so he decided he needed a chaperon." He stubbed his
cigarette out very carefully. "That's why I've been
hunting you, Prue. I thought of you at once. I hoped
that you'd be good enough to come and help us out."

"Are you crazy?"

"No. No. I realize, Prue, that this is not a very
graceful invitation. But won't you come?"

"Certainly not. I wouldn't consider it. Besides,
I've promised to help Rowena paint her house. You
may tell Bert Stires that I have a previous engagement. Did he ask you to get me, by the way?"

John hesitated. "He told me he'd be delighted to
have any one who could come," he said lamely.

"In other words, he promised to take anything you
could get. I'm sorry. You know he hates women, and
he bears me no particular love. I shouldn't think of
going. Even if I did, I'd not leave Rowena."

John banged his fist on the arm of the chair. "Won't the two of you come?"

Rowena laughed. "You recall the episode of Adelbert's teeth and my brick?"

"That makes no difference. You've simply listened to too many unkind things about Bert. He's a good sort. He doesn't dislike women. He's just scared to death of 'em. He'd be no end grateful if you'd help him out. It's going to be a good party. You'd enjoy the other men."

"Who's going to be there?" Rowena asked.

"Borden James, for one."

"Not," Rowena exclaimed delightfully, "not Prue's old beau Denny?"

"Yes. And the woolen Blakes. Victor himself and his son Junior. You've heard of them even if you don't know them,—they pay more income taxes than any other people in Massachusetts. Then there's Cary Hobart, the head of the Hobart Lumber Company. Greatest center rush they ever had at Harvard. Doesn't any one of 'em appeal to you? Denny's amusing,— Prue knows that. The Blakes have all the money in the world and Cary looks like Douglas Fairbanks. Rowena, haven't you any influence with Prue? Can't I bribe you to come? Prue, won't you come if Rena will?"

I nodded, feeling perfectly safe.

"Rena, what can I do to make you come?"

"I think," Rowena drawled, and I did not like the look in her eye, "I think that if you could make Blake sit to me, I might consider coming. But if you'd get Adelbert as well, I rather think I'd actually come."

I gasped.

"Done," John said without an instant's hesitation. "Done. Go and get your hats and coats and bags and I'll take you over before you change your respective minds."

"But——"

"No buts, Prue. Bert said he'd love to have any one who'd come, you said you'd come if Rena would, and she's said she'd come. You can't back out."

"But Ginger—the—cat——"

"Is he here? Well, bring him along. If he's out, I'll get him by the time you come down."

And in a state of complete confusion, I followed Rena into the bedroom.

"You know," she said, powdering her nose, "I think it must have been Fate that prompted me to buy some new clothes in New York. And I think, Prue, that we're going to have a very funny time."

"I agree," I told her, "with the last. I think that the noise of the Mantini machine-guns would have been considerably less nerve-racking than the grinding of Bert's false teeth when he catches sight of us."

"Where you goin'?" Phrone asked as we came out.

"We're going visiting," Rowena told her calmly.

"You stay right here. We'll be over every once in a while. Will you put Ginger into his basket? Thanks. Yes, we'll be over."

"Who you visitin'?"

"Mr. Stires."

Phrone raised her eyebrows, chuckled and glanced toward the telephone.

"Head-lines," Rowena whispered as we went out the door. "Head-lines, if only local ones. We'll be news very shortly."

She never, I reflected later, spoke truer words.

There were to be head-lines, but they were not going to be so restricted. And we *were* News, with a capital *N*.

CHAPTER TWO

THE LATE MR. STIRES

INSIDE of ten minutes, a harassed-looking butler was ushering us into the huge sun-room of Adelbert Stires's new house.

The four men sitting there greeted John vociferously, and while they slapped one another on the back I took the opportunity of sizing up the guests with whom I was to live for the next ten days.

At first they seemed remarkably alike. It took a second glance to show me how very different they actually were in spite of their dark gray suits and somber ties.

I recognized Denny James, of course, at once. He had a jaunty note about him that was lacking in the others, and not only his blue eyes, but his whole face, twinkled when he spoke.

Victor Blake I knew from the many pictures I'd seen of him. He stayed rather on the edge of the exuberant group and swung his eye-glasses back and forth on their wide black ribbon. He looked more like a professor of archeology than a financier. The young fellow beside him was obviously his son Junior. He had all the hallmarks of an expensive prep school and of Harvard,— and his exquisite spats annoyed me.

John had said that Cary Hobart resembled Douglas

Fairbanks, and he did. He had a tanned, out-of-door look, and even his little mustache was bleached by the sun.

Denny James caught sight of me and walked over.

"It's good to see you, Prue! I know I've put on weight, but you're just the same. Just as good-looking as you were twenty-seven years ago."

"Don't be ridiculous," I said, sensing rather than actually seeing Rowena's amused glance. "This is Rowena Fible."

Denny laughed. "And your mind works much the same way, too. Miss Fible, I knew your father and I still read the papers."

He introduced the other men.

"Mr. Blake," Rowena said as she shook hands with him, "I came on this party for two reasons, one of which was to have you sit to me. May I do a head of you? Or shall I put on my coat and go home?"

Blake laughed pleasantly. "My son's been at me for some time to have a portrait done and a bust will do just as well. I'd be delighted. What do you think, June?"

"Fine idea," June said. "And tell me, Miss Whitsby, aren't you Bill Porter's Snoodles?"

I shuddered as I always do whenever any one uses the absurd nickname that my niece and her husband evolved when they were children.

"She is," John said. "And even though she makes

faces, she loves the name. Tell me, where's Desire?"

"She's up-stairs." Denny chuckled. "Is her name really Desire? Cass Allerton was a prophet. What's the news of Bert?"

"He'll be here for dinner," John answered. "He's coming in the electric."

"He doesn't drive an electric," Rowena sounded incredulous.

"He does. It's an old brougham that he loves. He won't drive anything else. I've hoped for years that it would fall apart, but it doesn't seem to. He goes so slowly that he never has accidents and I don't think any one ever even bumped a fender of it. It leads a charmed life. Oh——"

He stopped short as Desire Allerton, followed by a small sniffing Pekinese, entered the room. I looked at Ginger, calmly sitting by my side, and wondered if anything would happen. Ginger dislikes Pekinese as much as I do, but apparently this beribboned object was beneath his notice. I breathed more freely and turned to the girl.

I think she was one of the most striking young women I've ever seen. Her hair was amber rather than red, and her eyes really were violet. Her finger-nails matched the bright blue dress that swirled around her ankles. She would have attracted attention anywhere, but here, with no competition, the effect was almost overpowering. The men had smiled when Denny joked about her name, but I noticed that they were unable to take their eyes off her. I did not blame them.

John introduced Rowena and me as her official chaperons, and she bowed formally.

"Won't you have tea?" I asked from my place at the table.

"No, thanks." She shook her head. "But Pup would love a cake. I hope your cat doesn't go for him."

"He won't," I assured her, "if he hasn't already." I was amazed by the girl's voice. It was hard and metallic and she had a certain accent which I couldn't place; then I remembered that she'd lived in France all her life. Rowena had shivered when she heard it, but Rowena always was inclined to exaggerate the Boston *a*.

"Don't you want to see your room?" John asked.

"I'll take them up," Denny offered. "I've just been over the place and I want to see if I can find my way around without having to call for help."

I picked up Ginger and we followed him out into the hall.

"That cavern you just passed through," he informed us, "is the living-room. It reminds me of the Grand Central Station. Dining-room and library on the right. Nice library. Red leather and enough ash-trays. Beyond them in the other wing are kitchens and all that. This," he opened a door at the farther end of the hall, "is the way to the game-room. It's built like a ship's cabin and it's got port-holes. Up-stairs," we mounted the curving staircase, "is confusion. John's here at the head of the stairs, Bert's rooms are on the front, here you are. The yellow room."

He opened the door to one of the most beautiful rooms I've ever been in.

"Yellow walls, yellow curtains, yellow everything. I'm willing to wager it's got a yellow tub and—er— yellow towels. Mine are all green and it makes me seasick. The rest of us are along the hall or in the other wing. Isn't this an establishment?"

"It is," Rowena said. "And there's another floor?"

"And more rooms and an attic and servants' quarters in the other wing and over the garage. Bert can always run a hotel if business flops. Dinner's at seven. I'll stop by for you. I say, what do you think of the girl Desire? I've finally decided her proper place in history."

"Where?" I demanded.

"She should have been a Sabine woman. Only if she had been, the situation with the Romans would have been reversed, if you see what I mean. How about some bridge after dinner, you two and Blake and I? Good. We'll side-track the rest."

And after dinner he side-tracked them very nicely. Adelbert had not turned up and the men speculated as to the number of times his battery had short-circuited. All of them knew the electric.

John and Hobart played billiards, and Desire and June sat in a corner and conversed in low tones. Denny called the girl's dress a Gunga Din model, but I noticed that both he and Victor Blake seemed to gravitate in its direction when either was dummy. It spoiled more than one shot at the billiard table, too.

At eleven o'clock, Rowena yawned. "I'm going to bed. Wonder where Bert is now?"

"I'm getting worried about him," Hobart answered. "I should think he'd call us if anything was wrong. He was to do some business for me and I want to hear about it."

"Well," Rowena said, "at least he's not had an accident. You always hear about them. So I——"

"Speaking of accidents," John interrupted, "I meant to have told you about the news broadcast before dinner. One of your late household was taken for a ride."

"One of the Mantinis?" Rowena demanded in mock horror. "My pals?"

"Yes. One of the henchmen was thrust in front of a machine-gun and held there. I've forgotten his name."

Rowena shook her head sadly. "I'm glad it didn't happen while I was around. And I do hope it wasn't the one I taught to say 'Thank-you-yes' and 'Thank-you-no.' He was sweet, and he had the nicest chest notes. Prue, let's run along. Coming, Miss Allerton?"

She glanced at us over her shoulder. "Not yet."

"Good night, then." And we left.

As I opened the window before slipping into bed I heard gales of laughter issuing from the game-room far below.

"What's that?" I asked.

"Shingle King returns," Rowena said sleepily. "He's been told who his chaperons are and that's the result. I hope he doesn't rout us out of the house. This bed's awfully comfortable. Prue, why didn't you ever marry Denny?"

I pretended not to hear.

"Oh, very well! But I think he's very nice. Are you really asleep? Go ahead and snore, if you want to. But he's very nice."

I did not disagree.

We woke up the next morning to find that snow was beginning to fall. Some had even drifted in on Ginger's basket; he was lying in front of the radiator and his tail waggled dejectedly.

At breakfast the seat at the head of the table was empty.

"Bert's a late sleeper," Rowena remarked.

"It's not that," John said, clearing his throat. "Fact is, he's not turned up yet."

"But I thought he came last night," I said. "We heard a lot of noise——"

"That was Denny's famous story about the Bishop

and the house-party," Hobart remarked. "But I'm worried. I think we should call Boston and see if Bert left and if he's still intending to come."

"He'll turn up around noon," John said confidently. "He probably made a late start and spent the night somewhere en route or else he started before daybreak this morning. If he doesn't get here by luncheon, we'll investigate."

"Eight jilted jests," June remarked. "I thought it was only debs who were late to their own parties. Snoodles,—I can't call you Miss Whitsby,—gobble down that pancake and we'll play some ping-pong. Won't you join us, Miss Fible?"

"Thank you, no. I'm going over to my house and get some plasteline I have packed away there. I'm going to compel your father to be sculpted."

It was so dark in the game-room we had to switch on lights. Outside the snow was falling in thick drifting flakes and the waves in the bay were almost black.

"I thought we might have a snow flurry," I commented, "but I'll admit I didn't take a northeast blizzard into account. I hope this doesn't turn into the sort of thing that will go down in history as that 'storm of thirty-two.' Bill Porter was down at his house here in the last blizzard and he couldn't set foot outside for three days. They were drifted in completely and there was nothing larger than a twelve-inch coal shovel to dig themselves out with."

"Fun," June said. "I've always wanted to be in a storm like that."

"You may yet," I told him, and by noon it seemed that I was right. After lunch John called in William and told him to lay in a stock of logs and to see that some stores in the garage were brought into the house.

"Now," Hobart said impatiently, "what about calling Bert's factory?"

John went up-stairs without answering. His face was long when he returned.

"He left yesterday around noon," he said. "Planned to come right down from there."

"Can't you call his mechanic and see if there's been any trouble?" Blake suggested.

"William's brother-in-law, Tom, does all the work on the electric. He drove Desire down yesterday. Bert would have called here."

"We've got to do something," Hobart insisted. "This business he was to do for me was important. It's a matter of considerable money, and I've got to know about it. I think you should call in the police. We've dallied long enough!"

William came in. "I beg your pardon, but do any of you gentlemen know anything about the electric system? It's off. Tom and Mr. Blake's man can't fix it, and we can't get the electricians by phone. It won't work."

"What's that mean?" John asked.

"Storm," Rowena told him. "The wires are down or else they've shut off the current."

John shook his head. "I don't know what we can do, William, if that's the case. You'll just have to manage."

William nodded dubiously and left.

"Now," Hobart said, "about Bert. I think we'd best call in the police."

"You seem to forget," Blake said, "that Bert has very definite ideas about publicity. He'd never forgive us if we put the police on his trail and it all got into the papers."

"I have an idea," Rowena announced. "Prue, where's Bill Porter's Man Friday? That Cape Codder who looks after him. Couldn't he help?"

"Asey Mayo's the very man," I said, feeling stupid not to have thought of him myself. "Asey Mayo'll find Bert for you, and he'll probably fix the electricity and the telephone to boot."

"What are Asey Mayo?" June asked.

"I remember," John said thoughtfully. "He's the the fellow that saved Bill Porter from being convicted in the Sanborn murder. He's the sort of person every one expects to find on Cape Cod and rarely does. A sort of jack of all trades, and he used to go to sea. How could we reach him, Prue?"

"Heaven only knows," I said. "But I wish Heaven would send him here."

William came back into the room.

"Miss Whitsby, there's a man here who wants to see you. Shall I show him in?"

I nodded, wondering who it could be. And the next minute in walked Asey Mayo, clad in hunting boots and corduroys, his rakish Stetson in hand.

He grinned pleasantly and came over to me.

"H'lo, Miss Prue. I heard in town that Phrone said you was here an' I kind of thought I'd run over an' see if you'd heard of Bill 'n' Betsey lately."

"I have," I said, shaking hands. I turned to the rest. "Let me present Asey Mayo."

There was a chuckle from Denny James. "Is it thought control, Prue, or does Heaven always send him when you're in need?"

"What's wrong?" Asey asked. "Who's in need?"

"Sit down," I said, "and take off your coat and I'll tell you."

He pulled off his wool-lined canvas coat with its innumerable pockets and took a seat before the fire. I told him about Adelbert, and he nodded when I got through.

"I shouldn't worry. If he's in the 'lectric, he's got bat'ry trouble or else flats. I drove one of them machines for Bill's father an' there ain't no end to the way they can act up."

"John," Hobart ignored Asey's opinions, "I'm still in favor of calling in the police."

"What p'lice you want?" Asey asked interestedly. "Town? State?"

"Any will do," Hobart said coldly.

"Then s'pose you tell me what you want done. You see, you sort of got the p'lice right here."

"What d'you mean?" I asked. "Where's Slough Sullivan?"

"He went up to Harwich to work an' the town 'lected me sheriff to fill his place. I didn't have that crazy Bill to look after, so I took the job. I'm sort of mixed up with the state an' county, too. They been havin' a crusade like on rum-runners an' they drafted a lot of us in. Yessir, you tell me what you want done an' I'll do it."

"What would you advise?" Blake asked.

" 'F I was you, I wouldn't do much of anything. Storm's bad an' it's goin' to be worse. 'Lectricity's gone already. Ain't much chance of Stires gettin' lost an' I don't think he'd of come to grief without you knowin'. Sure he left Boston?"

John nodded. "At eleven-thirty yesterday. And I don't think he would have changed his mind."

"Can't tell. He changed it ten times about that wharf I built him out front. Miss Prue says he was goin' to do some business. Now, he's a shrewd one. Sure he ain't playin' tricks?"

"If Bert Stires has dared to double-cross me," Hobart exploded.

"Calm down," Blake advised him. "You don't know that he has, Cary. I'd defer my outburst. I agree with Asey. The storm is bad and if Bert is on the road he'll have to wait over. There's really nothing we can do."

Asey nodded. "If the phones was goin' it might be dif'rent. I had a time gettin' over here an' I'm goin' to have a worse one goin' back. Miss Prue, I'll come over again to hear about them Porters."

He was putting on his coat when William entered. His face was smudged and his bald head gleamed with perspiration.

"What's the matter now?" John demanded. "Is the house on fire?"

"It's the stoves, sir. They don't work without the electricity and Lewis can't manage over a fireplace."

"Ain't you got no oil stove?" Asey asked.

"Everything's electric."

Rowena got up. "I'll go get my oil stove. Asey, will you drive me over? Phrone's got the wood stove and she doesn't need another."

"I'll get it," Asey said. "No need for you to bother."

"I want to go over anyway." And she went after her coat.

"What car have you?" I asked.

"The Monster, an' her windows is all up. Miss Fible'll be all right."

"The sixteen cylinder?"

Asey nodded. "Bill give her to me. She's good, but does she keep me poor! Four miles to a gallon of gas!"

"He," Denny said, after they had gone, "is one of the finer people. Does he always talk like that?"

"In the Cape dialect? Without any g's and t's and r's? Always. When he chews tobacco, you'll get one syllable in six instead of one in three. But he's got a brain like a steel trap. He's been everywhere and seen every one and done everything. Only, as Bill says, he's never been done."

"I love the way he treats us," June said. "Not as though he really approved, but more as though he accepted us because we were your friends."

"If you expected him to throw a fit at your names and your money," I retorted, "you're sadly mistaken. Ask John if the Mayos—they used to spell it Mayhew—have as many skeletons in the family closet as the Blakes."

"They're just as good," John said, "and maybe better."

"How old is Asey?" Blake asked with a chuckle.

"About sixty," I said. "But he's so tanned and lank that you'd take him for less."

Rowena and Asey returned. "Got that stove over," Asey said proudly, "an' never hurt it a mite. Well, I'll be gettin' along. I'm goin' to have trouble gettin', too. Roads is all driftin' over an'——"

From up-stairs somewhere there was a dull thud, then a series of small explosions.

"What——" John began.

"Stove," Asey said. "Dum fools! I told 'em how to light it." And he raced off up-stairs with the rest of us straggling after.

Lewis, the cook, had lost his eyebrows and some of his hair. But that was not the worst. His sleeves had been rolled up, and his arms were burned badly from the tips of his fingers to his elbows. Asey took command of the situation, put baking soda on the burns and directed William in putting out the small blaze.

"I'm goin' for the doctor," he announced. "You do what you can an' I'll get the doc here as soon as poss'ble. I may have trouble gettin' back, but you bear up, Lewis!"

It was almost an hour before he got back with a doctor whom I'd never seen before.

"Doctor Walker," Asey explained to me. "Taken Reynold's place. Likely young feller an' knows his business. Did we have a time gettin' over here! It's all drifts from the Golf Club up an' my lights wasn't no use. If it hadn't been for the Monster we'd be stuck back there right now."

"It's out of the question for you to go back," John said. "And we have more than enough room here. We can put the two of you up very comfortably. I wonder, though, what we're going to have to eat?"

Asey grinned. "Guess I can sing for my supper," he announced. "I'll get your food for you. Oil stove's gone, but I brought another from my house back in the car, an' I cal'late I've used one often enough t'be able to cook a dinner 'thout explodin'."

John looked faintly amused. "I didn't know you could cook, Asey."

" 'Member Porter's yacht, the *Roll an' Go?* I cooked on her for half the big-bugs on this coast. I'll show you."

And he did. We ate our dinner around the ping-pong table in the game-room, before the fire,—for the rest of the house was now freezing cold. It seemed that the oil heater worked by an electric attachment.

William served, and I noticed that he was not the only one to look on Asey with new respect. Even Cary Hobart was forced to admit that it was the best food he'd ever eaten. Up-stairs, Lewis was better. Even Ginger and the Pekinese sat before the fire in comfortable amity. And outside, the blizzard roared.

Suddenly Asey cocked his ear. "Some one come in your front door then," he said.

"Probably William shutting things up," John told him, but Asey shook his head.

"Some one come in," he insisted as he turned around and watched the door.

And down into the game-room walked Adelbert Stires, covered with snow and oozing water with every step.

For a moment no one spoke. Then John rushed forward and helped him take off his coat. The doctor picked up his bag.

"Man alive, how'd you get here?" Asey asked.

"I walked," Stires said. "Er——" He caught sight of Rowena and me, gulped, recovered himself and went on. "The battery gave out beyond the Golf Club. I followed the boundary fences from there. Prue, Rowena, I'm glad you could join us on such short notice."

I looked at Rowena. Her chin drooped.

"You hoofed it from there?" Asey said. "God A'mighty! In this storm! Doc, give him some whisky quick! I'll go up an' heat him some water an' get him some food. Mr. James, you're more his size. You take a candle an' get him some dry clothes. He's soaked through."

In the bustle I leaned over to Rowena. "What price revenge?" I whispered.

"After that sporting effort?" she whispered back. "Never. Doesn't the poor dear look like Winnie-the-Pooh? And think of him going all that distance in a derby!"

It occurred to me—afterward, of course—that not one of us asked him why he had been delayed. For over twenty-four hours we had expected him, waited for him and worried. And now that he had come, we were too surprised to see him to think of asking questions. He was so casual that no one gave it a thought. He might have been a guest dropping in for an evening of bridge.

After Adelbert had eaten and been dosed and dried out, and given a full account of all that had happened to Lewis and the various household systems, Walker and Asey propelled him off to bed, and Rowena and Desire and I followed.

Outside his door, Bert stopped. "I forgot," he said, "I wanted a word with Cary. Would one of you be so kind as to ask him to come up? Thank you, Asey. Er—I'm sorry," he said to Rowena and me, "that all this has happened. I—er—I didn't anticipate so much trouble."

"Don't be absurd," Rowena answered. "You're not accountable for the vagaries of a Cape blizzard. And, Bert, I'm truly sorry about those teeth. I always have been."

Adelbert smiled. I'd never seen him smile before and it made him look rather like a sleepy cherub. "It was my fault, Rena, as much as yours. I—er— I'm glad to have the opportunity of telling you I'm sorry for my part, too. I've wanted to tell you before, but, really, I never thought you'd care to see me after what I said."

Rowena laughed and they shook hands. Shivering, we took our candles and went to bed.

It was still dark when Asey roused me the next morning.

"Put on somethin'," he said softly, "an' come out into the hall, will you?"

I slipped on my fur coat and went out to find Walker and Asey waiting.

"What's the matter?" I asked sleepily.

"Stires," the doctor said briefly. "I—are you awake? Sure? Well, there's no use trying to break it to you gently, and I know you won't get too upset. But——"

"What's the matter?" I repeated, now fully awake.

"Mr. Stires is dead."

"Dead? What—how did it happen? Did that walk through the storm exhaust him?"

Walker shook his head slowly. "No. As a matter of fact, Miss Whitsby, Stires has been killed. Poisoned."

CHAPTER THREE

ASEY GETS TO WORK

ORDINARILY I am not easily upset. I was brought up to believe that in this world almost anything may happen—and usually does—and that it is wiser to accept events calmly than to get excited over them.

But the doctor's calm statement was a sledge-hammer blow. I was more than upset. I was, in the phraseology of my niece, in a jittering state. And somehow the absurd notion flashed through my mind that if I had bought my spool of orange silk and never bothered with Rowena Fible and her insane notions, none of this would have happened.

Asey and the doctor both had flash-lights and their long beams cast an uncanny light through the long corridor. I drew my fur coat more closely about me; it was bitterly cold. I glanced at my watch. It was nearly seven, though for all the light it might well have been two in the morning. Outside the wind howled around the corners of the house and somewhere a loose shutter banged.

They led me into Stires's room and Asey plumped me down in a chair, but not before I had a glimpse of a covered figure on the floor behind me.

"Tell me everything," I said, when I was finally able

to speak. "Everything. When did it happen? And how?"

"It was near two hours ago that I thought I heard a noise—sort of a thump-like, down here," Asey said. "My room's just above this an' I couldn't git to sleep somehow. I was colder'n Greenlands an' the bed was too soft. Anyhows, I wondered if Stires was all right; I'd been awful uneasy about that feller, an' so I routed the doc out, thinkin' he might be feelin' sick, an' we come down here. The door was locked, an' I had to go down cellar an' find some tools an' force the lock. Thought I'd have to bang in a panel of the door, but I finally got it open. We found him there on the floor. Maybe the noise I thought I heard was him tumblin' out of bed."

"But are you sure he was killed? Couldn't it have been that he tired himself out getting here, or weakened his heart, or something like that?"

Walker shook his head. "I went over him thoroughly last night, Miss Whitsby. His heart was all right. He was well, perfectly well. He wasn't sick. He was tired, of course, and after he struck the heat downstairs he got sleepy. He might have got a cold, but there wasn't a chance in the world of his dying. Not last night, anyway."

"But—but poisoned! How could he have been?"

"Well, I've examined him as well as I could. I'm medical examiner, you see, and I carry a lot of truck

around with me as I never know just when I'll be
needed on a case. I made the Marsh test, and there
is some arsenic in his vomit. But I'm puzzled about
the situation. It was arsenic that killed him, beyond
any shadow of a doubt. It wasn't any eccentric or
bizarre poison. Just plain arsenic. But I don't know
how he was given it."

"But arsenic works slowly, doesn't it? And if he
was poisoned, wasn't it in food?"

"Can't tell. You see, Miss Whitsby, there are any
number of ways of conveying arsenic into the system.
It can be given directly, in food, or it can be given
through the skin—through clothes. There are any
number of ways. If he'd been given a large dose
directly in food, he might have died in a few hours.
If it were a small dose, it would have taken longer.
If he'd been poisoned through the skin, only I'm convinced that he wasn't, it would have taken days. Now,
he was all right when we left him around ten last
night. And I think he died shortly before we broke
in, say, around five-thirty. But I'm not at all sure
he was given the arsenic in food. Different individuals
vary considerably in their reactions to poisons. It
would seem that he'd have to have been given a large
dose to have died in seven or eight hours. Yet from
what examinations I've been able to make, he wasn't
given a large dose. Not directly, anyway."

"An' I give him that food myself," Asey said mournfully. "But I give him the same food as the rest of us had. I don't see how it could of been anything he et, on account of what the rest of us would of died, too. Yessir, he had what the rest of us had. I fixed it myself an' put it on the tray an' brought it down an' watched him eat it. Even took a mouthful or two myself to see if things was plenty hot. Don't see why I shouldn't of died if they'd been anything wrong."

"Couldn't he have been poisoned before he came?" I asked.

"No." Walker was very emphatic. "No, I don't think so. I'm sure of it, in fact. I'd have found or noticed some symptoms last night. Or he would have felt sick."

"Couldn't it have been suicide?"

"I hardly think so. He didn't look like a man who was getting ready to kill himself when we saw him last night. He—well, he didn't appear to me to be the type that commits suicide." Walker thrust his hands deep into his pockets and hunched his shoulders. Restlessly he paced back and forth across the floor. "This is fishy. It's just as fishy as it can be. Listen, Asey, I've been thinking it over. Whoever did this didn't expect it to be found out."

"What you mean?"

"Just this. If you hadn't called me yesterday, but had phoned this morning and told me Stires was dead, that he'd been out in the storm, I shouldn't have looked for poison. I'd have rather been inclined to think that he'd died from a bad cold or exposure."

"But there'd have been an examination, wouldn't there?" I asked.

"Yes, and as I said I'm the medical examiner. But I wouldn't have been looking for poison. The outward signs—mottled skin, bloodshot eyes, vomiting and all that—they're not different from what you'd find in a case of death from a bad cold. I think, though I'm giving my personal opinion and I don't know whether another doctor would agree or not, I think that there would have been more than an even chance that under ordinary circumstances, this might have passed for a natural death."

"What made you think it wasn't?"

"Because I knew he was perfectly all right last night. I knew he was well; I knew that it couldn't be a natural death. I'll amend that: I felt sure that it wasn't. It could have been. Anything is possible, I suppose. But it wasn't natural and I've proved it. Then, too, he'd tried to get help. He got himself out of bed, you see, and collapsed completely on the way to that bell over there. Ironically enough, it wouldn't have helped him if he'd reached it and pushed the button, for the electricity's still off and it wouldn't have sounded. He made a superhuman effort to get help, but he was licked from the start. I wonder that he could move, even. I don't see how he managed to push himself off the bed."

"But are you sure," I asked pleadingly, "that he wasn't poisoned before he came? I mean, if he wasn't——"

"I know. If he wasn't poisoned before he came, he was poisoned after he got here. And if he was poisoned after he got here, that means that some one in this house did it. I'm afraid, Miss Whitsby, that there isn't any possibility of his being poisoned before he got here. I'm sure of it. He wolfed down Asey's meal, too, as though he hadn't eaten for a good long while, long enough so that if he had been, there'd have been some signs."

"But if Asey says his food was all right, how did it happen?"

Asey shrugged. "You got us there. The door was locked on the inside. There ain't no transom so that any one could of locked the door after comin' in an' then tossed the key back into the room. The key was in the lock anyway. An' that door's the only way to get into the room 'cept the windows, an' they was all shut an' locked from the inside, so that no one could of come in 'em, even if they was fools enough to go out in this storm an' try to scale up the front of the house. He didn't have no bags. They ain't even a tooth-brush in the bathroom. No medicine there, nothin'. Wasn't even a glass of water by his bed."

"It's awful. I can't see who—— Asey, shouldn't you wake up the rest and tell them?"

"What for? Wouldn't do no good. Ain't no use to wake 'em. I tried to open the front door an' the snow's drifted so that I couldn't. I flashed the light around an' we're pretty much drifted in. It's a cinch we can't get to town, an' no one's goin' to come out here to see how we be. The lights is off, the phone won't work, an' I'll wager we won't have lights or current until a good long while after the rest do, on account of prob'ly all the wires is down from town out here. Ain't no point in gettin' them folks up, Miss Prue. They'll have time 'nough to hear about it. We may get in touch with the rest of the world to-day, an' again we may not for two or three days."

"You mean, Asey Mayo, d'you mean we're marooned out here?"

"Yup. But there's one good thing about it. Whoever done this can't get away. He's goin' to be stuck right here with the rest of us. He can't do no runnin' anywheres."

My chin slumped. It had never occurred to me when I joked with June the day before that we might actually be snowed up. I had lived in the city so long that I had almost forgotten that such things happened. It might have been amusing, possibly, to be snowed up—if we had had heat and light and a telephone, and if Adelbert Stires were not lying dead on the floor beyond. But to be marooned in this great freezing barrack of a house with a murderer running loose, well, that was a different matter! My teeth began to chatter, and it was not from the cold. I remembered the time I'd visited near Danvers and a homicidal maniac escaped from the sanitarium. For one whole evening we had jumped every time the floor creaked. And it was possible that we were to be cooped up with this murderer for three days, and possibly longer! I began to shiver.

"But I called you," Asey continued, apparently oblivious of the fact that I was frightened out of my wits, "because, Miss Prue, I want you to help."

"You want me to what?"

"I know it won't be very pleasant-like, but you will, won't you?"

"But why? And whatever makes you think that I'll be able to help?"

"Because for one thing, you know these people better'n we do. The doc's the medical examiner an' he's done his duty. An' I'm sheriff of this town, an' till I can get hold of the county people an' till they can send some one here, well, it's my place to find out who done this. We got to run the guy down. Don't know's I figgered on havin' to turn detective when I took this job, but I guess I got to. Now, I know you, an' you're the only person in this place the doc an' I can trust. You could help us a lot, if you would."

"Of course I will," I said. "I'm not sure that I'll be of any great assistance, but I'll help if I can."

"Good. Now, doc, s'pose we sort of begin. Far's we know, Stires got poisoned by arsenic, given him we don't know how, an' by person or persons unknown, as they say, some time after he got to this house. That right?"

Walker nodded.

"I don't think 'twas anything in the food I give him. We can't find that he et or drank anything after we left him. You say there ain't no sores nor nothin' on him where he might of been poisoned by clothes."

"Right."

"Hobart was the only feller that saw him after we did. That is, he's the only one we know about. Now, what about this Mr. Hobart, Miss Prue?"

"I don't know much about him. I met him for the first time only yesterday. He's the head of the Hobart Lumber, he went to school with Adelbert and he was at Harvard with him. He was pretty wrought up when Bert didn't come last night and he fussed about and muttered about some business that Bert was to do for him."

Asey nodded. "When he come down-stairs last night after seein' Stires, he was happy an' cheerful as a basket of chips. He told Blake that Stires had put over a good deal for him. 'Course, he might of been bluffin', but I don't know. He'd have sense 'nough to know that we could pretty well find out about any business deals, 'cause they ain't things you can't trace. Well, anyways, he seemed plenty satisfied with Stires an' with life in gen'ral. Didn't have the look of a man that'd just give his host arsenic. Denny James, he lent Stires dry clothes, but he wasn't alone with him when Stires changed outside the game-room. What's Denny do?"

"He doesn't do much of anything; that is, I don't think he has any business unless you can call enjoying himself a business. He collects prints and books. That's about all."

"Lives on his income, does he? An' this girl, now? She's Stires's ward, is she? They didn't seem to be awful cordial."

"She'd only arrived from France yesterday," I said, and told him about Cass Allerton and Lucia Hammond. "Besides, you know Bert was not a ladies' man."

"What about the servants?" Walker asked. "How many are there?"

"There's William, and his wife, the housekeeper, and Lewis, the man you tended for the burns. They're the only ones I've seen, but there's Stires's chauffeur and I believe that the Blakes have one, too. Don't you think it must have been one of them?"

Asey smiled. "For your sake, Miss Prue, I'll hope so. But I got my doubts. The doc an' I sort of decided that some one pretty clever done this, an' from the glimpse I had of the hired help, I don't think that they're so dummed clever. Any fool that can't light an oil stove without lettin' it explode——"

The doctor grinned at his scorn.

"Have you examined the room?" I asked. "I mean, have you looked in corners and on the floor to see if there isn't some clue?"

"We give it a pretty thorough once-over," Asey said, "but we didn't find nothin'. Not even a cuff link or a cigar stub or anything else."

"Have you looked through Stires's clothes?"

Asey smiled. "I told you," he said to Walker, "that we needed a woman on this job. Nope, we ain't. The clothes he had on are all down-stairs. Miss Prue, s'pose you go get some clothes on. You must be nigh froze."

I admitted that I had been warmer. "But I'll probably wake Rena if I go into the room and she'll be sure to ask me what the trouble is—and then the house will be roused for sure."

"Then get your clothes quiet," Asey said, "an' you can dress down-stairs. The game-room's probably the warmest place, 'cause I made sure that the fire'd keep. You go in an' get your things. We'll lock this room up—I guess we can, an' wait for you outside an' then go down with you."

I literally sneaked into the yellow room and grabbed

the clothes I'd taken off the night before. I need not have feared that Rowena would wake. She was sleeping like a baby. Ginger, however, hopped out of his basket, and it was only with difficulty that I persuaded him to return.

The game-room was almost warm. I dressed with the dubious aid of a flash-light and discovered, as I slipped on my sweater, that I'd put on everything wrongside out. But remembering Olga's superstition about changing,—she said it brought trouble,—I left things as they were. There had already been, I decided, trouble enough.

I put on my fur coat as Asey knocked at the door.

"All set? Well, we went through Stires's pockets, an' here you are."

He passed over a silk handkerchief into which he had dumped the miscellaneous assortment. There was a full key ring, a small pocket-knife, a wallet and change purse, two small leather-covered note-books and a check-book. Then, with a grin, Asey produced a set of false teeth.

"Where on earth did you find these?" I asked.

"In his coat pocket. Kind of funny to carry spares along with you, ain't it?"

"Let me see them! But, Asey, these aren't spares! These are broken."

"Just as funny t' carry busted ones," Asey commented gravely.

There was something in his tone that made me laugh, and the doctor joined me.

"I suppose it's callous to snicker," Walker remarked, "but there is something funny about false teeth anyway,—and to find them in this situation is amusing. You know, I had a patient once who had a false eye and false teeth. He told me that people always laughed at his teeth because he had a peculiarly shaped jaw and he couldn't always make 'em stay put, and they felt awfully sorry about his eye. As a matter of fact, he said that the teeth hurt him a lot more. But it is a peculiar thing for Stires to lug around with him."

"He had teeth in, didn't he?" Asey asked.

The doctor nodded. "Uh-huh. He had a full set. I noticed them."

"Then don't you s'pose that the ones he had in was the spares, an' that he broke these here, the ones he had in his mouth, an' switched? That's the only way I can figger it out. These is his regulars an' them's his spares, an' prob'ly he was intendin' to get these mended. Well, so much for all that. What you findin' in them books, Miss Prue?"

"One's just full of addresses and phone numbers. The other is an engagement book, apparently. It's full of lists, too. See, here's one headed Tuesday. It's a list of things that some one was to get for the house here."

Asey glanced at the book. "Great boy for details,

wa'n't he? I'll look 'em over careful later. How about that check-book?"

I passed it to him.

"Huh, he kep' a bank balance, didn't he? Only used two checks in this book. Five hundred for cash, an' two thousand for cash." He picked up the wallet. "That's funny, too. They's only about seventy-five in bills in here, an' that check was dated yesterday. Wonder what he spent all that money for?"

"See here, Asey," I said, "where was he yesterday, and Tuesday night? Did you ask him?"

Asey shook his head. "Nope. Didn't he tell you while I was up gettin' his supper?"

"He did not. Asey, no one asked him! And he never offered to tell us. How stupid of us, after we'd waited and worried so long! Where do you suppose he could have been?"

"Dunno. Didn't he tell any one? Even Hobart when he saw him?"

"He must have, after all that dithering about Hobart's business. But it's funny he didn't tell the rest of us. He didn't even make any attempt to."

"Well." Asey pocketed the check-book and the note-books and, to my surprise, the teeth. "We got some exhibits t' conjecture about, anyhows. It don't look like they was goin' to do us such an awful lot of good, but we got 'em."

"I wish," Walker said, "that we could find out when

and where and how that arsenic was given him. If you prepared his food, Asey, and tasted some of it yourself, and if it was the same food that the rest of us had, I don't see how his supper could have been to blame. I don't quite see how he was killed by anything but a huge amount, either, but that's beside the point for the moment. We'll have to assume that the food was all right. How about the plates?"

"You mean, some one could of put arsenic on 'em? I don't see how. I got the plates kind of random-like out of the chiny closet. Couldn't of been in the sugar, neither, 'cause he didn't take no sugar in his coffee."

"Were any of the servants around?"

"Nope. That William was helpin' Stires get his clothes off an' his wife was up-stairs with the cook. The other fellers was in the other part of the cellar playin' cards. Kent told 'em not to sleep out over the g'rage for fear they might get stuck out there. He told William t' find room for 'em somewheres. No one was around attall."

"Well, are you sure that no one passed you on the way down there, Asey?"

Asey slapped his thigh. "God A'mighty," he said disgustedly, "but I'm gettin' old an' forgetful. Cal'late I'll be forgettin' my head one of these days if it wa'n't sewed on to my body. Doc, at the end of the hall they was only one of them bayb'ry candles for light.

You know how soft an' squashy the carpets is. Well,
just as I was goin' down-stairs, Blake come up. If
I hadn't sidestepped quick, I'd of knocked him over.
As 'twas, his sleeve got into the creamed chicken.
An' I s'pose that if his sleeve did——"

"His hand," Walker said quietly, "might well have
got into it, too."

CHAPTER FOUR

MISS ALLERTON

ASEY nodded. "I guess," he observed cheerfully, "that I'll run an' bring that gent down here."

As he disappeared up the stairs, Walker shook his head. "That man amazes me, Miss Whitsby. You know, I've always felt that it would be pretty exciting to be mixed up in an affair of this sort. I even had some idea that if I were, I'd be able to lay hands on the guilty party before you could say 'Eighteenth Amendment.' But I've seen as much as he has of this, and I admit that I'm sunk. But look at him—he's as calm and confident as he can be. I don't see how he's going to get anywhere, but, by George, I feel he's going to!"

I nodded. "I know what you mean. I rather have faith in Massachusetts myself."

Asey returned with Blake. His gray hair was rumpled and full of cow-licks and he was shivering with the cold. He yawned and seated himself before the fire.

"What's the matter, Asey?"

And very briefly, Asey told him.

"Look here, man alive," Blake said irritably, "this is not funny. I'm not one to protest against practical jokes, but this is going a bit far."

"I'm sorry, Mr. Blake," Walker said, "but Asey's not joking. He's telling you the Gospel truth."

Blake leaned back in his chair and for a second I thought that he was going to faint. Walker, watching him closely, even took a step toward him.

"But it's incredible! It's—oh, I can't believe it! Bert dead? Killed? Miss Whitsby, is it true?"

I nodded.

He was silent for a minute and I could see the effort he was making to control himself.

"Who did it?"

"That's what we're trying to find out," Asey informed him gently.

"But Bert had no enemies—and certainly none here in the house! All the servants have been with him for years. They're perfectly trustworthy. They loved him. And as for the rest of us, why, no one here could have killed him, Asey. They couldn't have!"

"But we're sure," Walker said, "that it must have been some one here. We know almost for a fact that it couldn't have been any one from outside."

"But who?"

Asey drew a long breath and started in without any preamble. "Mr. Blake, when I took Stires's supper down to him last night, I near bumped into you on the stairway. We sort of hit each other as it was."

"Yes. I didn't hear you coming and the light was bad."

"Well, Mr. Blake, we're pretty sure that nothin' in the food as it was when I left the kitchen hurt Stires. We sort of can't think of any other way except that it was food that poisoned him. Now, you was the only person I met from the time I left the kitchen until I got down-stairs."

"You don't think that I—that I put poison in the food? You're certainly not accusing me?"

"Before Asey answers," Walker spoke up, "I want to say something. We're snowed in here, Mr. Blake, and all of us are going to have a difficult and unpleasant time. Asey's job is going to be particularly hard. We're just trying to put together what we can before the rest are told. We're not accusing any one. We're only trying to get the facts straight. Now this has been a shock, but as one of Mr. Stires's friends, I know that you will want to help us all you can. Asey has got to find out a lot of things that he personally doesn't want to pry into. But it's his job, right now, and if you and the rest will understand and just try to help, the whole thing will be a lot easier."

"I understand, Doctor." From the pocket of his dressing-gown he drew out his glasses and commenced to swing them on their ribbon. "Asey, I was on my way up-stairs to get a handkerchief. It sounds absurd, but I'd forgotten one and I'd sniffed until I couldn't bear it any longer. June offered to go up for me, but I knew that he couldn't find one because he's never been known to find anything. I brushed by you, but I'll give you my word that I didn't poison Bert's food. I wish that you or the doctor would go up to my room now and search it thoroughly and see for yourselves that I have nothing there that might have hurt Stires."

There were footsteps on the stairs and William, with a heavy ulster over his black suit, came down. Asey glanced at him and turned to Blake.

"Thank you, Mr. Blake. The doc'll go up with you, an' I sort of wish you wouldn't say anything about this until later. Not even to your son."

"Is anything the matter, sir?" William asked after they had gone.

Asey looked at me pleadingly, and so I tried to break the news as gently as I could. Tears came into the man's eyes and he tried in vain to brush them away.

"I've worked for Mr. Stires twenty-seven years," he said. "I was even his servant in the army. He took Mrs. Boles into the house rather than lose me when I married, and you don't know how he disliked women, sir. I—I can't tell you how I feel. Who did it?"

"We don't know, William. Mr. Mayo's going to do his best to find out."

"If I can help you, sir, you just tell me what to do. My wife and I, we liked Mr. Stires as a friend and a gentleman as well as our boss. I don't know what she'll say to this."

"Don't tell her now," Asey said. "Don't tell any one until after breakfast. We're snowed in, William, an' I don't know when we'll get back to normal, an' things ain't goin' to be so happy. We'll wait till they all got breakfast before we tell 'em, 'cause they prob'ly won't feel like it if we tell 'em before. William, d'you know anythin' about this attall?"

"Not one thing, sir."

"Mr. Stires been havin' any fights with any of the men?"

"He never had fights with any one." I wondered for a moment about Rowena. "He'd get peeved if things wasn't just so, like his eggs being cooked three minutes by a stop-watch, and if we went over five seconds he knew it. He was fussy about things in the house and how they ran, but even when he got peeved, he forgot all about it in ten minutes. Same way with his friends. He'd get peeved with Mr. Kent or Mr. James and the rest, but he never got mad with any of 'em, and they never got mad with him, as far as I know."

Asey nodded. "Where was he yesterday and the day before? You know?"

"Why, no, sir. He didn't tell me last night, and with all the bustle I forgot to ask."

"Does he often go away an' not tell you where?"

"Never, sir. He always tells us where he's going and how long he'll be. And if he said he'd be some-where at a certain time, he was always there. He was very punctual. He left for the factory every day at eighteen minutes to nine as long as I've been with him and unless he told us different, we knew he'd be back at eighteen minutes past five."

"I see. All right, William. How's that cook?"

"Lewis? I looked in at him and he said he felt better, but I still don't think he can cook, sir."

"All right. I'll get breakfast. Miss Prue, you go up an' see if you can keep Miss Fible from askin' where you been an' what you're doin' up."

And I managed to get myself dressed all over again before Rena awoke.

"Are we all snowed up?" she asked cheerfully.

"We are."

"How perfectly marvelous! I say, wasn't Bert decent last night? I can't get over how I've maligned him all these years. What's the matter with you? You seem so glum!"

"Just cold," I lied. "I'm going to take Ginger down to be fed."

"I'll be down presently. Lord, it is cold, isn't it?"

I rummaged around and found two belts which I tied together for a leash for my cat. It occurred to me that it might not be healthy for him to roam about the house at large.

"Why all that?" Rowena wanted to know.

"I'm afraid he'll go for that Peke. Even if he didn't pay any attention to it yesterday, it doesn't mean that he won't to-day. He clawed the ear of Ada West's, you know, and nothing in the nature of a real reconciliation has ever taken place between us."—That at least, I reflected, was true.

"I see. And with Adelbert in such a good mood it would be a pity to have his niece rise up in wrath."

I shuddered at the casual mention of Adelbert, picked up Ginger and departed. I made my way out into the kitchen, and Asey smiled at the leash.

"Gettin' anxious for him? I've found a dozen tins of salmon there in the storeroom, so you needn't worry about his food none. But I shan't feel attall hurt if you want to feed him yourself." He presented me with a can opener and I stood over Ginger while he ate his fish.

Breakfast was probably the most awful meal I ever sat through. Asey, Blake, the doctor and I were so forcedly cheerful that it seemed to me the rest would surely ask questions. William put plates down and took them away, moving as automatically and jerkily as one of those mechanical toys one winds with a key.

"Bert still sleeping?" Denny asked. "That's good. He deserves a rest after that hike of his. Hasn't got cold or anything, has he, Doctor?"

Walker shook his head and changed the subject. "Snow's letting up," he said shortly. "But that doesn't mean that I'll be able to get to town."

"We're snowed in," Rowena explained proudly for

the benefit of the rest. They commented on it and June was particularly enthusiastic. Asey stoically drank four cups of coffee. Blake swallowed a glass of milk, made some pretense of eating, gave it up and took to swinging his glasses monotonously. He was pale and it seemed to me that he had added lines to his face in the last half-hour.

At last we were through. Asey spoke to William, glanced at the doctor and got up from the table.

"What'll we do for excitement?" June asked, and I saw his father wince.

"Guess we'll manage," Asey said dryly as William came back, followed by his wife and Lewis, who had put a coat on over his pajamas. Two chauffeurs, both in uniform, brought up in the rear.

"What's the matter?" John asked. "Why the—er— the parade?"

Asey cleared his throat. "I've waited until after breakfast to tell you what's happened. Mr. Stires is dead. He was poisoned after he got here last night, with arsenic, the doc says."

He hesitated and I followed his eyes around the group. Not a muscle of Hobart's face moved, but he was white underneath his tan. John looked as stunned as I had felt earlier in the day. June had been yawning, and the yawn was frozen in mid-air.

Rowena looked down at her plate, gulped and pushed the plate away. Her hand went out for her glass of water; she touched the glass, withdrew her hand. The twinkle had gone from Denny James's eyes. He leaned back in his chair and lighted a cigarette. I noticed that he made no attempt to smoke it.

Mrs. Boles was frankly crying, and Lewis's eyes glistened suspiciously. His face was too swathed in bandages for me to see more. I had not known which of the two chauffeurs was Tom, but now I knew, for the small man in gray walked over to Mrs. Boles and tried to comfort her. Blake's man, tall and hard-looking, with a scar on his left cheek, looked only faintly interested.

Desire Allerton was, however, the most unmoved and unconcerned of all. I marveled at it, then remembered that she had not set eyes on her guardian until two days before, and that there was no particular reason for her to feel any great grief over his death.

"It wasn't suicide," Asey went on slowly, as though he were picking his words, "we don't think 'twas any accident or anything like that. He was killed." He looked at the doctor.

"I've nothing to add," Walker said, "except that Asey is in charge. As I've already told Mr. Blake, we're going to be here for some time. How long, I don't know. But it will be a lot more pleasant for every one concerned if you'll try to help Asey and understand that he's trying only to do his duty."

"And I shouldn't ask for a better man," John said

promptly. "Asey, you go ahead. If we can help, we will, and you can bank on it."

Asey smiled wryly. "Thank you very kindly. Now——"

"Mr. Mayo." Tom had left his sister. "Did you say that Mr. Stires had been killed by arsenic?"

"Yup."

"Is arsenic a powder?"

"Usually," Walker said. "Why?"

"Would it be a white powder?"

"Yes."

"Then please can I talk to you, Mr. Mayo?"

Asey nodded. "Sure thing. Mrs. Boles, you'd better see that Lewis gets back into bed. The rest of you'll find the game-room warmest. We'll go into the library, Tom. Doc, you looked Lewis over? N'en that's all right. Miss Prue, will you come 'long?"

I followed them into the library, painfully conscious of Rowena's hurt look. It was obvious that she understood that I had known about Bert and not told her.

I still had Ginger on his leash. He made for the fireplace and Asey smiled. "Take the c'mfortable chair an' I'll put on another log an' try an' warm you an' your animule." He removed a cushion from the window-seat and placed it in front of the fire. "Here, Ginge, have a seat. Guess he don't need his leash in here, does he?"

"Thank you, Asey." I noticed, inconsequentially enough, that he had picked out a bright orange pillow which matched the ribbon bow on the cat's collar.

Tom stood and watched. He was, I thought, a perfectly nondescript person. He reminded me of the faces you see in news-reel crowds. There wasn't a single thing about him which impressed me unless it was his utter lack of any outstanding quality at all.

"Well, Tom," Asey said, "come over to the fire. What's on your mind?"

"I drove the young lady down Tuesday in the Cadillac, Mr. Mayo. I wouldn't of taken up your time if I hadn't thought of something I thought you might not know about. At Plymouth she rapped on the window and told me to stop at the next drug-store. I drew up at that one by the traffic lights on the main street and got out and asked her if there was anything I could get for her. She said that she'd get what she wanted herself. I needed cigarettes so I went in after her and the druggist was putting up some white powders for her. And then when you said Mr. Stires was poisoned by arsenic, it come to my mind. That's all."

Walker swung around in his chair and looked at him.

"What did you think the powders were then?"

"I didn't know. I never gave it a thought until Mr. Mayo spoke about arsenic and I'd read somewhere that it was a white powder. The left rear was shaky and I

was too busy wondering if we was going to have a blow-
out after that construction and crushed stone above
Plymouth to worry about the girl and her powders. I
just thought of it now."

"What you think of the girl?" Asey asked.

"I haven't thought about her. My sister—Mrs.
Boles, that is—she doesn't like her."

"Why not?"

"She covered the best towels with lipstick, and Clemmie says it won't come off. Then there was the tea
leaves."

"What tea leaves?"

"Well, Clemmie reads tea leaves. I didn't give it
much thought, but four or five times these last couple
of weeks, she's seen trouble in the tea leaves. Trouble
and a girl and a light. She's been real worried about it.
I didn't pay much attention, but there's been trouble,
and, well, the girl's here, and I guess that's all."

A smile hovered about Asey's lips. "I see, Tom.
Thank you for tellin' us."

"Not going to ask me anything else?" Tom sounded
disappointed.

"Got anything else you want to say?"

"No, sir, but I sort of thought that you'd be wanting
to know a lot of things."

"I do," Asey said. "They's a lot of things I'd give
all my ole collars an' cuffs to know about, but I'm
learnin' enough, little by little, t' keep me busy for one

good while. We'll call you in later if we want to ask
you anythin' more."

As he closed the door, Asey laughed. "I was hopin'
against hope that we wouldn't have to do any fiddlin'
around with that girl attall. She's too good-lookin' an'
besides, she's sort of the obvious one to bother about.
Ever notice how it's all the time the best-lookin' an'
the ugliest that causes the most trouble? Give me a
medium good-looker any day. They don't go around
confusin' things. Anyways, from what I seen of that
Allerton girl, she's a slippery cust'mer."

"What are you going to do about her?" I asked.

"Call her in an' ask her questions. I bet you she'll
lie like blazes if she ain't too bored to talk anyhow.
What about Blake's room, Doc? I ain't had a chance
t' ask you, what with scramblin' three dozen eggs an'
little odds an' ends like that."

"I couldn't find anything," Walker answered. "If
he had slipped poison into Stires's food it's pretty un-
likely that he'd have been foolish enough to leave it
around, anyway. He had a small bottle of medicine
that he presented me with very seriously. Arsenic and
strychnine that his doctor had given him: a drop in a
glass of water before meals as a tonic. But it wasn't
that compound that killed Stires. There wasn't enough
in the bottle when it was full to hurt any one, even if
it was taken in a single dose. It's a bitter-tasting mess,
anyway. Stires couldn't have taken it without knowing

it,—and I didn't find any traces of strychnine. So that's that."

"Well," Asey got up. "I'll go get little Sunshine an' see what she's got to say about her powders."

"Don't let her bring that dog," I added.

Asey laughed. "I won't."

Walker paced up and down the floor. It was the first time that I'd really seen him in anything that resembled daylight and I looked at him more closely than I had heretofore.

His clothes, now a little mussed, were good in a quietly professional way. He had put on a pair of thick tortoise-shell rimmed glasses that gave him a studious expression. He was young, about thirty-five, I decided, and I wondered why he had chosen to bury himself in a small town. I asked him.

"Wanted a chance to rest and write a book," he said. "So far I've got along famously. No one ever really gets sick down here. Once in a while some one cuts a finger or gets indigestion from too much fried food and I have a few regulars with rheumatism. I guess it's true that Cape Codders don't die. They just dry up and blow away. Why, even with this hot-and-cold weather, there've been only two colds. Which reminds me that I should have gone to see one of them, Mary Gross, yesterday and didn't."

"Is she the old lady that makes candles up on the Truro road?"

"Yes. But she was all right Tuesday, when I saw her last, and if she hasn't taken to doctoring herself with what she calls 'yarbs,' she'll be all right," the doctor answered.

Asey entered with Desire Allerton in tow. She wore to-day an orange corduroy suit and her finger-nails were a beautiful tangerine. I couldn't help wondering if she bought her dresses to match her nail polish, or the other way around.

"What kind of powders did you buy Tuesday in Plymouth?" Asey asked.

"Powders? Oh! Yes. Headache powders."

"Take 'em reg'lar, or what?"

"The doctor on the boat prescribed them for me. I was sick coming over and he gave me the prescription so that I could have them if I needed them. I felt sick coming down in the car—I still hadn't got over that crossing—and so I bought them."

"Mind if we have a look at 'em?"

"If you want to; go get them. They're on the shelf in my bathroom. In a pink box with a label."

Asey promptly left. The girl lighted a cigarette and looked out over the bay. We were silent until Asey came back with the pink box and gave it to Walker. I watched interestedly as the latter opened up a small kit which he took from his large black bag, and set to work. He fiddled around with test tubes and burners. Then he turned to the girl.

"This is the prescription that the doctor on shipboard gave you? How many powders have you taken?"

"Yes. It's the same one. I've taken four."

"There are only six powders here. The label says there were a dozen."

She shrugged her shoulders.

"And you're sure you took four?"

"Yes. Why?"

"Then," Walker smiled, "I congratulate you on your resistance. The powder I've just tested is pure arsenic."

CHAPTER FIVE

"PROBLEM:" Asey remarked pensively, "if A's got twelve powders an' takes four, why should six be left behind? What happens to the other two? An' why should they be arsenic?"

"I don't know where the other two went," Desire said shortly. "Probably they only gave me ten."

"Why arsenic?" Asey repeated.

"Those powders aren't arsenic. You can't get arsenic wholesale at drug-stores without something more than a prescription for headache powders. You're trying to be funny."

"I'm not," Walker informed her. "I've seldom been more serious. If I had a guinea-pig here, I could soon prove to you that I'm not fooling. This powder is arsenic. Pure arsenic. When did you take the last one?"

"Before dinner last evening."

"See here, are you sure that this is the same box? Are you positive it's the one you bought?"

She glanced at it casually. "It's the same as far as I can see."

"Possibly you're telling the truth," Walker said, "but how you could have taken four of those powders and not died an unhappy death before now, I can't understand."

"Listen." She stood up. "I took four of those powders. They're not arsenic. No more than you are."

And even though I wanted to believe otherwise, it seemed to me that she was telling the truth.

"Miss Allerton, come here. Look."

He opened one of the white slips, showed her the contents. "Here. Take this magnifying-glass. Were your powders like that?"

She looked at him disgustedly. "I didn't examine the others through any microscope. What makes you think I'd know if they were different?"

"Well, you can look, anyway." He forced the glass on her.

"They seem the same to me," she said after a few seconds. "These look more like crystals and the others were more grainy, if you know what I mean. But I may be wrong. I couldn't tell for sure. If you'd not said that they were different, I'd probably not noticed a thing about them. But are these arsenic? Really?"

"Yes."

She shrugged. "I don't understand it at all. It's lucky for me that you found out about them. I was planning to take another right now. I'd probably have taken it by this time."

"How d'you 'count for all this?" Asey asked curiously.

"I don't know. I suppose that some one thought I'd

have a hard time explaining them if Uncle was found poisoned by arsenic."

"You think some one planted it on you?"

"How else?"

"Who you think did it?"

"Should I know?"

"Where was you sittin' last night while Stires was eatin' supper? You remember?"

"Yes. I was sitting next to Denny James. He was next to Uncle."

Asey nodded. "You can go back. Only I'd 'vise you to go easy on what you eat an' what you take in the line of med'cine."

"What are you letting her get off so easily for?" I asked after she had gone.

Asey grinned. "I got an idea an' I don't want her around for a little while. Miss Prue, which one of them men d'you s'pose would know about her? If any of 'em does?"

"John Kent. He's the only one who lives in Boston and he'd probably know more of the details than the others. But why?"

"I'll tell you later. I guess we'll get Kent."

John's face was very long when he came in. "How are you progressing?" he asked perfunctorily.

"As well," Walker said, "as can be expected in the circumstances."

John smiled dutifully.

"Have you found out anything? Wasn't there any clue in his clothes? A letter or anything like that?"

I shook my head. "Only some checks made out to cash," I said. "There don't seem to be any clues at all."

"I wonder," Asey asked him, "if you could tell us more about this red-headed niece?"

"Desire?"

"Uh-huh. What was Mr. Stires exactly? I mean, was he her guardian? Or what? Did he have c'ntrol of her money? D'you know anything about her? Miss Prue says she turned up all of a sudden like. D'you know why?"

"Well," John laced his fingers together, "well, Bert was her guardian. He told me all about the situation after he got word of Cass Allerton's will. You see, Desire's mother was Bert's half-sister. There'd always been more or less of a feud between the Allertons and the Stireses—it was because of Old Amariah Allerton's comment about Amanda Stires—no! It wasn't Amanda. It was Amelia. Amariah told some one that Amelia was a tippler——"

Asey coughed discreetly. "So the Stireses an' the Allertons wasn't on the best of terms——"

"Yes. And when Cass Allerton eloped with Lucia Hammond, Bert was very upset. He'd never cared for Cass Allerton anyway, and Cass never was fond of him. I'm sure I don't know why he had provisions made for Bert to look after the girl. Perhaps he felt that Bert was the only one he could trust with her, but on the other hand I have a definite suspicion that he wanted to annoy Bert. Probably he thought she would be a burden. That was rather in keeping with Cass's sense of humor."

"What about money an' all that?"

"Allerton, from what Bert told me, had gone through the greater part of his fortune, but there was still enough left for Desire to live on very comfortably, providing, of course, that she was not too extravagant. Bert was to look out for her money, and for her, too, until she became of age. That's not far off, only seven or eight months. Some of the money was to be kept in trust until she was twenty-five. At that time she was to have complete control of it."

"An' if Stires was to die?"

"That's the peculiar part of the situation. If Bert died, she was to have complete control of it anyway. Evidently there was no one else Cass wanted to supervise the girl's money."

"So that now the girl comes into p'session of everything?"

"Just so."

"Now, how about her comin' when she did?"

"I haven't asked her about it and Bert didn't tell me the reason, but he did say that he'd not expected her until much later. As I understood it, he had wired for her to come over at once after her father died and he got no answer at all. Then, after much cabling back and forth, it came out that she didn't want to come to America at all. She wanted to stay in France. Bert told her he thought it was best for her to come and that she more or less had no choice in the matter at all. I think he had some idea of putting her into a good school until she came of age, then letting her go to France or do whatever she wanted. He'd never seen her, never knew anything about her, so possibly you can imagine how he felt when she descended upon him. He'd expected a meek schoolgirl with pigtails down her back——"

"An' he got Desire," Asey laughed.

"Yes, he got Desire. I know that he had wired money for her passage and I thought that she was scheduled to turn up in a month or so. They'd come to some agreement about her arrival and stay here. Why she came so suddenly, however, I don't know. Bert was too excited at her appearance at this particular time to be very logical about anything. I don't know when I've seen him more upset."

"Humpf." Asey considered. "Well, I guess the time's 'bout ripe to get her back again in here."

Desire trailed in wearily.

"More arsenic?"

John looked puzzled and I explained about the powders.

"Nope. We ain't found no more arsenic, Miss Allerton. How come you got here so soon when you hadn't planned to come until later?"

She lighted a cigarette before answering.

"I changed my mind."

"Fem'nine priv'lege. Why didn't you let Stires know about it?"

"We'd agreed that I was to come before the first week of May. I understood that I could arrive on that date, or come earlier if I chose to do so."

"You know that you're in charge of all your money, now your uncle's dead?"

She hesitated. "Am I?"

"I should think," Asey remarked, "that you'd know better'n me about it. Didn't you know?"

"I suppose I did. But it slipped my mind."

"Did, did it? Well, it wouldn't of slipped mine."

She yawned. "Probably not. I'm not accustomed to thinking about business matters."

Asey screwed up his mouth. "How'd you get from the Grand Central to Times Square?"

"Shuttle," she said without any hesitation. Then she stopped short and looked at Asey. He grinned. Walker was smiling. John's eyebrows were arched.

It occurred to me that this, supposedly, was the girl's first trip to America, that she had never been out of France, or on a New York subway, in all her life.

"I mean," she recovered herself hurriedly, "I suppose that that's the way. Of course I wouldn't know."

"I wonder why you'd s'pose that," Asey mused. "I can see how you might know about where Grant's Tomb is, an' maybe you've heard tell about the Bat'ry or the Bow'ry, but it seems kind of queer that you should be so glib about the Shuttle. Don't get me wrong. I ain't accusin' you of nothin'. I just think it's kind of cur'ous, that's all."

"There's nothing curious about it." But I noticed that her voice was not so casual as it had been. "I have read guide-books about New York. And I have heard all about the city even though I have never been there."

"Have, have you? What for did you read guide-books about New York for? I should think that if you was plannin' to come to Boston, you'd of learned a few facts about that first. Like how to get from Copley Square to Havvad Square. I s'pose you know how to do that, too?"

"Of course I don't."

"M'yes. Of course not." Asey stroked his chin pensively. "I s'pose you learned that Brooklyn accent out of a guide-book, too?"

"What do you mean, Brooklyn accent? I don't know what you're talking about."

"I think," Asey said, "that you do. Now s'pose we quit beatin' around the bush an' get right down t' brass tacks. You just tell us the whole story."

"There's nothing to tell!"

"What do you mean, Asey, about a Brooklyn accent?" I asked. "I don't understand."

"Miss Allerton does. An' Miss Fible does, too. She asked me when we went over to get that oil stove if I didn't think the girl had an awful American way of speakin' for some one that's supposed to of lived in France all her life. The minute this girl opened her mouth I knew she hadn't got to talk the way she does just stayin' in Yurrup. 'Course, with all you Bostonians an' all your civ'lized ways of talkin' like you had a mouthful of hot oatmeal, it might not 'cur to you that any accent is any dif'rent from any other. What I mean is, you sort of took the way she talked as bein' natural on account of what she was s'posed to of been brought up in France."

"But how did you know?"

"How? I had a mate once that come from Brooklyn. He didn't just talk all day. He talked in his sleep. He was the greatest talker I ever had t' sit an' listen to. You sort of got used to the way he spoke after a while, but you couldn't ever forget it."

"You're being absurd," Desire said angrily. "I've never been to Brooklyn. I don't know anything about this Brooklyn accent. I tell you, I——"

"Yup. I know. I know. But you give yourself away, young lady, an' I don't think you're goin' to be able t' crawl out of it. Now, are you Desire Allerton, or ain't you?"

"Of course I am. You know it."

"Mr. Kent." Asey turned to John. "You knew this Allerton feller, an' you knew the girl's mother. Does this young woman favor either of 'em, would you say?"

"She hasn't the Allerton nose," John answered. "I noticed it at once when I first saw her. All the Allertons, moreover, were dark, very dark. The Hammonds were a tall family. Even the women were unusually tall. This girl is light, and she's short, comparatively speaking. Of course, that does not prove anything."

"I should say it didn't," Desire commented scornfully.

"I wonder," John said slowly, "if you ever heard your mother or your father speak of their cousin Edward Rowan? He used to be called Neddy, as a rule."

"Cousin Neddy? Of course I've heard of him."

John turned to Asey. "You caught her up, Asey, and I rather think that I've tripped her again. There wasn't any cousin Edward Rowan, called Neddy as a rule."

The girl bit her underlip until I thought it would bleed.

"Come," Asey urged her. "You're not Desire Allerton, an' you know it. An' we know it. Who are you, an' what you doin' on this party?"

She did not answer. Asey repeated his question, and still she remained silent.

"Not goin' to answer me?"

She shook her head, stubbed out her cigarette, got up from her chair and left the room.

"Whew!" Walker whistled softly. "Asey, I hand it to you for finding things out, but what're you going to do about her now?"

Asey pulled a plug of chewing tobacco from the pocket of his gray flannel shirt and bit off a hunk before answering. He was, I reflected, getting down to business.

"What c'n I do?" he answered thickly. "Can't do nothin'. 'F I had my way I'd turn her over an' give her a good spankin', but I can't do no such thing. I'll put her on file, I guess, till the phones get goin'. 'N' then I'll call up that drug-store in Plymouth an' see what she really got there, an' then I'll call up Stires's lawyers an' get the address of Desire Allerton an' call her an' see what I can see."

"Then you don't think she's really Desire Allerton?"

" 'Course she ain't. I don't know who she is an' what she was after, an' right now I can't find out. Anyway, we know she ain't who she said she was, b'cause she wouldn't of made them breaks about Cousin Thing-ummy an' the Shuttle."

"She must have been the one that did it," John said earnestly. "If those powders are arsenic,—well, what more proof do you need?"

"Quite a lot," Asey told him. "F'r one thing, Mr. Kent, you could understand why she might of killed

Stires if he was her uncle; but why should she kill him if he wasn't anything to her anyway, an' if she'd never laid eyes on him till the other day? If she was Desire Allerton, why then there'd be some motive for her killin' him. But if she ain't, an' it's sort of clear she ain't, I don't see for why she'd do it. 'Course, she wasn't settin' far from him last night. She had a chance to put arsenic in the food, I s'pose."

John shrugged. "I suppose you know best, Asey, but I'm certain that she's the one you're after. Do you want anything more of me?"

"That's all, I guess."

John glanced interestedly at the doctor's kit on his way to the door. "You seem to have a lot of paraphernalia, Doctor. This is rather rough on you, isn't it? I hope you've no patients who need your attention."

"Thank heaven, I haven't. At least I didn't have last night. As I told Miss Whitsby, old Mary Gross was the only person I should have seen and didn't, but I'm not worried about her."

"Say," Asey asked after he'd gone, "did you tell your housekeeper where you was goin' when I picked you up yest'day?"

"Mrs. Howes? Oh, yes. I told her. It wouldn't have mattered much if I hadn't. She'd have found out anyway. She was very upset because I wouldn't wait to put on a clean shirt to come over here. I rather wish now that I had."

"Asey," I asked, "what are you going to do?"

"Well, Miss Prue, I wouldn't be a one to say. There's Blake, now. No matter if he didn't have any incrim-'natin' arsenic lyin' around, just the samey, he brushed by me an' he could have dosed Stires's food. Here's this niece that ain't a niece that's got arsenic, an' she had a chance to put arsenic in his food, too. I kind of don't think Blake's to blame, yet I wouldn't say for sure. An' as for the girl, well, we're sort of at a dead end. She's screwed up her tongue an' she ain't goin' to talk. We can't third degree her. She ain't the sort. We just got to wait for that. I guess we'll—what's the matter, William?"

"Nothing, sir. My wife says she'll get lunch, sir, if you don't want to."

Asey thought a moment. "That's real kind of her, but maybe I'd better do the cookin'. No r'flection, you understand, William. I just think it might be better, an' then if anything's wrong, I'll be to blame an' not her."

William nodded relievedly. "Thank you, sir. We hoped you'd feel that way."

"Might as well start to work, then. Here, I'll leash your cat, Miss Prue."

And the three of us started into the dining-room.

"I think that the first thing we'll do after lunch," Asey said as he held open the door for me, "is to do a little sleuthin' around for arsenic. I don't reckon that we'll find any, but on the other hand you never can tell."

In the dining-room Denny James was walking around aimlessly.

"Anything the matter?" Asey asked.

"I'm waiting for William to bring me a glass of water. I've caught cold and Cary gave me a couple of cold pills."

"Pills?" Walker asked. "Why didn't you come to me?"

"Oh, you were busy and all that. Didn't want to bother you when you had all this business on your mind."

"Mind if we take a look at 'em?" Asey asked.

"Of course not. But why?"

"There's been a little trouble about some powders," I said, "and Asey wants to be on the safe side."

Denny laughed. "I guess these are all right, but here—take 'em if you want 'em."

The doctor took three little white pills and disappeared into the library. His face, when he finally came back, was a study.

"Nothing wrong, is there?" Denny asked.

The doctor swallowed. "Mr. James,—God Almighty, man, you'd better say a prayer of thanks! Those pills were arsenic!"

CHAPTER SIX

MR. HOBART'S PILLS

DENNY'S mouth moved but no words came out. "Arsenic?" he said feebly at last. "Arsenic?"

"Yes."

"Listen here," Asey said. "Did you ask Hobart for cold pills, or did he offer to give 'em to you?"

"Why—I—let me see. I said that my throat was beginning to tickle and that I wished that I'd something to take so that I'd not get a cold. He said he had some pills his doctor had given him and that he'd give me some if I wanted 'em. He went up-stairs and got them and—well, that's all there is to it."

Asey nodded slowly.

"What are you going to do about it?" Denny asked. "It's incredible that Cary'd do anything like this—I'm sure it's all a mistake. It must be."

"Mistake 'r not, it's lucky for you, Mr. James, that we popped into this room when we did." He jerked his head toward William, who had just come in. He carried a glass of water on a small tray. "Took you a long time to get that water, William."

"Yes, sir. There's no more water, sir."

"How come? Tank empty?"

"Yes, Mr. Mayo. I thought there was a reserve tank, but Tom and Kelley say that's all used up too.

I'm sorry I took so much time, Mr. James. This is White Rock. We've got plenty of that and ginger ale and all in the storeroom."

"I see." Asey grinned. "Ain't goin' to be able t' wash your faces, I cal'late. Well, William, I'll mosey along an' get some lunch."

"Asey Mayo! Do you think that we could eat! That we *would* eat? I shan't dare touch a thing. Not until we get out of this place."

"Be reasn'ble, Miss Prue. You can eat boiled eggs, I s'pose; only if they ain't no water, you'll have to eat 'em raw. I'll guarantee that I'll lock myself up in the kitchen while I cook, an' I'll use canned things that ain't never been opened. They's no use goin' into this business of the pills right now. Fine thing about all this snowed-up business is that we don't have to hurry. Folks is goin' to be right where we can find them any time attall."

"But aren't you going to ask Hobart about the pills?"

"Sure. Only I want to get those folks fed first. I want to have a little time to think, too. Got a lot to think about. Doc, will you keep an eye on this Hobart? Keep an eye on all of 'em, for that matter. I think it kind of might be better if I let you eat one at a time in the kitchen, only I s'pose it won't do no good to get folks more upset than they are right now."

Lunch was a very sketchy affair. June and Asey alone seemed to have any appetite. Rowena confined herself to a box of English biscuits which she had taken from the storeroom. She opened the countless layers of tin and tin-foil herself and kept an eagle eye on the box while she ate. She was, apparently, taking no chances.

After we were through, Asey asked Hobart and Denny to come into the library. Walker and I trailed along after them.

"Now," Asey said after we were all seated as near the fireplace as we could manage, "now, Mr. Hobart, I'd like to ask you some questions about them pills you give Mr. James."

"What's the matter with them?" Hobart asked instantly.

"Have you got 'em with you?" Asey ignored his question.

Hobart drew a small bottle from his coat pocket.

"Here they are if you want them. My doctor gave them to me a few weeks ago. I'm susceptible to colds and they're the most efficient things I've ever found."

Denny winced at the word efficient. Asey took the bottle and handed it over to Walker, who set to work again with his kit.

"What's he doing that for?" Hobart demanded. "Those pills are all right. I took one myself this morning."

"Might have been all right then," Asey informed him, "but the ones you give Mr. James was arsenic."

"Nonsense!"

"No nonsense about it," Denny said. "I was stand-ing there, waiting to take 'em, and the doctor analyzed 'em and they were arsenic. And in a few minutes, I'd have taken them———"

"See here," Hobart said coldly. "You ought to know better, Denny, than to say things like that. The pills I gave you were perfectly all right. That is, they were all right when I gave them to you. What you might have done to them afterward, of course———"

"See here yourself," Denny replied hotly. "If you're insinuating that I substituted what the doctor found———"

"Why not? Aren't you insinuating that I tried to kill you? Mayo, those pills I gave him were all right. And if you've found out otherwise, there's only one explanation. He changed them—and he's trying to throw suspicion on me. I didn't offer him the pills anyway. He asked for them."

"I did not!" Denny's round face was very pink. "I did nothing of the kind. I said I was beginning to catch a cold and you practically forced 'em on me. You know you did."

Hobart got up from his chair and banged his fist emphatically on the table. Ginger jumped at the noise.

"That's a lie! You wanted to get those pills from me—then you changed 'em—and then you gave them to the doctor and told him I'd given them to you! You wanted to get me into trouble!"

"I didn't do anything of the sort! I don't say you had anything to do with the arsenic—the fact remains that if I'd taken your damn pills I'd have been dead as a door-knob by now and——"

"Round one," Asey interrupted wearily, "is over. Will you two please quit actin' like a couple of ten-year-olds an' keep quiet? Mr. Hobart, if you've finished your wranglin' bout, how was Mr. Stires when you left him last night?"

"Perfectly well."

"Did he tell you where he'd been Tuesday an' yest'-day?"

"No. I didn't ask him. Didn't he tell any one, any of you?"

"He did not. An' you, if I r'call rightly, was the one that set up such a hullabaloo when Stires didn't turn up when you thought he ought to. Seems funny you didn't ask him what kept him."

"Well, I didn't."

"Hm. Yes. You got somethin', Doc?"

"Yes. Look here, Asey, these pills are all right, except for one that was on top. That's a different shape and size from the rest—it's identical with the ones Mr. James had."

"You're crazy," Hobart said angrily. "If a pill in that bottle was arsenic, you put it there. I tell you, this thing has gone far enough! If John Kent—if any of you—had had sufficient common sense to get the police when I wanted you to get them, none of this would have happened anyway." He looked contemptuously at Asey. "You've got to get some one, I suppose. You've got it all figured out. I was the last one that saw Stires last night, so I'm the man you're after. You haven't any proof, so you get Denny to take those pills, then you plant another. I see! Well, have it your own way. The minute I can get out from this place, I'll——"

"I don't think," Asey said softly, "that you will do anything at all. An' right now, mister, you'll do what I say you'll do an' nothin' else. You seem pretty ready to put blame on top of other people. Maybe it wouldn't of been so funny if you'd took that top pill yourself. Ever consider that?"

Hobart looked startled. "Why, I——"

"Yup. Just so. Just so. Now, s'pose, if you didn't know all about this arsenic, you just thank the doc prettylike for savin' you from an early grave."

"Why—uh——"

"Thank him," Asey repeated firmly, "an' 'pologize to Miss Prue for actin' like a fo'mast hand."

"I'm sorry, Miss Whitsby. Er—thank you, Doctor."

"Now," Asey said serenely, "what was your business with Stires that you worried about so over?"

"Why, it was—er——"

"Don't say it's not important," Denny James interrupted, "because you spent hours telling us how important it was when Stires didn't turn up."

Asey looked at him. Denny subsided.

"Well," Hobart said, "if you must know all about it, I presume you must. I really don't see that it has any bearing on anything that you'd need. Bert was the head of a shingle company, as you may know. I'm in the lumber business. In the course of the last twenty-odd years we have together put through several deals which were of mutual benefit. There was a company here in New England which I wanted to get control of. I knew it was pretty much on the rocks, and I knew, furthermore, that if it became known that I wanted it, there'd be a great deal of haggling about the price. Bert had had dealings with the concern and he thought that he could help me out. We were to talk over the final details Tuesday. I got in early that morning. Everything was practically arranged. Then this niece turned up and there was trouble at the factory. Bert called me at the Club and told me that he'd look after things and for me to come down with Denny in his car as had been planned. When he didn't show up, I was naturally worried. As it turned out, though, he made a much better deal than I'd anticipated."

"When I suggested that he might of double-crossed you," Asey said, "was I right? I mean, could he have got his finger in the pie?"

"He could have, but he didn't. He got hold of Newell, the head of the company, and Newell was so glad to have an offer that he snapped it up."

"Feller know Stires was actin' for you?"

"Yes. Bert told him that morning, but it didn't seem to make any difference."

"I see." Asey put a log on the fire. "Then you let Stires go ahead an' do your business for you an' you didn't see him at all?"

"Why——"

"You must have seen him," Denny broke in calmly. "Where'd you get all that list of stuff we bought on the way down if you didn't see him?"

"I didn't say I didn't," Hobart retorted. "I wish, Denny, that you'd keep out of this. Asey, is there any need for him to be here?"

"I sort of like to have him around," Asey said. "So you saw Stires Tuesday mornin'?"

"Yes. After he called me at the Club, I took a cab and went over to his house for a few minutes. He said he had a list of things he was intending to get, but that it might be better for me to get them when Denny and I came. We didn't see each other very long. I just gave him my final figures and he gave me a list of things."

"What was this list?" Asey asked.

Denny pulled a wallet from his inside pocket and gave Asey a slip of paper without answering.

"Hm. Magazines, candy, cigarettes, lobsters, flash-lights, candles, flowers, at greenhouse. I see. I s'pose, Mr. Hobart, that you can check up on all this business Stires did for you?"

"Certainly. You could call Newell, of the Newell-Howard Company, or the manager of Stires's factory."

"You forget that the phones ain't workin'," Asey said.

Hobart shrugged. Denny took a pen from his pocket and wrote hurriedly on a piece of paper which he passed to me. I read it and smiled. It said, "Do you suppose Asey would let me speak?"

"Denny wants to say something," I told Asey.

"Say away."

"Thank you. I only thought that probably Vic would know about that company. I don't, because I don't know much about business anyway, but Vic knows about everything in the way of business. Perhaps he could say offhand what that company was worth."

"Bound to do me little favors, aren't you?" Hobart asked. "I don't see, Mayo, why Vic should know about this company. It's scarcely his field."

"Got 'ny objections to our askin' him?"

"Well, no."

"What was your final price?"

Hobart looked at Denny, then rather deliberately took a card from his pocket and wrote some figures on it. Asey took the card and whistled softly.

"Ho. Some money. Doc, will you get Blake?"

Denny took back the scrap of paper he had given me.

"What do you think of him?" he scrawled on it.

"I think he's guilty as hell."

"Remember," I wrote back, "that if he says the pills he gave you were all right and that you substituted the arsenic ones, you're in the same fix."

He made a face, but it was clear that the suggestion bothered him.

"Now," Asey said when Blake came back, "now, Mr. Blake, d'you know of a company called the—the Newell-Howard Company?"

"Yes. Indeed yes. I own quite a bit of stock in it. So did Bert."

"What?" Hobart fairly leaped from his chair. "Bert was a shareholder?"

"Yes, indeed. I'd say that between the two of us, we held thirty or forty per cent. of the stock. Why?"

"See here, Vic. Did you know that he was planning to sell—or bargain for the company—for some one?"

"Well, yes. In a way. I saw Newell a few weeks ago. He said that Bert had told him he'd got a buyer for the company and that if all went well, he and I would make up our losses. Why? You seem pretty excited."

"Excited! Good God, Vic, I'm the one who was taking over the company!"

Blake smiled. "How much?"

"Wait up." Asey gave Blake a paper and a pencil. "This ain't a game of questions an' answers. You write down what you think that comp'ny was worth."

Blake thought a moment, then wrote. "That's not accurate, Asey, but I don't think that's a bad offhand estimate. It's about what Newell figured on."

Asey compared the paper with the one Hobart had given him.

"Well?" Hobart demanded.

"Just about two hundred thousand dollars' dif'rence," Asey said cheerfully. "Can you explain that, Mr. Hobart?"

Hobart was too overcome to speak. I doubt if I've ever seen an angrier man. "Bert!" He exploded. "He—he was paying me back for——"

"For what?"

Hobart didn't answer.

"For that little affair about the Lassiter Company," Blake said quietly, swinging his glasses. "I don't think you have anything to say, Hobart. I think it's about quits. But I don't see why you made such a mistake in the first place."

"I honestly didn't know Bert was a shareholder. And I thought I had the thing lined up pretty well. I'd not gone into the matter myself. One of my men did."

"And you didn't know about this last night?" Asey asked. "Stires didn't tell you that he was doin' a little payback after he told you the price? He didn't let on that it was anything out of the ordinary?"

"No."

"But if you'd found out then," Asey went on, "what would of happened? Would you of got as mad as you just got? Would you have done anything about it? Would you of——"

"Have killed him? Certainly not. I'd probably have been angry at the moment, but as Vic says, I suppose that I deserve it."

"Repentant all of a sudden," Asey remarked. "Mr. Hobart, listen to me. You done Stires some dirt. Stires paid you back. You saw Stires after the rest of us saw him last night. To-day you give Denny James some pills. They're arsenic. They's another arsenic pill in the bottle that you got with you. Stires has double-crossed you in a nice business way, probably like you done him. Now, I ain't aimin' to accuse you, but it kind of seems to me like you was in a tough spot. You had a reason for killin' Stires, Hobart. That's more'n any one else has had so far. An' you can't say you didn't have no poison, b'cause you got it. An' you sure had every chance for usin' it."

I shall make no attempt to reproduce Hobart's tirade in reply to that.

For one thing, I was brought up in the days when *darn* was considered violent and uncouth for a lady to use. Of course, after my niece's first term in col-

lege, I became fairly well acquainted with a number
of expressions whose place I had hitherto considered
more or less confined to the stables and the dockyards.
But Betsey and her contemporaries swore cheerfully
and casually; they never meant much by it. Then,
too, Hobart used words which I never knew existed.
Their meaning, however, was painfully clear.

Boiled down, in simple Anglo-Saxon, Hobart had
no use for Asey, Asey's family, Asey's theories, Asey's
methods or his presence. He had, in fact, no use for
any of us. The doctor was a liar, Denny was a double-
crosser, Blake was another tool in the mammoth plot
afoot to convict him, Hobart, of Adelbert's murder.

Denny made a motion toward him, but Asey shook
his head. When Hobart glanced at me, however, Asey
stopped him short.

"That'll be about all from you for one good while,
mister."

"If I want to talk," Hobart blustered, "I'll talk.
And no two-for-a-cent hayseed like you is going to
stop me. I——"

With a sudden motion Asey flipped a bandanna
handkerchief out of his pocket, and before Hobart
knew what he was doing Asey had gagged him very
neatly.

The doctor obligingly pinioned his hands.

"There's six-inch adhesive in my bag," he suggested. "Do his hands up nicely."

Denny took out the long tin of tape, I helped him remove the covering, and Hobart's wrists were presently lashed together with the stickiest tape I ever handled. Asey wound it around and around.

"Now, Mr. Hobart," he said cheerfully, "you brought this all on yourself. If you'd of learned to keep your mouth closed, you'd of been all right. After that little speech of yours, you deserve to be gagged, an' to keep your gag in, we got to tie your hands. You can walk around, if you want to, but, by gorry, we won't have none of your talk."

I have never seen an angry lion, but Hobart's eyes approximated my idea of one.

"Now," Asey said, "we'll——"

The sound of shattering glass stopped him.

We looked toward the window. The snow had drifted up to all but the top row of small panes. Some one was hurling snowballs at those.

Asey ran to the window, undid the catch and started to force the top of the window down. The doctor picked up the coal shovel, and standing on a chair, scraped snow away until the window was half-open.

"For mercy's sakes," Phrone's voice howled shrilly, "for mercy's sakes won't some one let me in? Did you s'pose that I was goin' to stay all soul alone in that house in a blizzard? Let me in!"

CHAPTER SEVEN

AND STILL MORE ARSENIC

It was fifteen minutes before sufficient snow was scraped away for her to be hoisted throught the window. She was covered with snow and wringing wet.

"How'd you get here?" Asey asked.

"How'd you think I got here? I didn't fly, that's one sure thing! No, sir, I walked on my two feet, that's how. I've been on my way for a good hour an' a half. I don't mind stayin' alone, but I'm not goin' to be snowed up alone. No, sir!"

"But how'd you get through the drifts?"

"Ain't hardly no snow at all on the side of the hill from Miss Fible's down here. Ain't nowhere near so bad at her house as 'tis here. I been around to all your windows an' hollered 'cept the back ones. They're all drifted up like your doors. I went up to the second story at Miss Rena's an' took the glasses to see how the town was. The roads is all drifted, so far's I could see, an' I looked over to Lem Hill's, where they keep the snow-plow an' I couldn't see's they'd got it out. Seemed like 'twas snowed up. I think all the wires is down from the railroad tracks, too. Oh, Asey Mayo, you go git some rub' boots an' go out the window an' you'll find an oil can. I sort of figgered you'd run out of kerosene by now."

"You carried an oil can with you?"

"Matter of fact, I didn't carry it much. I rolled it down the hill. Rolled real easy, it did. Anyway, it's most full an' I guess you'll need it."

"I guess we will. Thank you kindly, Phrone. Say, Miss Prue, hadn't you better take her up an' git her into some dry clothes?"

"I certainly had," I said. "Come along, Phrone."

"What's the matter with that man?" She asked, pointing her angular forefinger toward Hobart. "What you got him all done up like that for?"

"Come along," I said, "and I'll tell you."

Out in the hallway we met Rowena.

"Phrone, you treasure! I've been wishing for you. Prue, now I can eat!"

"What do you mean, you can eat?"

"Phrone can cook for you and me—and the rest, for that matter. You will, won't you, Phrone?"

"Sure I'll cook. But what's the matter with Stires's cook? What's the matter around here anyway? An' what's Asey Mayo an' the doctor doin' here?"

Briefly, Rowena told her. "For the rest, you'll have to ask Miss Whitsby," she concluded somewhat bitterly. "She's in, as one of the Mantinis used to say, on the ground floor."

"Sakes alive," Phrone said, "Stires killed? My goodness me! Wait until the town hears of this! They was countin' on his bringin' so much money from taxes that the rate'd go down. Who done it?"

"We're trying to find out," I said. "Rena, I've got to go down-stairs. In the meantime, don't for the love of heaven, take any medicine or pills or anything."

"So that's the way it is," Rowena said. "I begin to see. You needn't worry, Prue. I wouldn't even drink a glass of water. There isn't any water anyway, I hear. What's all this going-on with Hobart?"

"I'll tell you later," I said, and went down-stairs.

In the game-room June was blandly sitting guard over Hobart. Desire sat in a corner, aimlessly playing solitaire. Kent and Blake were at the chess table.

"Where are the rest?" I asked June in a low voice.

"Denny's superintending William and Tom in the library. They're trying to repair that broken window with cardboard and brown paper. Asey and the doctor are hunting the house for arsenic. Say, Snoodles," he finished in a whisper, "what's the matter with the girl?"

"Why?"

"She hasn't spoken a word for hours. Can't get her to talk. What happened?"

"Lots of things. I'll tell you later."

John looked up from the chess-board. "Hullo, Prue. Can't we entertain you? How about some bridge?"

I shook my head. "I couldn't concentrate. How can you two play chess?"

Blake looked at me and smiled. "I can't. John, you've got me. See——" He pointed with his finger. "One, two, three. That's enough of that. What do you think of Miss Fible's work?" He nodded toward Rowena's stand on which the plasteline was already beginning to take some form.

"She's progressing, isn't she?"

"The woman works like chain lightning. I've never seen anything to compare with it. D'you suppose I could take some of that stuff and play with it? I've always had a feeling that I'd like to model, myself."

"Every one does," Rowena said, as she came down. "Even Mantini made elephants and cats while he watched me work. Here," she passed over a little roll of clay, "go ahead and play. It smells and it'll get your finger-nails full of dirt, but it's fun. Want some, John?"

And soon we were all pinching and pulling little messes of clay.

"See," Blake said, holding up a triangular gob. "See. Isn't that good?"

"What is it?" June asked. "The eternal triangle?"

"Nothing of the sort. It's a giraffe."

Rowena laughed. "Go sit in your model's chair, Epstein, and here—take his wire if you're going in for giraffes. I'd say it looked more like an ostrich. Giraffes have four legs."

"So they do. John, come over here.. I'll do a head of you in the modern style."

"Bunch of kindergarteners," June said. "What would the papers say of you now, Dad?"

"I neither know nor care," Blake replied cheerfully. "But I never had a better time."

"Come on and play games with me, Snoodles," June urged. "I'm getting pretty tired of sitting still."

I shook my head. "No. I've just remembered Ginger. Does any one know where he is?"

"Denny's got him up-stairs."

In the library William and Tom had just finished patching up the broken window.

"Isn't that a fine job?" Denny asked proudly.

"It would have been better," I said, "if you'd taken out the whole pane instead of patching over it."

"And I thought," Denny said mournfully, "that we were clever not to have taken it out. Shall we do it all over again?"

"Don't be silly. There's still a draft, though; William, get some burlap or some old cloths and put over it. That should do the trick."

William nodded, and he and Tom left.

"I'll take Ginger," I said, "and thanks for looking after him. Did Asey say where he was going first?"

"No. Prue, do you have to go chasing that man?"

"I'm not chasing him," I retorted indignantly. "He asked me to help him and I'm trying to help."

"And you're that tickled to have a finger in the pie that you can't sit still two minutes. Look here, Prue, let Asey be for the minute. I want to talk to you. You haven't given me a chance since you came."

"You're exact," I commented.

"What? Exact about what?"

"You want to talk 'to' me. Not with me. Go ahead. Only do hurry."

"Prue, will you stop being like that? I know you too well to be impressed by your bark. Why didn't you answer my last cable?"

"The last?"

"All right. Be vague. The cable I sent you from Italy when your niece married last fall. Why didn't you answer it?"

"Didn't I?"

"You know damn well you didn't. You——"

"Don't get like Cary Hobart," I said. "If I didn't answer that cable, I suppose it was because it—well, it slipped my mind. I'd have answered it eventually. Really. But you know what a bustle and hubbub there always is at weddings——"

"You," Denny interrupted coldly, "have certainly never given me any opportunity to know anything of the sort. Now, Prue, twenty-seven years ago——"

"Denny, must you delve into the past?" Mentally I wondered why it is that men must always go back to the beginnings of things. I suppose it's much the same theory that prompts a firm to reassure you that it has been established "Since 1776."

"I not only must," Denny said, "but I am. Now——"

June drifted in the door. "Snoodles, John says for you two to come and have some bridge. Or are you busy?"

"Not at all," I said gratefully.

"She is busy," Denny said firmly. "Run along, June."

"But she said——"

Denny took him by the elbow and propelled him to the door. "Go away. Go somewhere else." He came back to the fire. "Now——"

"D'you think that was a very polite way of treating him?"

"No. Neither was it polite for him to come bursting in here. Twenty-seven years ago, Prue, you said you couldn't marry me because you had to look after your father. After he died, you had to look after your niece. The minute I heard she was getting married, I cabled you from Rome, just the same way I've cabled you anyway every Christmas. Now, why didn't you answer?"

"I was busy. Really, Denny, it was sweet of you, and I did intend to do something about it, but I just never seemed to get the time."

"Of course," Denny said acidly, "Betsey was married about five months ago. Why——"

William knocked and came in carrying a piece of burlap. Denny looked at me disgustedly.

I superintended putting the burlap into place, then Phrone arrived on the scene.

"Asey says I'm to cook dinner," she announced, "an' he says that butler person will set a table somewhere. What'll I have for dinner? How long's Asey Mayo been callin' supper 'dinner' anyway?"

"I couldn't tell you that," I said. "I suppose he just picked it up. I'll go along with you, Phrone, and we'll see what we can find in the storeroom."

At dinner the doctor and Asey released Hobart, having secured his promise that there would be no more outbursts. He did not, in fact, say a word, and what with the girl as silent as an old-fashioned movie, the meal was not merry. Phrone came in from the kitchen and ate with us—and she and Asey bore most of the brunt of the table talk.

"I been thinkin'," she announced, "that maybe we could get into touch with town after all."

"How?" John Kent demanded.

"Well, you can't see the flag-pole here from town, but you can see Miss Fible's. I been thinkin' that we could rig up some sort of distress flag an' hoist it up, b'cause if I got over here, one of you men ought to be able to git back. If you couldn't use the flag-pole, you could put it out the upper window an' I should think that some one would see it."

Asey nodded. "That'd be all right. I sort of had some notion of doin' that myself. But how'd any one git out here?"

"Boat."

"By gorry," Asey said, "I never thought of that. Wonder if Stires had any signal flags. You know, William?"

"I don't think so, sir."

"I've got some," Rowena announced. "Grandfather Fible's flags are all up in my attic somewhere. But I wouldn't know one from the other."

"I would," Asey said, "an' I bet they's plenty uptown that would if they only saw 'em. We'll do that to-morrow mornin'."

"What are you going to do now?" Blake asked.

"Oh, we're meanderin' around."

And they meandered around until well after midnight when Asey called me into the library. The doctor, in shirt-sleeves, was clearing up his collection of bottles and tubes. In the dim candlelight he looked like some medieval alchemist.

"We've come," Asey said, "to a place that strikes me as bein' plumb funny."

"You haven't found more arsenic?"

"But ain't we!"

"Where?"

"Where?" the doctor repeated with a laugh. "Miss Prue, I've reached a state where I refuse to be amazed."

"I don't think," Asey added, "that there's anything left to find out but what this whole bunch is a pack of arsenic eaters."

"What do you mean, arsenic eaters?"

"People eat arsenic," Walker said. "Take it like a drug. Say it's a tonic. They take small amounts, not enough to do them any harm, then they enlarge the dose. You heard Blake say that he took arsenic and strychnine. Well, he takes very small doses. But he could enlarge the dose until the amount he could take would be sufficient to make another man, who wasn't used to it, extremely ill. Same way with arsenic eaters. Way back in the middle of the last century they found out that there were parts of Hungary and Styria where the peasants ate five or six grains of arsenic every day, and it didn't hurt 'em. It's perfectly possible for a man to make himself immune to arsenic that way. They say the Borgias did it. And the Emperor Justinian," he concluded in the precise tones of a lecturer, "was supposed to eat enough arsenic every morning to kill ten normal men. Believe it or not. And if you should ask me, I'd say that the guests in this house are a bunch of emperors."

"Tell me what you've found out!"

"Okay, Miss Prue. There was arsenic in the girl's powders. There was arsenic in Hobart's pills. There was arsenic in Blake's medicine, though that doesn't amount to much."

"I know all that," I said impatiently, "but what else?"

"Well," Asey drawled, "there was arsenic in the bottle that held Miss Fible's aspirin. There was a box in your suitcase labeled 'Headache'—an' that had arsenic in it too."

"But I never had any such box! Asey, where did it come from? Who put it there?"

"Should," Asey demanded, "should I know? I don't. Then Kent had a tin box of bicarb'nate of soda. That was arsenic."

"Asey!"

"An'," Asey continued, "this youngster June had a kit full of dyes an' things. I didn't know what they was but the doc says it was somethin' to do with dyes you put in clothes an' cloth an' all, an' we opened that up. They was a little bottle all labeled 'arsenic' in that, an' there was 'nough in that to do away with the bunch of us real easy."

"But, Asey!"

"Uh-huh. 'Tis kind of funny, ain't it? Only people ain't got no arsenic around is the hired help an' Denny James. An' for all we know the hired help may of got some out in the rooms over the g'rage."

"You can call it funny," I said, "but I—well, I don't know what to call it."

"I'll admit," Asey said gravely, "that it might not of been so funny if any one'd taken any of it, like

James an' those pills, an' Miss Fible an' her aspirin. But there you are. Laws of somethin' or other should prove that Denny James was guilty b'cause he didn't have any, an' law of somethin' else ought to prove that he isn't guilty b'cause he didn't have any. You can take your choice."

"But how did all this arsenic get about?"

"Planted," Asey said succinctly.

"But how? And what for?"

"Well, it was sort of dumb luck that the doc looked Stires over careful enough so as to think that there was somethin' funny about the way he died. It was sort of planned to look like it was a natural death, only the feller got fooled. We found out it was arsenic poisonin'. What then? He knew we'd go huntin' for arsenic, an' he put arsenic around for us to find. If he'd only put it on the girl, say, instead of scatterin' it around wholesale, it'd of been easier for us. But I sort of got it figgered out that he didn't want no one in partic'lar to be found out. That's why he planted it on every one."

"But can't you find out who did the planting?"

"How? Mrs. Boles's been in the bedrooms, makin' beds an' all. Every one's been in their rooms. No one's seen any one. You can't get no footprints in a case like this—not now—even if they'd do any good. There wasn't any finger-prints on anything—tins'd all been wiped off. We can't find out who planted it.

Even s'posin' we'd found a cuff link or a collar button lyin' around, it'd only prob'ly be another plant. We can't prove nothin'."

"But it's diabolical!"

"I guess 'tis. Feller did the plantin' didn't give one hang in hades what happened. He knows he's pretty well covered up. We can't trace this arsenic—not with these fellers here that trip around all over the globe. We don't know how long it was planned, how long this feller collected arsenic, as you might say. Prob'ly he didn't buy it himself—all these fellers has got servants around to do things for 'em. Yup, it kind of looks like we was stuck."

"But isn't there anything you can do?"

"What? Take it like this, Miss Prue, as if you was on the outside lookin' in. When you come right down to it, almost anybody had the chance to put arsenic in Stires's food. Every one was sort of excited an' bustlin' around last night. 'Course, Blake an' Hobart sort of had better chances than the others, but you can't get around the fact that they had chances too. Far's we know right now, Hobart's the only one that had a motive, but on the other hand, maybe Hobart's tellin' us the truth. Maybe he didn't know about how he was gettin' gypped by Stires. The girl business,— well, that's funny. She ain't who she was s'posed to be, but 'slong's she won't open her peep, well, that's that. We can do more about her when phones come on again. But as far as the arsenic's concerned, well, we're sort of in the same p'sition as the cat that got into a dog fight."

"What's that?"

"Up a tree, Miss Prue. Up a nice tall tree."

CHAPTER EIGHT

MR. JAMES FINDS A KEY

SOMEWHAT dejectedly, I picked up Ginger and went off to bed.

Rowena was still very much awake, and feeling that she rather deserved to know, I told her about her aspirin.

"My God!" Rowena's eyes bulged, and she got more expression into those two words than I had ever heard before. "My God! My God! And me with a headache! My aspirin? *My* aspirin? Prue, did I come from that gangster's palatial den to the peace and quiet of Cape Cod to be confronted with a murder and arsenic in my aspirin?"

"Apparently," I said, "you did. But you've no one but yourself to blame. It's all your fault that we embarked on this adventure. I, if you recall, had no intention of doing anything of the sort. I set out Tuesday morning to buy a spool of orange silk. I'm sorry I didn't get it. I have a horrid feeling that I may never get it at all, now." I told her about the rest of the arsenic that had been found, and got her caught up, in general, with all that she had missed.

"Then every one's in the same fix? What's Asey going to do? When do you suppose the arsenic was planted?"

"Some time after the doctor announced that Stires was poisoned by arsenic and the time they found it last night. Don't talk any more about it, Rena. I've had enough for one day. I'm miserably cold and terribly sleepy and I'm scared out of my wits."

"So'm I. But I haven't even the courage to go to sleep. Prue, I'm going to barricade that door. Oh, I know it's locked. But with a murderer like this one around, I have no faith in locks." And she got out of bed and proceeded to put three chairs and a table in front of the door. Her last move was to take two empty tumblers from the bathroom and put them by the side of her bed.

"What are those for?"

"So that if any one starts to come in or if I begin to feel as though I were poisoned, I can throw one at the window and make a noise. Prue, I don't see how any one could have gone about this house and left arsenic everywhere without any one seeing him. It seems to me that Asey should be able to find some clue."

"He says that if he did, who would be able to tell but what it was planted, too? Did you notice any one wandering around this morning after breakfast?"

She shook her head. "No. No one in particular. Every one was restless and jumpy and more or less in and out. But I didn't think that any one could really enter a room and not leave any traces."

"Well," I said sleepily, "how many people would you diagnose had been into this room, besides you and me and Mrs. Boles? You never can really tell if any one's been in a room or in a certain place unless something you left in a definite spot has been tampered with. At least, I can't. I'd know in a minute if any one had touched my desk or my books at home, because I've kept things in the same way and the same place for years. Same way with my brush and comb. I always leave them at a certain angle on my dressing-table. But even if I noticed that they'd been moved, it wouldn't mean much."

"I suppose not." Rowena got out of bed, and picked up the candle. "But you've given me an idea."

"What's that?"

This morning just before breakfast I took some things out of my suitcase. There was a bottle of ink, you know, that funny kind of bottle that's supposed not to spill. With a screw top. I started to make a note about a telegram I wanted to send to-day, and found I didn't have any ink in my pen, so I opened the bottle. I never remember to put the tops back on ink bottles, and it just occurred to me that it was screwed on tight now."

"Is it?"

"Yes. Screwed on tighter than I'd ever screw it."

"But that probably means that Mrs. Boles noticed it and feared for the table cover."

"I don't think so. I was up here after she'd made the beds and the stopper was still off. I thought of putting it on at the time, but you know how those things are. You just never get around to doing them, somehow."

"Then you think that the person who fooled around our room here put the cover on your ink bottle?"

"If you didn't, who else did but that person?"

"But where does it get us, even if all our suppositions are true?"

"Easy," Rowena said. "This person is just one of those people who can't help putting the covers on ink bottles. It's as plain as the nose on your face. Don't you know how some people are always going around emptying ash-trays so they won't spill over and dirty things, and sneaking around putting the covers on ink bottles so that the ink won't spill? It's the same type that does both those things."

"You're crazy," I said with a yawn.

"No. Prue, I have an idea!"

"Don't tell me. Please, please, Rena, don't tell me. I followed an idea of yours Tuesday."

"No. But listen. All we've got to do is to put an ink bottle on the edge of a table down-stairs and take the stopper out, and then wait and see who dashes to it and puts the stopper back. See? Then you'll be sure that the person who does that is the one who put mine back on, and he's the person who did the planting and the one who did the planting is the one who killed Bert. There," she finished complacently. "That's sensible, isn't it?"

"Maybe," I said. "But I wish you'd let me go to sleep. I don't want to, but I feel I should."

"I know I'm a nuisance, but you must remember that you've been roistering around all day finding out things and I've been playing with a lump of sticky clay. Somehow the whole affair seemed remote until to-night. If a person would put arsenic in my aspirin, he wouldn't hesitate at a knife or a boa constrictor. At least, there's something material about all that, but poison is so—so elusive, somehow. I tell you, Prue, I'm a nervous wreck. I've some allonal pills in my hand-bag and I'd take one if I weren't so certain that there was some fiendish poison lurking in it. I'm beginning to feel like a guest at a Borgia dinner party."

"Remember," I said, smiling in spite of myself, "that there are two of us here, and I don't think, with Asey and the doctor in the house, that we need be awfully fearful. It's just the same theory I have about lightning. I don't like it much, but if it strikes you, you'll never live to tell the tale, and if it doesn't, it doesn't. If some one's going to kill us, there's not really a lot we can do about it at this point. We're as safe as we can be."

"I know," Rowena said as she blew out the candle,

"I know. Like the poor benighted Hindoo who does the best he kin'doo, and when he something or other— what is that rhyme? Anyway, he has to make his skindoo. We've just got to make our skindoo, too, I suppose. You can be blasé about it if you want to, but I'm scared stiff right now."

And, actually, I was too. I was considerably relieved to find myself whole and hale and hearty in the morning.

Down-stairs there was rejoicing, for in some unknown way, the electricity had been restored again; we had heat, light, water—and the electric stoves were going.

"Darn lucky," Asey said cheerfully. "That means the phone should get going soon. An' we didn't have a drop of kerosene left in the place—an' I don't think that there was more'n half a candle left."

"What you goin' to do about tryin' to signal town?" Phrone asked.

"I'm goin' to go over to Miss Fible's right after breakfast," Asey replied.

But after breakfast, William rushed in excitedly.

"There's a boat, Mr. Mayo. A boat coming from town. It's coming here. Tom saw it. It's coming in to the wharf."

Asey dashed into the library and peered out the window through the binoculars.

"Josiah Cummin's boat," he reported. "Only one

could of got up here anyway. Got that back door opened, William?"

"Yes, sir. Tom and Kelley finished digging it out like you said."

"Good. You go get my coat, will you? I'm goin' down an' investigate."

The rest of us watched while Asey and the doctor clambered through the snow-drifts to the wharf.

They came back on a dead run.

"What's the matter?" I asked.

"Doc's wanted. Hurry call. Lyddy Howes, his housekeeper, she made Josiah come up for him. Seems like Pete Barradio's wife—they're that Portygee family near Truro way—she's havin' another baby, an' they couldn't get no other doctor."

Walker got his things together hurriedly.

"Are you going back with him?" I asked.

"Guess not. Walker'll call the county folks, an' he'll send telegrams to that Plymouth drug-store an' Stires's lawyers an' put in all the calls I want. I don't think I'd better leave here right now. Not with things the way they are. He can do everything just's well, or git some one to do it, an' Josiah'll come back with his boat an' stay here so's we'll have some way of gittin' places. He says they won't be able to get the road out here cleared before to-morrow, if they can do it then. Seems like everything was pretty well stopped up. Hey, William, make me a list of food you need—quick. Josiah'll bring back supplies. Nope, I got a better idea. Where's Phrone? Phrone, you go up an' get things at the store an' bring 'em back with him in the boat. Mind goin'?"

Phrone's eyes glistened. I knew she was thinking of the sensation she could create by her news.

"I'll go," she said briefly. "They ain't much in the line of supplies we don't need. Who'll pay for 'em?"

"Charge 'em to Stires. Some one'll pay for 'em some time. Oh, an' get me some tobacco, will you? Sailor's Pal Cut Plug. Chewin'. I always get it, an' they'll know it." He scribbled quickly on a slip of paper. "Here, Doc, this is for you. You know what to do, anyway. Here, Phrone. Any one else want anything?"

"Luckies," June said. "Razor blades."

"There. That'll do for one time. Tell Josiah to come back as soon as Phrone's done, an' tell him to hang around the telegraph office an' bring back any news to me."

We watched the boat as it lurched down the bay.

"Thank God," Asey said, "for Pete Barradio an' his wife. Lord knows I never thought much of 'em, but I can't say they ain't done us a good turn to-day. Well, we're in touch with civ'lization once more. Funny, civ'lization don't seem such a swell thing when you're in it, but when you ain't got it, it begins t' appear like there was somethin' in it after all."

The rest drifted off to the sun-room, and Asey and I were left alone in the library.

"Asey," I said, "just between you and me, what do you think of all this?"

"What I think, Miss Prue, I just couldn't tell you. It'd take Mr. Hobart of the big vocab'lary to describe it. Say, I been wonderin' about those false teeth.— And lissen. In one of those note-books we took from Stires's pockets, I found a slip of paper that's funny. It just said 'J. J.—Tuesday—$500' on it. 'Member that one of them checks was for five hundred to cash? Well, apparently it had somethin' to do with some one named J. J."

"J. J.," I said. "James Johnson. John Jackson."

"Uh-huh. What's Denny James's real name?"

"Borden. No *J* there."

"I guess not. Well, we'll——"

There was a knock on the door and Asey jumped up to admit Denny.

"Asey," he said, looking from me to Asey and back again, "did you ever notice that peculiar bowl in the hallway? The blue one on the pie-crust table?"

"The one with all the dragons chasin' each other an' playin' tag? Yup. I seen it when I first come in an' it kind of took my fancy. Why?"

"There's always a pile of paper match flaps there. Bert hated to run out of matches and so he always had a lot of bowls of them around, just the same way he had a lot of ash-trays, because he hated to have to hunt for 'em."

"Uh-huh," Asey said.

"Well, I just went to the bowl for some matches and in the bottom, I found this." He held up a key with a small tag attached. "It's been here, for all I know, ever since we arrived. I just happened to dig down into the bottom and find it. Thought you might like to have it."

Asey took the key and read the inscription on the tag. " 'A. Stires. Private. W. H.' "

" 'W. H.,' " Denny suggested, "probably stands for 'Wellfleet House,' don't you suppose?"

"I'd imagine so. Uh-huh."

Denny's enthusiasm was considerably dampened by Asey's apparent lack of interest.

"I only thought," he said almost apologetically, "that it might lead to something. Er—Prue, don't you want to play some bridge? We need a fourth."

"Run along," I said, quoting his remark to June. "Run along."

Denny swallowed twice. "Very well. I'll leave you with your—well, I'll leave."

Asey looked at me and grinned after he had left.

"So that's it? Kind of rough on him, wasn't you?"

"What about the key?"

He dangled it on his finger. " 'Tis kind of int'restin', ain't it? A perfectly good key. One of them things you open doors with. B'longs to a small Yale lock, I shouldn't wonder. Bill's got one like it on his boat-house. I wonder how it got there?"

He called William in.

"Ever see this key before?"

"No, sir." William shook his head. "But there's a couple of closets down-stairs that it might belong to. In the cellar. There's another closet up attic, too."

"How come he'd have locks on closets?"

"Because there's always a lot of burglaring around in the summer-houses after the people go home in the fall. Mr. Stires had had considerable trouble in the Orleans house. He made it a point not to have any-thing particularly valuable here for that reason. But there are a lot of small things, like blankets and sheets and some silver and dishes and so on, that were to be left here, and so he had those closets put in. They have sort of steel-like doors so that they can't be broken in."

"How often do you put matches into that blue bowl? The one on the hall table?"

William looked his surprise. "Why, every morning, sir. I go around every morning to see that they're full. I put new packages there this morning and dusted the bowl, too. I hope there's nothing wrong? Some-times the matches get damp and won't light, but I thought that the ones we have now were all right. They'd ought to be. They're new."

"Nothing's the matter with 'em. Only this key was in the bowl."

"It wasn't there at eight o'clock this morning," William said stoutly. "I can swear to that. Whoever put that key in there, sir, has put it in since then. Who found it?"

"Mr. James. Just now."

"Very curious," William said. "I don't know who'd have one of those keys but Mr. Stires. He had them all himself. I hadn't one, even, nor Mrs. Boles."

Asey nodded. "Okay, William. Thanks."

Asey took Stires's key ring from his pocket and compared the keys there with the one Denny had found.

"He ain't got no duplicate. Well, I guess it might be a good idea to do a little investigatin'. Only I don't want all that crowd around. I kind of wish they wasn't so dummed many people in this house, anyway. Sort of a convention, that's what it is. Miss Prue, would you go an' peek an' see where they all are?"

I went out and obediently peeked.

"They're all in the sun-room," I reported. "Rowena's working on Blake's head. He's sitting like a ramrod and playing bridge with June and Denny and Hobart. The girl's reading a book."

"Good. Now, Miss Prue, you go in an' take a little vacation while I prowl around."

"I want to come too."

"Nope. Ain't no place for first assistants, cellars an' attics ain't. You go into the other room an' med'-tate. I need a little med'tatin' done for me about now."

"I'm going where you go," I said.

"Nope."

"Yes. Asey, I'm going to go with you."

"Whither I goest, you'll trail along too?" He grinned. "Mr. James won't like it."

"I don't care what Mr. James thinks or likes. I'm going to prowl with you."

Asey laughed. "All right. I ain't a one to do a lot of arguin'. Like Sol Mayo, a cousin of mine that went to a town meetin' a long while ago while they was arguin' about whether the town should have a flag-pole or not. Sol, he listened to 'em argue till he got tired. Half the town wanted a flag-pole an' the other half said it was a sinful waste of money. Finally Sol got up an' shifted his cud from one cheek to the other an' said in a quiet sort of way, 'All I got to say's this. I'm tired of all your argifyin'. 'F you want a flag-pole, I say, have a flag-pole. 'F you don't want a flag-pole, I say, don't have a flag-pole. Only I'm tired of all this careenin' back an' forth.' Well, if you want to come 'long, come 'long."

Out in the hallway we met Rowena. "Where are you going?" she demanded.

"Sleuthin'," Asey said. "But you can't come, so's

you needn't ask. You med'tate instead. I wanted Miss Prue to, but she wouldn't."

"You," Rowena said, "are—well, Mr. Mantini's phrases would fit the case, but I'm a lady. I hope you get lost."

"We probably will," I said. "Come and find us if we don't show up in an hour or so. You might turn it into hare and hounds, Rena."

"Will you leave a paper trail?"

"No. You just use your imagination. After all, you'll probably have an idea."

She made a face at me. "All right. I'll hunt you if you don't turn up. In the interim, I'll work on poor Mr. Blake. That man is taking an awful lot of punishment, just sitting and sitting."

"Where to first?" I asked after she had gone.

"Cellar," Asey said promptly.

So we went down the steps into the game-room and Asey opened a little door which I'd not noticed before.

"How'd you know that was here?"

"I helped build some of this house, an' besides, the doc an' I could draw pictures of it after our hunt yest'day. You can get into the cellar this way or from the kitchen."

"What's that infernal machine? It looks like a dream I had last night."

"That's Stires's fancy oil burner. It's kind of a cross between a Mogul-mallet engine an' black magic.

I thought I was a mechanic, but I'd be scared to touch it. It cleans the air an' pumps cold an' hot air an' I don't know what all. There's the closets, way over in the corner. Darkish, ain't it? I wish I'd brought my flash."

"Why don't you go back?"

"I'd prob'ly run into Miss Fible or Denny or some one who'd want to come with me. Here," he tried his key in the first closet. "Nope. No go. Must be the other."

And the key did fit the other lock.

"Good," I said with a laugh. "I wish I had brought some paper for a trail. If Rowena could find this, she'd be doing well. What's it like inside?"

"Black as the inside of a nigger's pocket an' twice as stuffy. I thought there'd be a light here, but there don't seem to be. Well, a match will have to do, I guess."

He lighted a match and we peered around. The closet was just big enough for the two of us to stand in without touching each other. The walls were lined with shelves, all empty.

"There ain't nothin' here so far's I can see," Asey remarked. "Guess we drew a blank."

He turned around, but as he did, the door slammed to and his match went out.

"I should have brought my 'lectric torch," he said regretfully. "Well," he lighted another match, "here we are. Be a nasty place to get cooped up in, wouldn't it?"

His hand wandered around the knob and he twisted it back and forth.

"Open it quickly," I begged. "It's awfully stuffy."

"Miss Prue," he said, and his voice was puzzled and flat, "I kind of hate to tell you, but——"

"But what?"

"Well, the key's on the outside an' this is a spring lock. We're here until some one, Miss Fible if she remembers us, comes an' gets us out!"

CHAPTER NINE

THE CLOSET

"Can't you make a noise? Scream or something? Wouldn't that help?"

"Dunno's it would," Asey said. "These doors is all metal. An' they ain't no one around. They don't have to pay any attention to that oil burner nor to anything else down here so long's the 'lectricity goes, so I don't s'pose they come down much. An' if we did make a noise I s'pose they'd think we was playin' one of them fool games in the game-room. But I can bellow an' see what happens."

And he bellowed until I begged him to stop.

But no one came.

"Funny thing that door closed so all of a sudden-like," Asey remarked. "Miss Prue, I got a handful of matches an' I think I'll look around an' see if they ain't some light here. Funny that they isn't. All of the rest of the closets in the house is full of 'em."

At last he located a switch, but repeated attempts at snapping it on produced no results.

"Out of order," he said disgustedly. "Guess we don't get to have no light."

"Wait a minute," I said, as he was about to blow out the match, "there's a candle on the shelf there."

I gave it to him and he lighted it.

"This is somethin'," he said. "Always feel better when I can see what I'm doin'. Y'know, I should think you could sit on one of them shelves. I can't b'cause I'm too tall, but if you was to sit forward like so's your head didn't strike the shelf above, you'd be all right."

Somewhat gingerly I seated myself on a lower shelf.

"I could kick myself," Asey muttered, "for gettin' you into this mess. I stuck a piece of wood under that door, though, an' I don't see why it should of shut."

"It did slam hard," I replied. "I suppose the wood slipped out."

"Prob'ly. But this is a concrete floor an' I don't see why blocks of wood should go slippin' around. You know, I kind of think——" he hesitated.

"D'you think some one slammed it?"

He nodded. "I dunno but what I do. I was foolish to come lumberin' down here without a torch an' I was foolisher not to of left you outside or else to of taken the key out with me."

"But who could have slammed the door? And why?"

"Dunno."

"And what good would it do for any one to lock us in here anyway? They'd know that we'd be sure to get out sooner or later."

"Uh-huh. Only it maybe perhaps might be later."

"You don't think we'll suffocate or anything like that?"

"Nun-no. Dunno's we will. Only it ain't such a big closet. I guess Miss Fible'll come after us pretty soon. Or else Jósiah'll come back."

"But Josiah won't be back for hours! And we were only joking with Rowena. She didn't take us seriously. She's probably forgotten all about us by now. And if she's working, she's surely forgotten. She loses all conception of time and people when she works. I wish this place had a window."

"It would be nice," Asey agreed. "It's lucky that candle was here. I think Stires must of bought out a candle factory. We been usin' bayb'ry candles ever since the 'lectricity was off an' we used a powerful lot of 'em. You know, Miss Prue, the more I think of this key, the more I think of it."

"What do you mean?"

"Well, here's what I been figgerin' these last few seconds. Some one, some time early this mornin', stuck that key into that bowl, knowin' it was a pretty good chance that some one would find it an', bein' curious, bring it to me. I might even of found it myself. Anyway, I got it. An' bein' an ole plum-dum fool, I ups an' runs head first into some one's plan. I don't know whether they wanted me out of the way temp'rarily, or permanent, but whatever they wanted, they got it."

"I wish," I said bitterly, "that I'd stayed up-stairs."

"Feel that way myself. I don't see how shuttin'

us up down here's goin' to get any one any place. That I don't. They couldn't be plannin' a getaway. I'd give a lot to know what was in the back of their—or his—or her—head."

"Her? What do you mean, her?"

"Figger of speech, that's all." But I had rather more than a meager suspicion that he was thinking of Rowena. It occurred to me that she, after all, was the only one who knew that we were going "sleuthing."

"That door shutting might have been purely accidental," I said.

"Yup. So might a lot of things. 'Member the poems about Little Willie an' the dynamite?"

"I wish," I said, shivering, "that you'd not be so ominous."

"All right." He pulled off his boot. "I'm goin' to bang on the door with this," he announced. "Easier than usin' up lung power. Wisht I'd taken my p'lice whistle with me. I left it up in my room."

He banged on the door until the paint came off. But no one heard.

"Does your nose feel queer?" I asked suddenly.

"Does, sort of."

"Funny smell from that candle."

"Uh-huh. It's just the bayb'ry, though. They all smell funny."

"I know that they do, Asey Mayo! Hasn't the whole house smelled of bayberry for the last two days? But

this is different. I wonder who left that candle here
in the first place?"

" 'Tis funny. P'ticularly if Stires had this key—or
was s'posed to be the only one that had it. Don't see
how any one could of got into this place at all."

"But we know Stires didn't have it."

"Ghosts," Asey said succinctly. "Ghosts. I'm
comin' to the c'nclusion that ghosts is the only reas'nble
answer to all of this anyway. Say," he looked at the
candle as though he'd never seen one before, "say, look
at the way that's burnin', will you?"

"It flickers a lot."

"Yup, it's ter'ble bright even though it flickers, too."

"Well, it's burning," I said, "and that's something
to be thankful for."

"I cal'late so." He sat down suddenly on the floor.

"What's the matter?"

"I guess," he said cheerfully, "that I et too many
of Phrone's eggs. Or else I didn't eat enough. My
legs is weak. Say, did I ever tell you about Issachar
Hurd?"

"No. Are you trying to take my mind up?"

"Iss Hurd," he ignored my question, "he was a friend
of Barney Gould. I guess you heard of Barney Gould
an' his express, ain't you? He was the dippy feller
that used t' walk around collectin' road taxes. Walked
'nough so's he figgered he deserved t' collect 'em. He
walked t' Boston once an' brought back a dozen hay-

rakes an' a keg of nails, all for a quarter. N'en once,— say, do your legs feel funny?"

"They're asleep."

"So're mine. Well, where was I? Oh, yes. Iss Hurd had a wife that was a great one for neatness an' cleanliness. She was godly as all get-out, but she was even cleanlier an' neater'n that. Every time Iss come into the house, he had t' take his boots off, an' everythin' in that house run by clockwork. At five-thirty every evenin' Iss had to fill the wood-box. One night he went out, an' when he wa'n't back by seven, Charity—wife's name was Charity—she began to— say, there's somethin' more'n funny about that candle. Look! Look at it! There's a sort of mist comin' off it!"

"Nonsense!"

"Yessir. Every time it flickers, that mist comes off it!" With a sudden motion he picked it up and stubbed it out.

"What are you putting that out for?" I cried. "I hate to be left in the dark. Light it again!"

"Not on your life!"

"Why not?"

"B'cause, Miss Prue, 'less I'm mighty much mistaken, it's that candle that's makin' us feel sick."

"But how?"

"Dunno. I kind of wonder, Miss Prue, if this wasn't that light that William's wife seen in the tea leaves?

Yessireebob, this is just another one of them plants,
an' what a plant! Yessir, I give this guy credit."

"What are you babbling about?"

"Lissen. Some one left that key hopin' I'd come in
here. We did. Some one waited till we got in, an'
then slammed the door on us. They'd been in here
before an' fixed it so's the light wouldn't work, an' left
this candle. 'Twas a long shot we wouldn't have a light
of our own, but we didn't. We found the candle an'
lit it. N'en we begun to feel sick—hey, what you
doin'?"

"I think," I said drowsily, "I'll join you on the
floor." And I slid off the shelf and landed with a
thud on the cement. "But how can the candle make
us so groggy? Sure it isn't that the air's bad or giving
out?"

"Don't think so. Some one thought I was beginnin'
to find out too much, or else they didn't like me—
anyway, they got me in here, an' they didn't want
me to come out on two feet. That's certain. How long
we been in here? I ain't got my watch."

"I have. Give me a match." I peered at the tiny
dial. "We've been here forty or fifty minutes, I'd say."

"Humpf. Well, Miss Fible or Josiah'll be here
any minute now." His voice was not so convincing as
his words. "About Iss Hurd, now. His wife went out
an' looked around, an' she couldn't find him anywhere. . . ."

I listened half-heartedly as his voice droned on. I was limp. My nose seemed about to burst. My hands wouldn't move. I understood the whole situation, my brain was clear enough, but I could make no connection between what I wanted to do and what I did. My left ankle, doubled under me, was uncomfortable. I wanted to move it, but I was finally forced to take my hand and push it into another position.

I began to think of that spool of orange silk—and my niece Betsey and her husband. Suppose I didn't get out of the closet on two feet, as Asey had insinuated? Suppose I never got out alive; suppose I died! I wondered if Betsey and Bill would come home. Too bad to spoil their honeymoon. Too bad, if I had to die, it couldn't be over with all at once. Why, if some one wanted to kill Asey, did I have to be included?

I thought about Denny James. I was sorry that I'd treated him as I had the night before. I really might have answered his telegram when it came last fall. I might have told him last night what I'd intended to answer. I might at least have explained to him that Betsey would have felt badly if she'd known that it was because of her that I'd never answered his yearly telegrams, that it would have been too obvious to go dashing off the very instant she was married——

"Fifteen years later," Asey said with a chuckle, "Iss turned up at six o'clock with an armful of wood. 'Where you been?' Charity asks. 'Been gittin' that wood,' says he. 'Got 'ny huckleberry pie?' 'In the pantry,' says she. 'What kep' you so long?' 'Oh,' says Iss, casual, 'I got tired of runnin' like a clock. Thought I'd just bring that wood in by 'nother route, for once.' "

I tried to laugh appreciatively, but it was a very weak effort indeed. Asey began another yarn, finished it and began another. And I think that it was some time during that one that I mercifully went to sleep,— or became unconscious. I never quite knew which.

At any rate, the next thing I remember with any degree of clarity was the doctor bending over me. I was on the sofa in the game-room, and Asey was stretched out on the floor.

"How is he?" I whispered.

"He's fine," the doctor said cheerfully. "Most of his trouble was worrying about you. Here, drink this and go to sleep. You're all right."

"But I feel sick."

"You can't possibly feel sick," Rowena said firmly, looking down at me. "You've been sick. Quite a lot. Go ahead and go to sleep. Asey's all right and so are you. And it was only by the grace of God and the doctor coming back and William's incoherent talk of keys and closets that we found you. And Ginger. That blonde beast sat outside that closet and howled till we opened it. I'm going to make a medal for him. Go to sleep!"

Obediently, I went to sleep.

It was dark when I woke up. Asey and the doctor were talking quietly together in front of the fireplace. The rest were nowhere to be seen.

"I'm hungry," I said.

"How do you feel besides that?" the doctor asked.

"All right. Really. Tell me what happened."

"Wait until you've had some soup. Asey, will you get it? And tell Mr. James that she's awake and whole. Actually I've been more worried about your boy fr—about him, that is, than about you. I'll wager he's lost ten pounds to-day."

I made no comment.

"And that cat of yours, say, he's a whiz. I came back and no one knew where you were, then Miss Fible remembered that you were bound somewhere, and William jabbered about keys. And closets. Unfortunately, we started in the attic and worked down, and when we arrived here, Ginger was in front of your black hole, mewing away for dear life. And we opened the door to find Asey talking about shipwrecks off the Sandwich Islands, and you fast asleep. Here," Walker took the cup of soup from Asey, "d'you want me to feed you or will you dribble it down your neck yourself?"

"I'll do it myself; what about that candle?"

"That," Walker said, "is a story. There are bayberry candles all over the house. In all the bedrooms.

Everywhere. Seems Stires used nothing else. We noticed it, but after all, it didn't seem important. Well, when Asey came out of the closet, he was gripping that candle you had in there as though it were a million dollars in bearer bonds. Told me to analyze it, and I thought he was crazy. But he insisted, and I did."

"And what did you find? Hurry up!"

"Outwardly it was the same as all the rest. But I discovered that this one had a specially prepared wick. It had been dipped, I'm pretty sure, in a paste of Paris green and water. When it burned, it would give off that white vapor Asey noticed. Arsenious oxide vapor, and probably, though I'm not so sure of this, arseniureted hydrogen."

"I still don't understand."

"Well, did you ever hear of any one getting sick from green wall-paper?"

"Heavens, no!"

"Well, in some cheap green wall-papers, they used to use Paris green to hold the dye. When I was an intern we had a couple of cases of it at the M. G. H. People lived in cheap houses built on filled-in land, and when it began to get damp, as it did of course, the green wall-paper gave out a mild form of what this candle did. Arsenious oxide vapor. I'd never have known if we hadn't been puzzled about those cases. People had a mild form of arsenic poisoning, and we couldn't find out for a good long time what caused it. See?"

"I begin to."

"And if Asey hadn't doused that candle when he did, you'd have been on another plane right now. People would have thought that you'd suffocated. But the symptoms would have been arsenic poisoning, just like Stires."

I dropped the empty soup cup on the floor with a crash.

"You mean that a candle—a candle was the cause of his death?"

"Uh-huh. And the beauty of it all is that we can't prove it."

"I won't say 'why' and 'what for' again. Tell me."

"All right. William says that Stires always went to bed with a lighted candle on the table beside him. Always has, as long as William's known him. Probably his friends know of his little idiosyncrasy. Lots of people do keep lights at night, though they don't usually keep candles. There's a five-branch candlestick in Stires's room. Stires lighted his candles when he went to bed Wednesday night. Now they're just puddles of wax in the sockets. So we can conclude that he let them burn all night."

"An' what's left," Asey said, "don't show any trace of poison in the wicks at all. An' the last inch of the candle from the closet is okay. The guy prob'ly left the first few an' the last few inches of the wick all good an' proper, an' poisoned the in-between part. So that you wouldn't notice anything wrong when the candle was first lighted, an' after it burned down you can't find anythin' wrong with it either."

"But how did Bert——?"

"It was like this," the doctor said. "Stires lighted the candles and went to sleep. He was pretty tired and he probably dropped off in no time. If he smelled any odor at all, he assumed, of course, that it was the bayberries. He wouldn't have given it a thought. Now, those candles were on his bedside table. The windows were closed. See, there are five candles directly next him. He's breathing that vapor into his lungs. Good arsenious oxide vapor and the possible arseniureted hydrogen."

"But it's diabolical!"

"It's all of that. Now, perhaps Stires wakes up. Feels sick. Decides he'd better get some one. He's probably pretty well paralyzed. I don't see how he moved the few feet he managed to move from the bed. You and Asey couldn't move much—and you didn't get such a dose of it. His brain is probably clear enough, but he can't talk. Or if he can, not above a whisper. He can't call out. He probably hasn't the slightest notion of what's wrong with him. He only knows that he's sick, and he's trying to get help. From eleven or so Wednesday night until the candles finally went out—during all that time he's been breathing in that vapor. He can't get to the bell—and even if he had, it wouldn't have worked. There, Miss Prue, is the story as it probably happened. That's how Stires died."

"But you found arsenic in his stomach!"

"Many explanations of that. Breathed with his mouth open——"

"Where did the candles come from?"

"That," Asey said with a grin, "is still another story. You remember Mary Gross, the old lady on the Truro road?"

"Did she—was she the one that made them?"

"Yes. She always made them for Stires, William says. But she didn't kill Stires,—that is, she prob'ly made the candles, but she made 'em for some one else."

"How do you know?"

"Because," Walker said, "I went around to see her after I finished with Pete Barradio's wife. I didn't have much to do there and I stopped in at Mary's on the way back. Mary is dead."

"Then she died from her cold?"

Walker shook his head. "She was killed the same way Stires was killed. By the candles she'd made for some one else."

CHAPTER TEN

AND THE CANDLES

"Good heavens! How? And when?"

"She died Wednesday night, I think, or Thursday morning. You see, she didn't have electricity in her house. She used old-fashioned kerosene lamps; apparently she ran out of oil and had to resort to candles. She was in that little sitting-room. There were two candles—or stumps of 'em—on the table beside her, four more about the room in holders. And her symptoms are the same as Stires's—arsenic poisoning."

"Look here," I said, "I don't see how, if she made the candles, she'd have been killed by them. But tell me. If you're sure that the candles are the cause of all this trouble, does that mean that all the things we've found out about the arsenic up till now are useless?"

Asey nodded. "Cal'late that they are. Some one had this all figgered out. If we found out that Stires was poisoned by arsenic, he had it fixed so's we'd find arsenic. He planned to git me out of the way an' that slipped up. Now by sort of dumb luck we found out about the candles—and whee! Mary Gross is dead! Ain't no doubt but what she made them candles, but if she made 'em an' knew what she was makin', she'd never of used 'em."

"But she might, Asey. She might have killed herself."

"I don't think so, Miss Prue. I don't think that there's a chance in this world that she did. Mary was a little mite crazy, but she wouldn't of hurt a fly. She had a collection of sick cats an' dogs she looked after all the time, an' she was just the same way about human bein's. There never was a kinder ole lady goin' than Mary Gross. She couldn't of killed Stires. But she could of made those candles with the poisoned wicks without knowin' what they was. Then she could of been asked to try 'em—or mebbe she just made a mistake."

"But if she made those poisoned wicks——"

"I figger it this way," Asey said. "Whoever planned this wanted to use the same kind of candles that Stires always used. He must of known about Stires's habit of sleepin' with the candles next him an' planned it out from there. Well, the av'rage person don't know much about dippin' candles. These is all hand dipped. An' you can't go dippin' candles casual-like, just the way you'd bake a cake. What I think is that this guy fixed the wicks himself, an' sent 'em to Mary an' she dipped the candles usin' them wicks."

"But why did this person want to get rid of Mary, if she didn't know? And what about you? And me?"

Asey shrugged. "Wouldn't be a one to know about you 'n' me. I don't much understand about Mary,

either. With all these nifty plans, seems funny he'd
go about deliberately tryin' to kill Mary. Two deaths
of arsenic poisonin' here would kind of be more'n a
funny coinc'dence. Might pass off without any trouble
in N'York or Boston or some place like that, but not
in Wellfleet. Folks'd begin wonderin'. An' no feller
that's done as much thinkin' out as this one has would
ever slip up like that. Y'see, it wouldn't matter so
much about me. In what y'might call the ord'nary
course of events, I'd of been fished out of that closet
nice 'n' dead. An' it's dollars to doughnuts it'd of
been a verdict of suf'cation. An' even then they
wouldn't of found out about the candles. 'Cause even
if some one'd thought of it, that stump'd of been all
right."

"The exquisite part of all this, Miss Prue," the doctor said, "is that the weapon which deals out death
destroys itself. It destroys its evidence as it works.
The victim,—well, his death looks equally like suffoca-
tion or death from a bad cold, or arsenic poisoning.
Actually it is arsenic poisoning. But even if that's discovered, the logical inference is that the arsenic was
taken in food."

"I never heard anything like it before in my life,"
I said. "It's just beyond me."

"It's nothing new," Walker said. "They tried to
do away with Leopold of Austria like this centuries
ago. And it was a favorite way of killing off popes and

cardinals in the Middle Ages. Easy to send them
holy candles, you see. I've read about such cases. It
was a good way of murdering people in the Renaissance,
and if you should ask me, I'd say that it comes as
near to being a perfect manner of killing any one as
I've ever seen or heard about. For in destroying its
victim, the candle destroys itself. We know now what
killed Stires and Mary Gross. But I'd hate to have
the job of trying to prove it in court."

"Then all this dithering around and finding arsenic
isn't going to get us anywhere?"

"Nope." Asey shook his head. "We got to make
another beginnin'. This is sort of like the King of
France marchin' up the hill an' then traipsin' back
again. The arsenic idea is out. What we're after
now is candles. An' I think we'll begin with William."

"But did you find out anything? Didn't the doctor
get any answers to his telegrams?"

"Yup. The druggist in Plymouth says those powders
was headache powders, good an' plain an' simple. The
lawyers say that they got a cable day before yest'day
from Desire Allerton in Cannes. She's comin' next
week. So that sort of finishes with this girl for the
time bein'. If she's a stranger, she wouldn't of known
about the candles an' Mary makin' 'em. An' Stires's
manager at the fac'try says the same thing about that
Newell Comp'ny that Blake said. Says Hobart got
gypped an' he don't see why Hobart didn't know it."

"All of which," I commented, "is not a lot of help. Did I tell you about Rowena and her ink-bottle top?"

Asey grinned. "Nope."

So I told him Rowena's idea for finding the murderer by the ink bottle, and he laughed.

"If she wants to set an ink bottle in a good c'nspicuous place an' wait for some one to put the top on, she can. If the guy that planted the arsenic did put it on, he'll get the idea in a minute an' never touch it, if he's the feller I take him for. An' prob'ly every one'll put it on, just to make matters good an' mixed. But let her try it if she wants to."

He went off and returned with William.

"Some more things I want to ask you about them candles," he said. "I know Stires always used 'em an' Mary Gross always made 'em, but who got 'em? Who brought 'em this time? Where'd the ones in the house come from?"

"Some of them, sir, came from the Orleans house. The rest Mr. Hobart and Mr. James brought with them when they came on Tuesday."

"Who put the candles around in the rooms?"

"I did. Usually my wife does, but she was very busy that day."

" 'Member which you used?"

"Oh, yes. The ones we had here from the other house. The new ones we used in the candelabras that night and we've been using them since."

"All of 'em look alike? The new ones wasn't any dif'rent?"

"Not that I noticed, sir. They're always bigger than ordinary candles, because all of Mr. Stires's holders were old ones and needed big candles. They were hand made, so of course they weren't exactly the same size always."

Asey nodded. "Okay, William. That's all for now, thanks. Doc, I'm goin' up an' see what I can d'scover about the rest of these fellers an' candles an' one thing an' another."

"Good idea," the doctor said. "I'm going to go and supervise Phrone while she gets some food for Miss Prue. Be all right alone here?"

"Of course I will. And I'm perfectly able to get up and eat. There's no point in my staying here longer."

"You'll do nothing of the kind. You stay put until you've had something to eat. If you want anything, sing out."

They had no sooner disappeared up the stairs than Denny came down.

"How are you, Prue?" he asked anxiously.

"Flourishing," I said. "Flourishing."

"Look here, Prue, I want you to promise me something. I want you to promise that you won't go wandering off into strange places with Asey Mayo again. Not that I don't like Asey. I do. I think Asey's a fine man. A——"

"I know. An upstanding citizen. A diamond in the rough. One of nature's noblemen."

"That's not what I mean at all. What I mean is, he's all right, but you can't tell how many more closets he might shut himself up in."

"*Shut* himself up——" Then I stopped, realizing that the rest probably had not been told about the candles and about our being locked in.

"Yes. So, Prue, won't you be careful? I mean, if Mayo decided to investigate a meat chopper or a hand grenade or something of the sort, won't you please let him do it alone? Won't you promise me that?"

"Yes. Yes, I'll promise not to help him if he opens a bomb. I'll be careful."

"Thank God. Now, Prue, twenty-seven years ago——"

I covered my ears. "Dear lord, Denny, not that. Please, don't let's start that now. I—really, I've been through enough for one day."

"Very well," he said stiffly, and left as Walker came down the stairs with Phrone.

She bustled around with a trayful of food and generally made me feel as though I were recovering from a siege of double pneumonia.

"I'm certainly glad," she said, "that Darlin' got here at last."

"Darling who?"

"Darlin', the undertaker. He's takin' Stires up to

town. Miss Whitsby, you don't know how stirred up folks is about Mr. Stires. Wouldn't b'lieve it, at first. Don't know when I've seen people more upset."

"I can imagine," I said dryly. "Doctor, did you notify the county officials and all that sort of thing?"

"Yes. I called up all the people Asey told me to."

"Are they going to send down men, or what?"

"No. Burnett, the head push, seems to have a lot of faith in Asey. He said that Asey had been in on it all and probably could do as much as any one else, right now. He's sending down some men to help Asey, though. The road will be cleared out by to-morrow and I suppose they'll be here then. I had a notion that they'd put some one else in charge."

"I guess you forget," Phrone said, "that Asey Mayo's got to the bottom of one murder an' if he's done it once, he can do it again. That's what they said uptown, that it was lucky Asey was around."

It was fully an hour before Asey returned.

He sat down in one of the big leather armchairs, bit a hunk from his plug and chewed viciously.

"What have you found out?" Walker asked amusedly.

"Wait a minute."

"What for?"

"I'm countin' to five hundred by ones an' I ain't quite through yet." His lips moved noiselessly.

"There. Jehostophat! Jehostophat! Jumpin' Je-hostophat!"

"What's the matter?" I asked laughingly.

"Matter? Matter! Huh. I set out t' see if any of these people knew anything about candles. I didn't expect any one of 'em would. An' what do you think?"

"All of 'em do, I suppose," the doctor sighed.

"All of 'em, 'cept the Blakes, every dum one of 'em, mind you, got candles from Mary Gross at one time or another. They admit it. They more'n admit it. They told me stories about candles till I wanted to howl like a dog."

"Even the girl?"

"No. Not her, either, far's I know. She's gone off to bed an' I sort of didn't think it was worth it to get her up. Wouldn't that jar you?"

"It would and it does," I said. "Tell us."

"Well, your friend Denny James got the candles when him an' Hobart stopped there Tuesday when they was gettin' things on Stires's list. N'en he had a friend who had an old house an' so he got candles made to fit some old candlesticks so's he could give 'em to the friend. That was last fall. He often got candles from Mary through Stires."

The doctor raised his eyebrows.

"An' John Kent, he got some around Christmas. Often went there with Stires, too. Hobart got some, by way of Kent b'cause he'd got so many before through

Stires for his sister—that is, Hobart's sister—that he didn't want to bother Stires again."

"What did they all get them through Stires for?"

"B'cause Mary was sort of temp'r'mental an' she'd only make candles for her good customers, not for every Tom, Dick an' Harry that wanted 'em. Guess she found out, too, that these fellers would pay more for 'em. Anyway, she'd always fill orders for Stires an' for Kent. Denny an' Hobart had a harder time."

"And the Blakes never knew her, or bought candles?"

"That's their story. An' Miss Fible says she used the ole lady's menagerie to model animals from for somethin' or other she was makin', an' she got in Mary's good graces an' so Mary made candles for her. So that's that."

"Then any one of them might have ordered the poisoned candles?"

"Looks that way. Mebbe the Blakes did, for all we know. The others all admit gettin' 'em."

"What about the servants, Asey?" I asked. "Are you sure that they haven't something to do with all of this?"

"I'm pretty sure an' I'll tell you why. This job ain't somethin' that any one of these hired help could think up, let alone carry out. Lewis is okay, he's a good cook, I shouldn't wonder, but he ain't no mental whiz. Can't even light a kerosene stove. William, well, him an' his wife is more int'rested in what Evan-

geline Adams says the stars'll do an' what the tea
leaves say than they are in anything else. Tom's all
right, but he's the sort of feller that you have to tell
what to do; he can do it all right, but he wouldn't
never think of doin' it if you hadn't of told him. An'
that hatchet-faced Kelley, well, he never even saw
Stires. I'm rulin' them servants out. It wasn't one
of them."

"Did you find out where every one was just after
we were locked up? Can't you find out who slammed
that closet door?"

"I asked Miss Fible. She says she left the room
not long after we went down-stairs. Wanted a nail
file on account of that clay gettin' under her nails an'
botherin' her. Says Hobart went out in the hall to
get some matches, she remembers that because she
wanted some herself. Says June an' the girl was scrib-
blin' notes back an' forth on a piece of paper an' that
Kent an' Denny wandered around. Says they was
playin' bridge, but that they stopped just after she met
us in the hall."

"Which means," the doctor said, "that any one of
'em could have gone down-stairs."

"Uh-huh. An' I found out how the feller slammed
the door without me hearin' him come in. I wondered
about that b'cause I got a sort of sharp set of ears. He
follered us down an' on his way into the cellar he
picked up a billiard cue an' then he slunk around an'

pushed the door shut with that. Probably jerked that little piece of wood out of the way beforehand."

"What makes you think the person used the cue?"

"Found a little blue chalk mark on the door where the tip of it was."

"Couldn't it have been one of the servants?"

"Tom an' Kelley an' Lewis was up in Lewis's room playin' cards an' didn't stir out of there. Mrs. Boles was up in her room markin' linen. William was puttin' the storeroom to rights."

"Then couldn't it have been William? We asked him about the key. It's possible that he put it there himself."

"Uh-huh. But it ain't any more poss'ble than that Denny James put it there. He found it, he says. But we only got his say-so. An' William didn't have no more chance than Miss Fible, or Hobart, or Blake, or Kent. Or any one. Golly, this sort of beats me, this does. What with Mary dead an' gone—we prob'ly shan't know who she made these for. It's all so anybody-might-of. I'd give my shirt to get an honest-to-God suspect, I would. This candle business may of cleared up how Stires got killed, but it sure robbed me of a couple of def'nite ideas."

"Asey," I said thoughtfully, "I have an idea."

"Constant 'sociation with Miss Fible, I shouldn't wonder," he replied with a chuckle.

I laughed. "But, Asey, why did some one want to

kill you so much that they didn't care if they did away
with me in the bargain? I mean, it seems to me that
you must have found out something that this person
thinks is important, so important that he'd rather have
murdered the two of us than let it come out."

Asey rubbed the back of his ear reflectively. "I
didn't ever think of it that way, Miss Prue. No, sir,
I didn't. Maybe this feller knows of somethin' I've
found out that's important, but, by golly, I'm dummed
if I know what it's all about."

"On the other hand," Walker suggested, "it's just
as possible the other way around. I mean, it's just
as logical to assume that Miss Prue knows something,
even if the full significance of it has escaped her, that's
dangerous to this person."

I shook my head. "That's impossible."

"Walker," Asey said suddenly, "I just thought of
somethin' I forgot to ask you about. When you come
back an' couldn't find us, how did they all take it?"

"Well, Mr. James," with a sidelong glance at me,
"Mr. James was fit to be tied. Miss Fible was pretty
worried. They all were. Then William came forward
with this closet-and-key theory, and we promptly went
to the attic."

"But why the attic?"

"Why, I don't remember. Let me see. James said
he'd found a key. William said you'd asked him about
it and that he told you it probably belonged either to

the attic or the cellar closets. Miss Fible said she
hadn't noticed which way you went when she left you
in the hall, she thought you'd gone up-stairs. Kent—
yes, Kent said that we'd better try the cellar closets,
and some one said it would be better to start at the top
of the house and work down. We broke in the attic
closet after considerable fuss and bother and then
some one suggested—Asey, you'd better ask some one
else. I was in such a state, all primed to tell you the
news about Mary and then not able to find you, that I
really don't remember who did all that suggesting that
delayed us so long."

"Miss Fible," Asey said, "will know. I'm sure of it."

And Rowena did. "Who suggested the attic first
and then rambled around opening every door on the
second floor? Denny James. I could have boxed his
ears at the way he held us all up. We'd have got you
out of the closet an hour sooner if it hadn't been for
him."

CHAPTER ELEVEN

I DID not pass a happy night.

When I awoke Saturday morning Rowena's bed was empty, but before I finished dressing, she came into the room.

"The road's been opened," she informed me, "and some burly gentlemen have been sent down to help Asey. They're stationed around the doors and William tells me there's a motorcycle cop at either end of the road. The phones are in order and there've been so many calls that they've had to warn the operator to put through calls only from certain people. Phrone says that they've had to corral extra girls to handle things. And the place was swarming with reporters, but Asey got rid of 'em."

"Did they see you?" I asked, raising my eyebrows.

"I regret to say that they did. Head-lines again, Prue. 'Spinster Sculptress at Stires Killing. From Chicago to Cape Cod, Says Miss Fible, is from Frying-Pan to Fire.' I know it'll be something like that. I can feel it coming. I tried to hide, but that obnoxious Johnson man saw me and pounced on me. We,—well, we've met before. There wasn't any use trying to evade him. But Asey was marvelous. He sent them on some wild-goose chase after a man with a white beard.

I didn't get the whole story, but it was good enough to make them go. The motorcycle cops have orders not to let 'em back. Asey gave out a list of the guests and those reporters just gasped. Said it sounded like a conference to cancel the national debt."

"Asey is still in charge?"

"Yes, thank goodness. I was rather afraid that they'd put in some bull-necked individual, but they're showing unusual intelligence. Oh, yes. The lawyer is coming some time this afternoon, Phrone tells me. That woman's a marvel. She knows more that goes on in this house than the rest of us combined. I'll wager she could even give Asey points. How d'you feel this morning, by the way?"

"Practically normal, thank you."

"Um. Prue, will you tell me something?"

"Depends."

"Prue, was that closet episode yesterday accidental, or intentional?"

I shrugged. "What do you think?"

"I don't think it was accidental. I don't think Asey's the sort to let a spring lock fool him. Who locked you in?"

"That's something I'd give a lot to know."

She nodded. "Then you *were* locked in. I see. Come along and get some breakfast. Lewis is up, superintending Phrone, and she's furious. I'm interested to see just how the meal is going to turn out."

As far as the food was concerned, the meal was a huge success. Socially, it was a failure. Denny contented himself with an orange, and even June's appetite was beginning to fade. The weather was the sole topic of conversation.

Just as we were getting up from the table, one of Asey's new assistants appeared in the doorway.

"There's a woman here, and she won't go away. She says she's got to see you. The state cops couldn't keep her away."

"Who is it?"

"Name of Howes, she says."

Asey laughed. "Lyddy, huh? Well, let her in. If she's got by the crowd of you, she deserves to be let in."

"Isn't she the doctor's housekeeper?" I asked as we went into the library.

"Yup. She is. But that ain't what she's here for. The doc's gone back to town an' she'd of seen him most likely. She's some r'lation of Mary Gross, an' I was plannin' on goin' up an' seein' her to-day about Mary anyway. H'lo, Mis' Howes!"

She bustled into the room, her galoshes flopping and her red knitted muffler streaming out behind. She was one of those women whose clothes always seem to be making a tremendous effort to catch up with the rest of her.

"Well," she greeted us, "well! Why, hullo, Miss Whitsby. I hadn't heard that you was here. Well, if

I didn't have a time gettin' here! I says to all those fellers outside, I says, I guess I got the right to see the sheriff of this town if I want to. I'm a taxpayer, I told 'em, an' just as good as anybody else. I guess that took the starch out of 'em."

"Take off your coat," Asey said hospitably. "Take off your coat an' set a while. How'd you come over here?"

She unwound the red muffler. "Come in the flivver, an' if I didn't have a time with it! Now, I want to know all about Mary Gross. I was workin' so hard yest'day afternoon paintin' my settin'-room floor that I didn't go up-town at all. Just this mornin' I was startin' up for my mail an' the doctor come and told me about her. 'What's the matter with her?' says I. 'She's been poisoned,' says he. So I told him I was goin' to come right over to see you an' get to the bottom of it all. Mary Gross was as good a woman as ever lived an' what a body'd want to poison her for, I for one don't know. And," she took the first breath she'd drawn since she started, "and I'm the only livin' relation she's got in this world. Her great-great-grandfather an' my great-great-grandfather was half——"

"I know they was," Asey said, unfeelingly stemming the flow of words. "I was goin' up an' see you this mornin'."

"Was you? Ain't it lucky I come! Doctor Walker

says that Mary an' Mr. Stires both was killed by arsenic. Is that a fact? I think it's a terrible thing, I do, losin' Mary, but losin' Mr. Stires is even worse, you might say. He was goin' to be a great help to the town with his money. They said that they reckoned that the tax rate'd go down because of his comin' here an' I'd sort of planned to have a new picket fence on the strength of it."

" 'Tis a pity," Asey said. " 'Tis a pity an' that's a fact. Now, Mis' Howes, I wonder if you'd answer some questions for me?"

She nodded vigorously. "I'd be glad to, if they're about Mary. I guess I knew's much about Mary Gross as any one in this whole town. Used to go up to see her three times a week anyway, regular. There's not a better woman ever lived than Mary, even if she was a little mite queer sometimes. An' even at that, I don't think she was half as queer as some folks tried to make her out to be."

"Did she keep any record of who she sold candles to," Asey asked, "or how much she got for 'em an' when she sold 'em?"

"No, siree. She just took the money an' popped it into the Savin's Bank as fast's she could. Many's the good time I've said to her, 'Mary,' I've said, 'you should ought to keep some records of all you make. S'pose there's a mistake,' I said. But she never would. I told her that there wasn't ever a better bookkeeper

than her father, but she just never would keep any
books attall."

"Made a lot of candles, did she?"

"Land's sakes, yes. The minute she'd see the berries
fillin' out she'd start in an' take her pail an' begin to
pick. She'd go around the Gull Pond way an' over
back of the islands an' I don't know how many tons
of berries that woman's c'lected. Takes about a bushel
to make five or six pounds of wax, an' it takes a good
thirty or forty dippin's to make the big candles. Yes,
she made a lot of candles an' she put in a whole lot
of hard work on 'em."

"Did she make 'em all at once?"

Mrs. Howes shook her head. "Most usually she just
boiled down her wax an' then kep' it an' dipped the
candles to order. That was because some people wanted
one size an' others wanted another. When I was over
there Tuesday she was havin' to——"

"You was over there Tuesday? What time?"

"In the afternoon, right after dinner. I'd made
some sugar gingerbread an' some caramel custards an'
they come out so nice that I guessed I'd take some
over."

"Any one come in while you was there?"

"Yup. That Mr. Hobart that was a friend of Mr
Stires an' another man I'd never seen before."

"What'd they say? Was you in the room with 'em?"

She nodded. "Uh-huh. This man I never saw be-

fore come in first an' asked for Mr. Stires's candles,
an' Mary wrapped up all she had on hand for him in
a paper bag. Then Mr. Hobart come in an' asked
again if they was Stires's candles, and she said they
was an' he picked 'em up an' they both went."

"Mary say anything about 'em after they left?"

"Nary a word. She wasn't a one to talk a lot."

"Did she send a lot of candles by mail?"

"Yes."

"Register 'em or insure 'em, or how'd she send 'em?"

"She just sent 'em off plain. Time after time I
told her that she'd ought to be more careful an' do
something in case the candles should get lost or broke.
But she never did. She used to get old corrugated boxes
from the A. & P. an' cut 'em down to suit her. I don't
know's she ever lost any by breakin', either."

"D'you know any one she sent candles to?"

"Well, there was Mr. Stires. He was her best customer. Then there was some people over to South
Wellfleet an' a lot of the summer folks here in town,
an' some artists from Provincetown an' a lot of folks
that stayed at the Inn, an' all that."

"Who mailed her bundles?"

"She did. She went up to the P. O. every day, 'cept
once in a while when it was awful stormy an' it happened to be my day for comin'."

"Then you wouldn't know who she sent things to, or
who sent her letters?"

"Dunno's I would. She used to have a lot of mail. Catalogues in the main. Like Sears, Roebuck an' seed catalogues an' all that. She," Mrs. Howes added reminiscently, "she was very fond of catalogues, particularly Sears, Roebuck's. Used to read it by the hour, even to tires an' bicycles. She was plannin' on buyin' a silk coat with fur around the bottom of it that she saw under negligées. She was goin' to buy it last year, but with prices comin' down all the time she thought she'd wait until it got cheaper."

"Then you wouldn't know any names of people she wrote to?"

"Guess not. If only she'd registered her parcels like I always told her to, you might of been able to find out. But she wouldn't. She said that if you couldn't trust the U. S. mails—only she used to call it the 'penny post'—she didn't know who you could trust."

"Did she get parcels?" I knew that Asey was thinking of the wicks.

"Land's sakes, yes. Did all the shoppin' she could out of mail-order catalogues. Used to buy a pound of rock candy from Sears every other week. On strings, 'twas. She was real fond of rock candy."

"Did she," Asey tried to make his question casual, "did she ever say anythin' about makin' special candles for any one?"

Mrs. Howes considered. "Well, now you mention

it, seems to me like I did hear her say somethin' about
it. Along last fall some time, I guess it was. They
were for Stires."

"Stires?" I was amazed.

"Yup. That was what I understood. I might of
been wrong, but I don't think so."

Asey nodded. "Who you think done this?"

"I wouldn't know. Down-town they was sayin' that
it was funny that two folks should die of arsenic poison
at the same time, even if they was so far dif'rent as
Mary an' Mr. Stires. 'Tis funny, when you think of
it. Ain't you goin' up to Mary's to look around?"

"We're goin' up later on this mornin'. Would you
want to come along too?"

She looked very pleased. "I would. Shall I take
the flivver over an' meet you?"

"We'll pick you up at your house when we get up
to town. No need of tantalizin' that flivver any more'n
you can help."

Mrs. Howes grinned. "Wish you'd tinker with that
timer when you get a chance, Asey."

"I'll do that," Asey promised, as he escorted her to
the door.

"How about it?" I asked when he returned.

"This feller," he said, shaking his head, "this feller,
he ain't human. He's even got it fixed so's if we got
the candle idea worked out an' got back to Mary, we
couldn't get back any farther, if she was 'live or dead."

"Of course we could find out if she were alive."

"Nope.   Hear what Lyddy said?   She said it was
Stires that ordered the special candles.   That means
that this guy used Stires's name, prob'ly, knowin' that
Stires gave her enough orders from his friends so that
if he'd do anything strange, like sendin' her wicks an'
givin' a lot of directions, it wouldn't mean much to
her.   Mary was sort of like a kid.   She'd never of
thought anything was wrong, an' I don't blame her
much in this case.   See, he's got it all planned out, step
by step, like.   We don't know who wrote Mary, who
Mary wrote; if we did find anything, it'd be in a false
name.   All we know is that some one, some time last
fall, got this idea an' she made the candles."

"But she'd have had to send these candles to a
different address, wouldn't she?"

"Yup.   But what of it?   She'd taken other orders
from Stires that was sent to dif'rent addresses.   We
know that, from all these fellers here gettin' 'em.   Far's
I can see, there's only been two slip-ups in this feller's
plans.   Real slip-ups, that is.   One's that Mary run out
of oil, an' prob'ly candles, too,—that is, all but the
poisoned ones.   The other's that two of us went into
that closet.   If it'd happened that I'd gone in alone,
I'd never of suspected that candle was wrong.   If there
hadn't been some one there feelin' as funny as I did,
I'd never of given it a thought."

He got up from his chair.   "Well, we'll mosey up

an' go through Mary's belongin's. Dunno's I want to but there's a chance she might of kept a letter or else made some notes that Lyddy didn't know about."

He turned around as June stuck his head in the door.

"Hey, Asey, I don't like to bother you, but would it be all right if I were to go out? I'm sick and tired of being cooped up and if I don't get out I'll roll over and die of boredom."

"Where you plannin' on goin'?"

"Well," June hesitated, "I thought I could take the car and go for a little ride."

"Nun-no," said Asey decidedly. "You can't go for no ride. You can walk, though. Better for you, anyway. Give you exercise an' you'll get a lot more fresh air. Only take one of them fellers at the door with you."

"Think I'm going to run away?"

"Nope. Only I don't want you to get into any trouble. Never can tell what might happen, an' you don't want it to happen to you."

"Okay. Can—can Miss Allerton come, too?"

"Miss Allerton," Asey said, "in a pig's eye! Is she talkin' again?"

"Well, no. We've sort of been carrying on a conversation in pencil, and she said she'd like to go out if you didn't mind."

"She goin' to tell me who she really is?"

"She won't talk," June said, "and she doesn't answer anything like that. I've tried to find out. Can she come?"

"Sure."

"And John and Denny and Cary——"

"Father says they can all go," Asey grinned. "Mind that they wrap up, an' lissen, youngster, if you walk along the beach, don't fall into any holes an' don't go an' get stuck somewhere where the tide'll soak you. Be kind of an awful let-down to have pneumony after all that's gone on, but you might 's well be careful."

"Junior'll make 'em toe the mark," June announced. "Thanks, Asey. I'll tell 'em to get ready. Can I pick my own guard? Yes? I want that one with the purple shirt. He appeals to me."

Asey called William in.

"We're goin' up-town. Got a list of stuff? I'll take it. An' now the road's all open, you might get Tom to bring Stires's 'lectric over. Tell him to tow it."

"Have you the keys to it, sir?"

Asey took Stires's key ring out of his pocket. "Know which they are? Take 'em off. Oh, yes. An' take his bags out an' put 'em somewhere where no one can get at 'em. You see anything you think is funny, an' you let me know."

"Yes, sir."

Asey put the key ring back into his pocket. He felt

something, grinned. "William, did Mr. Stires always wear false teeth?"

William looked at me and smiled faintly. "Yes, sir. Ever since Miss Fible knocked them out."

Asey turned to me. "Whyn't you tell me your friend c'mitted assault an' bat'ry on Stires?"

"I never thought of telling you," I answered honestly. "But I'll tell you the whole story right now."

At its conclusion, he laughed heartily. "I see. William, would you know if Mr. Stires'd busted his spare set of teeth before he come down here?"

William frowned. "I don't think so, sir. He was, well, he was rather sensitive about those teeth, sir. He was always terribly afraid that he'd have to go without them somewhere. I think I'd have known, because he'd have said something about them. I packed an extra set in his bags. I'm sure he didn't have any trouble before Tuesday, Mr. Mayo."

Asey nodded.

He gave some instructions to his men; Tom brought around the long gleaming Monster, and we set out for town.

"What makes you so curious about those teeth?" I asked.

"Dunno. They sort of take my fancy. That kind of looks nice, don't it?" He pointed a mittened hand toward the row of white hills, where the snow-laden boughs of the stubby pine-trees were bent down to the ground. Beyond the hills the blue of the bay and the blue of the sky blended together so perfectly that I wondered where one began and the other left off.

"It is gorgeous," I said. "I'm feeling better than I have since Tuesday."

"I know how 'tis. You know, Miss Prue, I been a lot of places, but days like this I'm always glad I come back to Wellfleet. I always had a sneakin' kind of hope that I wouldn't never get to no pearly-gated Heaven when I die. Heaven may be all right for some folks, but like I told that feller from California that bragged so about his ole state, Heaven an' California may be all right, but give me the backside of Cape Cod any day." He waved at a motorcycle cop, and we sped on over the snow-crusted road.

"Asey," I said thoughtfully, "d'you suppose that you'll ever find out who killed Stires and Mary?"

"I dunno." He glanced over the bay. "I dunno."

"But what do you think?"

"You can't," he observed, "most always generally sometimes tell. I'd sort of hoped we c'd find out by Monday. Dunno's we can, but I was sort of aimin' to."

"What?"

He grinned and adjusted the brim of his rakish Stetson.

"I tell you, Miss Prue. I want to see a feller in Prov'dence about a boat for Bill on Tuesday, an' I got somethin' I want to do Monday night real bad."

"What is it that's so important?"

"Well, I dunno's it's so important, Miss Prue. I was plannin'," he touched the button on the musical horn as we turned the corner on to the main street, "I was sort of plannin' to go to the movies Monday night. It's Greeter Garbo, an' it's the only chance I got to see her."

CHAPTER TWELVE

AT MARY GROSS'S

I was still speechless by the time we drew up in front of the little white house where Mrs. Howes "looked after" the doctor.

Lyddy was waiting for us at the door.

"I been waitin' with my things on for half an hour," she announced. "An' I'm all of a twit. Some car, ain't it? Bill give it to you, Asey?"

Asey nodded briefly.

"Well," Mrs. Howes continued, "I should think he would of given it to you. After savin' his life like you did."

Asey looked as though he could have bitten her head off with considerable pleasure.

"Come from Bill's fac'try?" Mrs. Howes went on. "Awful expensive-lookin'."

"Yes," I said, since Asey did not seem inclined to answer, "it came from the Porter factory. It's a special that Jimmy Porter had made for Bill, but Bill never liked it. He said it had too much aluminum."

"Nothin' flashy about Bill," Mrs. Howes agreed. "Found out anything since I left you?"

"Not a thing."

"Dear, dear. But Rome wasn't built in a day, I s'pose, wǎs it? My husband always used to say that it was slow an' steady that wins the race an' I don't know but what he was right."

Asey turned the car up the lane where Mary Gross's weather-beaten house stood. I call it a house, but it was more like a box. It was a Cape Cod cottage on a miniature scale, and the kitchen ell did not look large enough to hold a coal hod.

The doctor was waiting there. "Darling—isn't that a name for an undertaker?—Darling's just gone," he said, "and he told me that you'd be up, so I hung around. He left the keys with me."

In the kitchen Mrs. Howes pointed to a "patent" rocker and began to cry.

"Right there," she said, "right there was where I seen her sittin' last. Knittin', she was; socks for my cousin Edith's boy."

We entered the tiny living-room. A Franklin stove was the only heating apparatus that Mary Gross had had. It was backed up crookedly against the boarded-up fireplace. I wondered that the woman had not frozen to death, for the east wind was fairly pouring up between the cracks of the wide beamed floor. The room was damp and bitterly cold.

The wall ornaments took my eye. There were three crayon portraits of very anemic men, and two wax funeral wreaths in wide walnut frames.

"Them wreaths," Mrs. Howes caught my glance, "was her Great-Uncle Uriah's and her Great-Aunt

Sophy's. Lived over in Chatham, they did. Stage Harbor way."

In the corner was a parlor organ with three hymnals placed precisely on the music rack.

"Mary loved a good hymn," Mrs. Howes murmured.

On a what-not in the corner were piles of pamphlets and papers. There was a gleam in Asey's eyes as he brought them over to the light.

I had not believed that so many patent-medicine advertisements existed. There were literally thousands of them, mixed up with farmer's almanacs of years back. Asey came on a picture of Rudy Vallee and held it up with a laugh.

"She heard him over my radio once," Mrs. Howes explained, "an' when I was writin' for my picture of him, I got one for her too. She didn't like it as much as I thought she would. Said that yeast was made for bread, not folks' innards, an' it was a mercy that they didn't rise like a lot of biscuits if they ate it."

The doctor sat down in a ladder-backed chair and laughed. I helped Asey sort out the papers. There were bills from mail-order stores, tattered catalogues, and a number of dog-eared recipes cut out from the woman's page of a Boston newspaper. But there was not a single letter in the whole lot.

In the next hour we went over that house from the tiny one-room and open-space attic to the small round cellar under the kitchen. Asey and the doctor tackled

the barn while Mrs. Howes and I flipped open the
pages of every book in the house from the family Bible
to old tracts like *Hannah Hawkins, the Drunkard's
Daughter,* in an effort to find something which would
lead to the identity of the person who had ordered the
poisoned candles.

We found book-markers of faded yarn, newspaper
clippings of Lincoln's death, marriage certificates and
deeds and receipted bills of fifty years back. We went
through albums filled with spotted tintypes and time-
stained photographs.

At last, dirty and disheveled, we had to admit failure.

"One thing," Mrs. Howes remarked briskly, "we
won't have to take the carpets up, 'cause they ain't
any, an' I looked under the rugs. They used to be
a real pretty carpet in here, sort of a tan color, it
was, with nice red peonies. It wore out so around the
edges that Mary was scared of trippin' over it an'
fallin', so she took it up last year."

"Nothin' doin'?" Asey asked as he and the doctor,
both looking rather the worse for wear, came in.

"Not a thing. Mrs. Howes, what in the world
could Mary have done with all her papers and letters
and things like that?"

"Prob'ly used 'em to start fires with," Mrs. Howes
replied promptly. "I sort of thought you wouldn't find
much. You see, she didn't take a daily paper, or
any other, for that matter. She never was a one to

care much about what was goin' on in the world.
Sometimes I'd bring her over a paper, but she mostly
used it for fires. She saw a picture of that Gandhi
man in the last one I brought over, an' she burned it
right away. I can hear her now. 'An' him a grown
man,' that's just what she said when she saw his clothes.
'An' him a grown man.' "

"I guess," Asey sighed, "that it's sort of like I suspected. We just come to a dead end."

The kitchen door slammed suddenly and we all
jumped.

Joe Bump, the village half-wit, stood in the doorway.

"H'lo," Asey said, "h'lo, Joe. How're you?"

"Fine. Where's Mary?"

"You want her?"

He nodded. "Yup. Where's Mary?"

"She's not here," I said.

"I want her."

"She's gone away, Joe," the doctor said patiently.
"She won't be back."

"Of course," Joe said fretfully. "I forgot she was
dead. What'll I do with the kit?" And from the
pocket of his worn leather coat he pulled a small black
kitten whose eyes were barely opened.

"Where'd you get her?" Asey wanted to know.

"Him," Joe corrected. "Him. They was goin' to
drown him, so I brung him to Mary."

"He's sweet," I said, picking up the furry little ball.

"Nice cat." Joe nodded his head. "Nice cat. Mother come from fish store, father come from Poor's barn. Nice cat. Double paws."

"What are you going to do with him?" I asked.

Joe shrugged. "Give him away. Too good to kill. Shouldn't kill kittens."

"See here," I said, "I'll take him. Ginger's getting sort of set in his ways and he likes kittens. This one'll cheer him up and stop him from being lazy. I'll take him home with me to Boston, Joe."

Joe nodded his approval. "Ginger's a good cat. I seen him. This cat'll be as good even if he ain't got long fur. Shouldn't kill cats. Shouldn't kill anything, even people."

"What you mean, Joe?" Asey asked slowly.

"Some one killed Mary," he explained, waving a casual hand. "He drives a black car. Saw him Tuesday."

"Joe!" My arms were all goose-flesh and a shiver ran down my back. "What man? Tell us?"

"Know a lot that goes on in this town," Joe announced proudly. "Man came up here Tuesday." He counted on his fingers. "To-day's Sat'dy, yest'dy Friday, next day Thursday, next day Wednesday. Next day to that I saw the man that killed Mary. He had a shiny car."

"Who was he? Ever see him before?" Asey demanded.

"Yup. I come to give Mary some clams. Stopped on the way. Got here late. Real late."

"He d'livers for some of the stores," Asey murmured, "so that part's most likely right. Go on, Joe."

"Come up here an' give 'em to Mary, went away. Just then I hear a car. I hid behind the bushes. Big black car comes up. Man drivin'. Bad face."

"Joe, you say you seen him before. Where?"

"Drivin' cars."

"Where? In this town?"

"In this town an' lots of other places," Joe told him. "He's out to the new house. Stires's house. Man got killed there, too."

"He drives a big black car, an' he's out to Stires's, an' you seen him drivin' cars in this town an' lots of other places? I don't get you, Joe. What other places?"

"Movies. He drives a car in the movies, too."

"What movie?"

"Last one."

"Humpf." Asey thought for a moment. Then he smiled. "Uh-huh. I was there. Big feller with a barrel chest?" He demonstrated a barrel chest. "Hard face, like an ax?"

Joe nodded delightedly.

"Who is it?" The doctor and I spoke in unison.

"Kelley," Asey said. "He's a dead ringer for the feller that drove a car in that picture. I don't remember his name, but him an' Kelley could of been twins. I thought when I saw him the other day that I'd seen him somewhere before."

"Kelley," Joe cooed, scratching the kitten behind its tiny ears, "shouldn't kill anything, not even cats."

I shivered.

"How you so sure he killed Mary?" Asey asked.

"Killed people in the movies," Joe returned with finality.

"Yup, he did. But what makes you think he killed Mary?"

"Who else would of?" Joe was getting tired of answering Asey's questions. He shifted from one foot to the other and looked longingly at the door.

"You saw him go in? Did he go in?"

"He banged on the door an' Mary let him in."

"When'd he come out?"

"I don't know. I went off."

"Whyn't you wait until he come out?" Asey asked, more in desperation, I think, than anything else.

"Cold."

"An' you're sure it was the same man that went to Stires's, the one you saw drivin' a car in town?"

"Yup. I guess I'll go now."

"We'll drive you back," Asey said.

"In a car?" Joe beamed.

"Yup. Doc, when you get through, come over. Joe, you ride in the rumble."

"Rum-ble rum-ble." Joe laughed. He appeared to enjoy the sound of the word.

"What about the kitten?" Asey asked.

Mrs. Howes unwound her red scarf. "This'll do for him. Keep him comfy. Don't it beat all, what Joe told us? I don't s'pose he'd ever of told if Asey hadn't pumped him. I hope Joe ain't makin' this up. Sometimes he means to tell the truth, but he gets it all mixed up an' twisted so's you can't always depend on him."

The black kitten was wrapped up until only his nose protruded from the scarf. He mewed once or twice when the horn sounded, but on the whole he behaved himself very well.

We dropped Mrs. Howes at her gate, even though she plainly indicated that there was nothing she would have liked better than to accompany us, and we left Joe on the main street of the town. The bus, it seemed, was due, and he "always had t' watch it." We gave William's list to the grocery clerk and hastened home.

Asey called for Kelley before he had taken off his coat and hat. Blake overheard him. "Nothing wrong, I hope?"

Asey shook his head, and it seemed to me that Blake looked relieved. "Kelley's a good man," he said almost apologetically, "but he will fight. He gets into scrapes very easily."

Kelley came into the library. "Want me?"

"Where was you Tuesday night?"

"Nowheres."

Asey narrowed his eyes. "Where was you Tuesday night, Kelley?"

"Oh, I went up-town. Had to have some oil put into the car. They had some here in the garage but it wasn't the kind I use."

"An' then?"

"I come right back an' went to bed."

"Kelley," Asey said smoothly, "just stop beatin' around the bush. We got you. We know you went places an' done things. You just break down an' tell us about 'em."

"Well," Kelley looked at the ceiling, "after I got the oil put in, I went up to the pool-room an' asked where I could get a drink. They told me some place out of town an' I tried to find it."

"Up on the Truro road?"

"I guess so. It was on the road that goes down the Cape. They told me I had to turn to the left an' I made a wrong turn an' got into some ole lady's house an' the next left, it landed me into some swamp. Then I come back."

"Ever see the ole lady before?"

"No."

"What she look like? What you say to her?"

"Heavy built dame, she was. Had a lot of gray hair down her back in a braid. I banged on the door for a long while before she answered. She called out first an' asked who it was an' I told her it was a customer. I thought I'd got to the right place. Then she come an' opened the door an' asked me what I wanted an' I told her she ought to know."

"What she say to that?"

"Asked me if I wanted candles. I thought it was some sort of a code so I said sure. Then she let me in, an' I looked around an' saw her bringin' out candles, so I left. I backed out an' beat it."

"An' you didn't buy candles?"

"Say, what would I do with 'em? Of course I didn't buy candles. I beat it. Then after I got in that swamp I decided that the boys was just havin' fun with me an' so I give it up an' come back here."

"You wasn't sent there?"

"No, sir!"

"Never heard of the woman before?"

Kelley shook his head.

"Didn't know she was killed the next night?"

"No. Was she?"

"That's your story an' you stick to it?"

Kelley looked blank. "That's the truth. I just went in an' come out again. I didn't get candles for any one. I didn't get any candles at all. I—I never saw the old lady before. I didn't get anything for any one. I just wanted a drink."

Asey leaned back in his chair and smiled sweetly at Kelley, who shuffled his feet nervously.

"Honest, Mr. Mayo, I didn't get anything for anybody. I didn't."

Asey grinned and then he laughed.

"I tell you I didn't get anything," Kelley said, and he was beginning to get angry. "That's the truth."

"I know," Asey murmured. "I know. Mama, I never touched the jam. Who said you touched it? Well, I didn't. Sure, Kelley. You didn't get anything for anybody. I didn't even ask you if you did, 'f you rec'lect as much. Go on an' tell me what else you didn't do. I kind of enjoy this."

Kelley's face was very red.

"Go on," Asey urged. "You didn't get candles for any one."

"Well, I didn't get any candles or anything else for any one. An' whoever's been sayin' that I did is a liar and a——"

"Cal'late so," Asey said, "I cal'late so. Now——"

There was a knock on the door, and Blake came in. He and Kelley exchanged a look.

"Mr. Blake," Kelley said pleadingly, "this guy says I bought candles for some one from an ole lady that got killed. I don't know what he's tryin' to accuse me of, but I wish you'd tell him it ain't true."

Blake turned inquiringly to Asey.

"I'm sure," he said, and he almost purred, "I'm sure that Kelley's telling you the truth. I've already told you that I never bought any candles from this woman who made Bert's for him, and I assure you that Kelley never bought any for me, either. Really, Asey, I don't see what all this bother about candles has to do with Bert in the first place. I think that some more direct action really might be advisable."

He sat down and commenced his eternal twisting of his glasses.

"Make haste an' stumble," Asey replied cheerfully. "D'rect action's all very well in its place, Mr. Blake. Maybe you just got a dif'rent idea of d'rect action than I have. Just what did you send Kelley after on Tuesday night to Mary Gross's, Mr. Blake?"

"I did not send——" Blake began, but he was interrupted by the advent of Asey's purple-shirted assistant, who rushed in, breathless, dripping wet and shivering with the cold.

CHAPTER THIRTEEN

A FIGHT

Asey got up from his chair and went to the door.

"Hey, Robbins! Kelley, you go stay with Robbins till I want you. Mr. Blake, I'll see you later. Now, Pike, what's the matter?"

"You said those fellers an' all could take a walk, an'——"

"Wait up! Anybody beat it?"

"No. They ain't beat it. They been beatin' each other."

"What? Who?"

"Yessir. The youngster an' the girl an' the tall lean one an' the big feller an' the one they call Denny, they all walked up the beach. We was nearly home again—just down there by the wharf when I looks up an' sees the youngster an' the lean one scramblin' all over each other for dear life. Reg'lar rough an' tumble."

"June an' Kent," Asey said. "How'd it start?"

"Couldn't say. The girl an' the other man was ahead, then come these two, then me an' the Denny one. We was about fifty feet behind. I'd dropped back to light a cig'ret, an' when I looked up, they was goin' at each other hammer an' tongs. I tried to pry 'em apart——"

"Didn't the other fellers help you?"

"Well, maybe they wanted to, but they didn't do anything about it. An' from what those two give me, I'd say that they didn't want to be parted much. I told 'em to lay off, but they wouldn't pay any attention to me. An' after they'd bashed me a few, I got out of it. But I stopped 'em easy, after then."

"How?"

"I bided my time, like, an' tripped the young one an' he went into the water. They was real close to the waves. Kind of worked down from high-water mark, like. Then the big feller went after the kid, an' I tripped him as he went. Got wet gettin' 'em in, but after a dousin' they seemed to cool off a lot."

Asey chuckled. "Fightin', huh? Miss Prue, that makes me cheerful. I didn't think any of these fellers except Hobart had the kind of polish that works off, but it kind of looks like they was all like the rest of us in spite of their clothes an' their talk. Not as civ'lized as I'd thought. Did you get 'em back okay?"

"Yeah. I grabbed the youngster an' told him I'd give him hell if he didn't quiet down an' then I told the older one to keep his distance. They come home all right. Both of 'em was soused under. They'd got soaked an' I guess they was chilly enough to want to come back quick an' peaceful by then." He shivered. "I could do with some dry things myself."

"Go get the butler an' tell him to dig you up a dry outfit," Asey directed. "Tell him to go to any wardrobe he thinks'll fit an' fix you up. Then take a good drink. An' then tell William—no. Tell him as soon as he gets your clothes that I want to see that young feller down here pronto."

The man departed; there was a little puddle of water on the floor where he had been standing.

"Wonder why those two should fight?" Asey mused. "I didn't think Kent was the kind that'd go in for hammerin' people, an' somehow I didn't think the kid had enough gumption. Say, what does that Kent feller do, anyway? He got a business?"

"I don't know that you'd call it a business. His particular hobby is ancestry, genealogy, and all that. He's hunted the Kent family over most of the civilized world. The last I heard, he'd traced it back to some prophet or other. I never asked him because he'll talk for hours when he gets started."

"But don't he do nothin'? I mean, how's he live?"

"His family had a lot of money. His father owned the *Clarion*."

"The newspaper?"

"Yes. But I don't know if John has anything to do with it. I never gave it a thought, and I'm sure he's never mentioned it."

"Them reporters this mornin' sort of bowed down on all fours to him," Asey remarked, "so I guess he has. I kind of wondered at it then. Funny, now you come to think of it, he ain't been mixed up in this at all."

"What about Blake and Kelley, Asey?"

He shook his head. "I was bluffin' Kelley, first. It never 'curred to me that there was anythin' in it, not until he started denyin' things so hearty. An' then Blake was just sort of too smooth. There's somethin' up there. I wonder if it wouldn't have something to do with this here fight."

There was a hurried knock on the door and June entered. He wore a vivid silk dressing-gown over his trousers, and a silk scarf was tied carelessly about his neck.

"Sorry, Snoodles," he said with a grin, "but William told me Asey wanted me in a hurry and I didn't take time out to clothe myself properly."

His lip was cut and he dabbed at it with a handkerchief. There were two strips of adhesive plaster on his forehead and his left eye looked as though it were going to be beautifully black in a very short time indeed.

Asey looked at him, sniffed, and called William.

"Store boy brought up the groceries? Well, bring in a hunk of beefsteak."

June tried to laugh, but his cut lip bothered him. Expertly Asey applied the steak.

"There," he said. "Feel better?"

"Feel all well now," June said facetiously, picking up the little black kitten. "Where'd you get this, Snoodles? Miss Fible's got Ginger down in the game-room modeling him. Now she can make it into a family group. Asey, don't scold Junior. He's taken one beating."

"What," Asey drawled, "what was Junior doin', brawlin' around like a common person on the beach?"

June tweaked the kitten's tail. "Asey," he said seriously, "I'm darned if I know what the trouble was all about. I was talking with John, and all of a sudden he turned around and just made for me. He called me names and I lost my temper, and that's the way it began. I'd never have hit back, ordinarily, but this— this house and all had sort of got me down. So when he sailed into me, I just sailed back. Really, I'm awf'ly sorry about the whole thing. I mean, I don't go brawling around as a rule, and I like John a lot. We always got along awf'ly well. I don't know what got into me—and I'm sure I don't know what got into him."

"What were you talking about?" Asey asked.

"Why, I was talking about the girl. She was ahead of us, walking with Cary. John had said that Cary seemed to be falling for her, and I agreed. You haven't been around with the crowd, but he has seemed to hang around her the last day or so. I laughed about it——"

" 'Member just what you said?"

"Well, not exactly. I think I said that I hoped Cary wasn't serious, because after all, he was old enough to be the girl's father. Then I remembered that John was the same vintage, so I thought I'd better coat it over a little. I said that after all, Cary didn't look old now, but by the time that Desire was thirty, he'd be brushing his hair even more carefully over the back of his head than he does now, if he had any to brush. I think I quoted a cartoon of a sweet young thing and an aged and—er—nightcapped husband. I tried to make the whole thing silly, so that I wouldn't hurt John's feelings. What's the phrase I want, Snoodles?"

"Reductio ad absurdum, maybe?"

"That's it. But I guess I must have annoyed him; he called me a few choice words, and then he just upped and atted me."

I looked at the boy closely as he sat there and played with the sleepy kitten. His wet and rumpled hair was drying into little curls and, except for his beefsteaked eye, he looked very peaceable and blameless.

"What's your father's hobby?" asked Asey suddenly. "I mean, does he have some crazy fool thing that he goes around collectin'?"

"Does he?" June shook his head. "Ask me! Yes, Asey, the man collects pewter. And old prints. Between the two of 'em he drives me wild."

"Has he got any since he come down here, d'you know?"

June nodded. "He—no, he couldn't have. I guess he got that pewter plate in New York. I forgot he couldn't have had a chance to get any since he came here, and I know he had a plate in his closet when I was hunting for a trick coat hanger Wednesday. I didn't come all the way from New York with him; I was in New Hampshire and I caught up with him and Kelley in Springfield, you see. Probably he got the plate on the way."

"I see. What about Kelley, June?"

"He's more of a body-guard than a chauffeur. Dad's had trouble once or twice and so he has to have Kelley around. He's not so hard as he looks."

"June, your father don't look like a business man."

"He doesn't. But you should see him in action. That old boy's a planner, that's what he is. Give him a stiff problem that'd knock any given ten men for a loop, and watch him plan his way out. I get proud of him."

Asey's eyes gleamed. "Okay, June. Run along. An' send John down, will you?"

"So Blake's a planner, is he?" Asey said softly after June had gone. "Just an old planner. Huh. I been huntin' a planner."

"What about this hobby and old plate business?"

"When Walker an' me was goin' through Blake's stuff on our arsenic hunt, I found what I thought was an ash-tray tucked away on the top shelf of Blake's closet. Walker, he said it wasn't an ash-tray, 'twas a pewter plate. I didn't think much of it at the time, but t'-day while we was prowlin' around Mary's, I noticed some plates just like it, only bigger, in the closet. There was two of 'em. Walker said that there'd been three, on account of what he'd tried to buy 'em from her when he first saw 'em, only she wouldn't sell. N'en when I tried to think of what Kelley might of bought or got from Mary's besides candles, I remembered that plate of Blake's. That's why I asked June."

"You think Blake sent Kelley there to get that plate? But how would Blake have known about it in the first place?"

"He could of asked Stires if they was any old pewter around down here. An' if this here's the way I think it is, it'll work another way."

"What do you mean?"

"Well, if Blake did send Kelley to get that plate, then he an' Kelley had a good an' sufficient reason for goin' to see Mary. They could really of got candles, an' said that they was gettin' that plate."

"And if you'd found that plate, and Blake knew about it, that would be a reason for his thinking you might connect Mary and the candles,—it would have been a reason for shutting you in the closet!"

Asey nodded.

"But if that was the case, I wonder why he and Kelley lied about that trip to Mary's?"

"B'cause we can't prove he got that plate from Mary. He might of got it somewheres else, like June said. An' we can't prove that Kelley ain't tellin' the truth. An' it's sure an' certain that Kelley'll say what Blake tells him to."

"Asey, don't you think we've really got on the track of something at last?"

"Kind of looks that way."

A timid knock sounded on the door. Asey grinned.

"Mr. Kent," he said in a low voice. "Mr. Kent comin' in to do a little explainin'."

But it wasn't John Kent. It was the girl.

"Oho," Asey raised his eyebrows. "Come in."

I noticed that her finger-nails were a natural pink and wondered if that meant that she had given up her part.

"Have you found out about me?" she asked.

Asey shook his head. "The lawyers are doin' that. I know now that you prob'ly didn't have anything to do with Stires's killin' anyway, so I left it to them. But I'd be glad to know it all now."

"I—I suppose you think I've been silly. Have you—have you seen June? Is he all right?"

"Little black eye," Asey told her. "Otherwise all safe an' sound."

She nodded. "Well, you were right about Brooklyn. My name's Hoffman. Rachel Hoffman. I knew Cass Allerton. I was in France with a vaudeville troupe that got sunk. He was very friendly with a woman in it, a friend of mine, and after we busted up, she went to live with him. She was with him when he died, and she knew that his daughter was going to come over here. Allerton had told her all about it. Desire was in school, you see. She never saw much of her father anyway. Anyway, Leah got a job and I couldn't find anything to do at all. I was busted, flat. She got money enough for me to come over, and then she remembered about Desire Allerton. You see, even if I came over here, I'd still be out of a job and broke. So she got a passport fixed up and I came over as Desire Allerton. I was only going to stay with Stires for a week or so. Just until I got in touch with a man I knew in New York who'd get me a job. But Stires shunted me down here the minute I got in Boston. I didn't have a chance to do a thing. I was going to call Jack from that drug-store in Plymouth, but that chauffeur followed me in and I knew he'd tell Stires if I did any phoning. So I just got my powders and left. It—I guess it sounds thin, but that's the truth."

"Whyn't you tell us all this in the first place? Don't you know that mask'radin' under another name's sort of dang'rous? Whyn't you tell us?"

"Because," she smiled, and her voice somehow seemed less harsh, "because I thought you'd be sure to find out I wasn't the one you were after, and I hoped I could get away if you didn't. I had some idea that if I didn't say anything, you wouldn't have anything against me. And besides——"

"Besides what?" Asey demanded.

"Well, I rather thought I'd get out of it. I mean, usually I can manage men—that is, I mean, people—"

"Sex 'peal," Asey murmured. "I see. What made you tell us now?"

"I don't know." She lighted a cigarette. "Yes, I do. Of course I do. June kept after me. He said if I told you the truth, then I'd be out of it all, and if I didn't, then you'd keep on suspecting me. That's all. Going to arrest me for going under a false name?"

Asey grinned. "Did you get any money from Stires?"

"Here." She passed over a ten-dollar bill that she took from her sweater pocket. "That's what he gave me. I had just money enough to buy those powders."

"How much you got now?"

"Nothing."

Asey pocketed the bill and nodded. "When we git this ironed out, Miss Hoffman, you come to me, an' I'll finance your trip to New York. Shouldn't wonder if I didn't stake you to a couple weeks' rent, too."

"You're a swell!"

"No, I ain't. You ain't out of the woods yet, young lady."

"I suppose not. But," she rose, "I'll tell you one thing. I feel a lot better than I have for the last three days."

She smiled and left.

"You believe her?" I asked.

He nodded. "It's the sort of story that's silly enough to be true. It'll be easy enough to check up on, anyway. I told Crump to find out all about her."

"Crump? You mean Stephen Crump? Is he Stires's lawyer? He's mine."

"He's Bill's, too, an' mine, on the two 'casions I ever needed one. He'll be down some time to-day. I talked with him this mornin'. Miss Prue, what do you think of Denny James delayin' the search an' gen'ral hunt for us yest'day? I sort of don't like to ask you, but what do you think?"

"It's hard for me to believe that Denny held things up on purpose, Asey. I can't believe anything of the sort. But if Rowena and the doctor say he did, he did. It's possible that he wanted to be sure that they didn't miss any place where we might be. Perhaps he was acting in perfect faith. On the other hand, whoever shut us in that closet wanted us to be there just as long as we could be there."

Asey picked up the black kitten and played with it thoughtfully. "Denny James is a nice feller, an' if you was to ask me, he's the most amiable one of this lot of chaps here. But that holdin' up the hunt stuff is a big black mark against him. An' he got candles from Mary. An' he was there Tuesday. Those candles was in a paper bag. He could of got the poisoned ones then an' changed 'em."

"So could Hobart."

Asey smiled. "Uh-huh. But we're statin' the case versus James. I sort of wish he wasn't so amiable. Makes me more s'picious than if he wasn't. So much for Mr. Denny James right now. Say, did you notice we ain't had no food?"

He went out and got William. "Whyn't you tell us we hadn't et?"

"I'm sorry," William said apologetically, "but you seemed to be busy. Shall I bring food in here?"

"Yup. An' where in blazes is Mr. Kent?"

"Speak of the devil," John said, walking in, "here I am, Asey. Sorry if I've kept you waiting, but I stopped to get a bath and a shower and Cary gave me a rub-down. You can't get a wetting at my age and not take precautions. I'd have come down half-dressed, as June did, but I thought that a few minutes wouldn't make a lot of difference."

Unlike June, John was fully dressed in a dry suit. I noticed that he bore no marks of the conflict at all.

Asey remarked as much and John nodded.

"I used to box at college and I still keep in shape. I—I can't say as much for June. I don't think he has any ideas of how to defend himself."

"I sort of gathered that," Asey said dryly.

"Foolish of him to go for me in the first place," John continued casually.

William brought in trays of lunch, and Asey and I hungrily set to work on them.

"So he made for you?" Asey commented.

"Yes. Yes, he did. He's made no apology, either, and I rather think that an apology is due."

"How'd it all happen?"

Asey buttered a roll.

"Most amazing thing," John said, lighting a cigarette. "Cary and the girl—I notice she's talking again. Has she told you who she is?"

"Yup." Asey gave him the details.

"A friend of a friend of Cass's. Hm. The Allertons went in for friendships. Cass's father—but I mustn't run on. Cary and the girl were walking ahead of June and me. I remarked that Cary seemed to be paying attention to the girl. It was not anything suggestive. The girl, whoever she is and whatever she may be, is good-looking, and Cary is always susceptible. June laughed in an unpleasant fashion and made a rather ugly remark about Cary. I told him that I thought he'd better amend his statement, and he started in to fight. I wasn't prepared for anything of the sort, but I jumped aside as well as I could in all the snow, and told him to stop. He wouldn't, and—well, my nerves had been a bit on edge, and I'm afraid I hit harder than I should have. Lost my temper. We'd all been more keyed up than we realized, I think, and I suppose that there is some excuse, in a general way. But June's attack was quite unprovoked."

"He hit you first?"

"Yes."

"You don't," Asey took a sip of milk, "you don't look like the feller that got hit first."

John smiled. "I side-stepped and ducked his first lunge. Then he led with his right."

"Is kind of a raw recruit, ain't he? Led with his right an' you stepped in an' let him have it?"

"That," John said, "is about the size of it. Asey, I hear by way of Miss Fible's engaging housekeeper that Mary Gross is dead. Is it really arsenic poisoning?"

"Guess it is."

"Strange," John said. "Very strange. Two cases of arsenic poisoning in a small town like this are a coin——"

Rowena burst into the room.

"I want to talk to you, Asey."

"I'll go," John rose and obligingly departed.

"Asey! Prue told you about the ink bottle, didn't she? Well, what do you suppose?"

"You really want me to s'pose, Miss Fible, or will I just say what?"

"Don't joke, Asey. Listen. I took that ink bottle down-stairs with me and put it on a table where I kept my spare clay. I put the top beside it and a pen, so it would seem that I'd been writing and just forgotten to put the cover on. And what do you think?"

"What?" Asey asked obediently.

"Well, June and the girl have been down. They never noticed it. Denny looked at it, but he didn't make any move to touch it. Blake said that I'd better put the top on and John suggested it, too. But just this moment, Cary Hobart came down and began to fiddle around with a billiard cue."

Asey and I exchanged a look.

"He was showing June some trick shots. And he stopped right in the middle of a shot and came over to the table and put the top on that ink bottle. Did it just the way you'd,—well, the way you'd do any casual little thing. Perfectly unconscious of it. Then he went back and finished his shot."

"So-ho?" Asey whistled.

"Yes. And when I asked him why he did it, he looked amazed and said, 'Oh, did I put it on? I'm sorry, if you were using the ink. But I spoiled one of my father's best Persian rugs with a bottle of ink when I was a boy, and I've never forgotten the whipping he gave me. I never have seen an ink bottle without a top since that time that I haven't unconsciously put the top on it.' "

CHAPTER FOURTEEN

MR. BLAKE EXPLAINS

ASEY tucked his thumbs into his belt and grinned.

"Well," Rowena said proudly, "what do you think of that? Don't you think it's something?"

"It *is* somethin'," Asey told her. "Miss Fible, I'm much obliged."

"I may not," Rowena remarked as she left, "be sufficiently worthy to play Doctor Watson like Prue, but I think that my idea in this particular case turned out to be brilliant. I've got another idea, too."

"What is it?"

"I'll tell you after I've got some results."

"What now?" I asked Asey.

He sighed. "We'll look into this later. I want to get our loose ends done up proper now. That ink bottle seemed sort of foolish when you first told me about it, Miss Prue, but now, I dunno. If Hobart's so good at billiards that he can do trick shots——"

"He was playing Tuesday night," I said.

"Well, if he's a player, it might come natural to him to pick up a cue to bang that door shut with. An' he's got as good a motive's any one we found out about so far. This fight business, now. This's int'restin', ain't it? Both of 'em tell the same story, but they's just 'nough dif'rence so's they can put the blame on the other feller. June says he was crawlin' out of callin' Cary an' ole duffer, an' John ups an' ats him. John says June made cracks about Hobart, an' when he tells the kid to take it back, June goes for him. What you make of it, Miss Prue?"

"I don't know," I said honestly. "Isn't it possible that each of them is telling what he really thinks is the truth? Both admitted that they were rather keyed up."

"Uh-huh. But I'd give that alibi more of a ratin' if they'd had this fight when they started out. They'd plowed way up the beach an' was nearly home Walkin' on a beach in any kind of weather is as good as sawin' wood. It'd of taken the edge that they claim they had on their nerves right off an' made it's blunt as an old razor blade. They might of been wrought up when they set out, but after hikin' up the beach an' back, their tempers had ought to of calmed down."

"I don't think it's important, is it?"

"Well," Asey drawled, "it might be that Kent said somethin' about Blake. Maybe he suspected somethin'. Might be that June suspected Kent. I dunno. They's somethin' just fishy 'nough about it that kind of 'peals to me. I'm goin' to get Kelley an' see how much more I can bluff."

Kelley came in. He had lost a lot of his nonchalance and he eyed Asey warily.

"About this little trip of yours the other night,"

Asey began, "I wonder, Kelley, 'f you realize just how much of a hole you're in?"

"What do you mean, hole?"

"Hole or cav'ty," Asey explained cheerfully. "Sort of thing you tumble into an' don't have much fun gettin' out of. Hole."

"Why am I in a hole, huh?"

"Kelley, that ole lady you went to see Tuesday night was killed on Wednesday. You're goin' to get mixed up in a murder if you don't tell us about that plate."

"What did that tin plate have to do with her bein' killed?" Kelley asked.

Asey looked at me and smiled.

"Had a lot to do with it. Now, Kelley, I don't blame you for lyin' for Blake. Blake pays you to work for him an' I s'pose that you got to do what he wants you to. But I'll tell you this, feller, he's puttin' you in a tough place. I ain't a one to go around tellin' people it's their duty to squeal about things, but I'm tellin' you this much, Kelley. You can tell me the truth an' save your skin, or you can lie some more an' get jailed for somethin' you prob'ly didn't do."

"You mean that Blake had something to do with this woman's bein' killed, an' he's goin' to blame me?" Kelley's eyes narrowed.

"I ain't makin' no ac'usations about Blake. Maybe he'll blame you an' maybe he won't. You know him better than I do. You know if he'd let you down or not.

If you think he'll get you out of this, why, prob'ly he will."

Kelley ran his finger around the inside of his collar.

"You know best. Up to you, that's what it is." Asey picked up a book-end and tossed it from one hand to the other. " 'Course, if you'll tell me about that tin plate, an' why Blake told you not to talk about it, why it's a dif'rent matter."

"Look here," Kelley said suddenly, "look here, I don't want to get mixed up in anything. I went to Blake Tuesday an' told him I needed some money for oil an' gas. He gave it to me an' asked me if I'd do an errand. I said sure. He told me to go up to the pool-room an' ask where I could get a drink. Then he told me to go up to that place I went, an' if any one was there, I was to say I was huntin' a drink. If there wasn't any one around, I was to get that little tin plate I got for him."

"Did he give you any money to give her?"

"Nope. I asked him if there wasn't money due on it an' he said that everything was paid for."

"Get anything else besides that plate?"

Asey put the book-end back on the table. He seemed to be paying no attention to Kelley, but I noticed that he was watching his every movement in the mirror over the mantel.

Kelley's reply was prompt. "No. Not a thing. I told the old lady what I come for after I see that she was alone, an' she give me the plate an' I put it up in Blake's room when I come home."

"What'd you tell me about them candles for, first of all?"

"Because that's what she asked me."

"Did Blake tell you just why he didn't want you to talk about the plate?"

Kelley shook his head.

"You didn't ask?"

"No. You see, I been on errands like that before for him. He's always gettin' those tin things."

"An' what d'you s'pose he told you to ask in the pool-room about a drink, first, for?"

"So's I'd have an excuse, I guess, for bein' where I was. Mr. Blake sort of plans things out."

"Did he ever have a fight with Stires?"

"Not that I'd know about. No. No, he never fought with Stires. He had a couple of run-ins with James."

"What over?"

"Well, Blake collects pictures, an' so does James. An' they both go after this tin stuff. Once or twice they run up against the same things an' then they have a grand squabble as to which one gets it."

Asey nodded. "I b'gin to see. Uh-huh. That's all, Kelley. If Blake says anything to you about this plate, let me know. If he has any more plans, you kind of might let me know, too. An' you needn't tell him what you told us."

"Yes, sir." Kelley went out.

"An'," Asey went on, "if Blake's such an all-fired planner, he knows that if we wormed out about the plate, he's got a reason for keepin' it quiet b'cause of Denny James. Miss Prue, this beats me. I seen a lot of high an' mighty people when I went around with Bill Porter's father, but by gorry, I never saw folks like these. No, sir. I'm beginnin' to b'lieve that if they wanted to go from Boston to Los Ang'les, they'd take a boat an' get there by way of Greenland an' South Africa. Nope, they ain't what you'd call simple folks."

He went out and returned with Blake.

"I hope," Blake said quietly, "that you are convinced that Kelley is not involved in all this."

"I guess," Asey returned, "that we'll leave Kelley out of this. You wanted d'rect action, Mr. Blake. You're goin' to get it."

Blake looked faintly hurt. "Why, really, Asey——"

"Yup. Really. Now you sent Kelley up to Mary Gross's for a pewter plate. You told him to say he was after a drink, if there was any one around. You didn't want Denny James to know about the plate, an' so you go to all this meanderin'."

Blake shook his head. "Asey, what has Kelley been saying?"

"Don't," said Asey wearily, "don't go an' tell me that he's lyin', b'cause I know he ain't an' you know it too. D'rect action, Mr. Blake. It's what you ordered."

"All right." Blake took out a handkerchief and began to polish his glasses. "I did as you say. Continue."

"You're a great planner, Mr. Blake. I ain't told any one official, but Stires an' Mary Gross was both killed by the fumes of pois'nous candles that Mary made for some one."

Blake let his glasses fall.

"An'," Asey went on coolly, "I'm tryin' to find out who had Mary make 'em. If you used Kelley's gettin' a drink to cover up that plate business, I think that it's more'n likely that you used this plate business to cover up gettin' them candles that you had Mary make."

Not a muscle of Blake's face moved. Suddenly he leaned over and picked up his glasses and put them away in a case.

"There's no reason," he said at last, "why you shouldn't think that way. You're perfectly justified. I've brought it on myself. But it's not true, Asey. You asked me if I had ever bought any candles from Mary Gross and I told you that I hadn't. You asked me if I knew her, and I told you the truth when I said that I'd heard of her but that I didn't know her."

"You was tellin' the truth," Asey commented, "with inward res'vations, like the feller that ate all the apples he stole."

"Yes." Blake smiled wryly. "I didn't tell about the plate. You see, I had a set of eleven plates all made by a particular man. They ranged in size, and I had only to get the smallest plate to finish my set. I had asked Bert often if he knew of any pewter down here, but he said that people had pretty well scoured the Cape. Then last fall he told me that Mary Gross had a few plates. She let him see them, and from what he told me, I had a feeling that the smallest one was the one I wanted. So I wrote her, and we had a lot of dickering back and forth. I offered her an exorbitant price, but only a few weeks ago did she accept."

"Where does Denny James come in?"

"About a month ago Denny wrote me and told me that he had come across a find. Ten plates of the same sort I had. He wanted a very small one and a very large one to complete his set. He found the large one in New York. He and I have had several run-ins, and he did me very neatly the last time, so I thought I was perfectly justified in getting ahead of him in this. I wrote Bert and asked him not to tell Denny about Mary Gross's plates. Denny was coming to visit me after we left here, and I was going to spring the set on him— and tell him where I got the smallest. That's the whole story, Asey. I'd sent Mary the money and told her that I'd get the plate when I was down here. I wanted to see it, so I sent Kelley after it Tuesday night."

"Why all the cock-an'-bull story of Kelley an' the drink?"

"Because I didn't want it to leak out about the plate if Denny went there for candles while he was here. I'd told Mary not to tell, you see, and I didn't want it to circulate any other way. If Kelley had gone there and some other native saw him take away a pewter plate, the story would go around that some one at Stires's was buying pewter, and any loose pewter would promptly be brought over here. At least, that is what has happened in other towns."

Asey nodded.

"I—well it sounds absurd," Blake said rather nervously. "I know it sounds absurd. But that's the truth, Asey, without any inward reservations."

"I hope," Asey said, "that it is."

"Is that all?"

Asey drew a long breath. "Yes."

William came in. "Mr. Mayo, did you forget about Mr. Stires's bags? I've put them up in my wife's room, and she's seen to it that no one disturbed them."

"We'll go take a look," Asey said.

I picked up the black kitten and took him down to the game-room. To my relief, Ginger seemed to approve of it, and the kitten promptly started to chew Ginger's tail. Rowena was annoyed.

"After I've worked for hours to make that cat sit so that he'd be quiet and picturesque at the same time, you have to do this!"

"Make it a Laocoon group," I suggested, and went up the stairs with Asey.

Mrs. Boles was sitting in a rocker reading a confession magazine, and Stires's three bags were piled directly in front of her. She jumped when we came in.

"I've been nervous," she said, "just as nervous as I could be. I'm glad you come. Do you want me to go?"

"No need," Asey said, "you may be able to help us." He took Stires's key ring from his pocket and unlocked the bags.

Mrs. Boles helped him remove the piles of underclothes.

"See here," she held up a pair of heavy silk pajamas, "these have been slept in. I packed all his things myself, because William was so busy, and everything in these bags was spandy clean. See, here's a dirty shirt, too."

"Seems," Asey said, "that he spent the night somewhere an' put on a clean shirt Wednesday mornin'. That's about all that means. Nothin' else been touched attall 'cept his shavin' things. Huh."

"Did you ever find out, Mr. Mayo," Mrs. Boles wanted to know, "where Mr. Stires was Tuesday night?"

Asey thumped his fist down on the table. "By golly, I knew there was somethin' I meant to do an' didn't, but so many things's been happenin' lately that it plumb slipped out of my mind. Say, didn't he give you any idea at all where he was goin'?"

"No." Mrs. Boles shook her head energetically and

the great coils of black hair on the back of her head fairly bounced. I wondered, inadvertently enough, how any woman with such masses of hair could ever find hats to fit. I was forced to have my own hair cut long ago because, as I told my niece, it was all very well for queens to tee their hats high on their heads, but I was not a queen.

"No," Mrs. Boles continued, "he didn't tell us. As far as we knew when we left Tuesday morning, he was coming right straight down here."

"Who came to see him Tuesday mornin'?" Asey asked.

"I wouldn't know. That girl came just as William and Lewis and I were leaving. Will went back to see if there was anything he could do, but Mr. Stires told him to go right ahead, and to get a room ready for her and for a chaperon."

"Then there was only Stires an' Tom there when the girl come?"

"Yes. I'd left everything for Mr. Stires's breakfast, even to the toast in the toaster and the egg ready for the electric boiler. Tom said he could manage to get things, because I'd left a time table of how long everything was to stay in. All he had to do was plug in a switch and watch the stop watch."

Asey laughed. "Mrs. Boles, do you know of any hard feelin's, as you might say, between Mr. Stires an' the rest of the men here?"

"Well, I wouldn't be the sort to get any one into trouble, Mr. Mayo, but he and Mr. Hobart had two fights I know of about business. Not that I blame Mr. Stires one bit. Mr. Hobart is a very hard person to satisfy, Mr. Mayo. It's not my place to make any comments about the guests Mr. Stires saw fit to bring into the house, but like I told him the last time Mr. Hobart was here, Will and I do the best we can, and if Mr. Hobart finds fault, it's not because we haven't tried to do our best for him."

"What was the matter? Was he fussy?"

"Fussy?" Mrs. Boles pursed her lips. "You can't suit him. He must have his bed so's the upper sheet is just twelve inches from the top of the bed. He sends his boots to Tom to polish, and if Tom doesn't spend an hour on 'em, he sends them back. Too high polish, or too little. Always fussing. Always wanting something different from what it is. Mr. Stires had Will stop at the greenhouse in Yarmouth on the way down to get flowers. I put two nice red roses in Mr. Hobart's room, and what do you suppose? The minute he sees them he calls Will to take them away. He doesn't like the smell of that kind of rose, if you please!"

"What about him an' Mr. Stires an' the business?"

"That was last year. Mr. Hobart, Will says, got very mad and said dreadful things."

"I can imagine," Asey murmured.

"I don't like Mr. Hobart," Mrs. Boles concluded,

"and I won't make any bones about saying as much. I *will* say, too, that if it isn't that girl that killed Mr. Stires, it was Mr. Hobart. All the others are very nice gentlemen."

"Any of them ever fight with Stires?"

"No, indeed. The Blakes and Mr. James and Mr. Kent always was on the the best of terms with him. The Blakes wasn't around as much as the other two. But Mr. Kent and Mr. James and Mr. Stires, why, they used to have a great time. I don't think that Mr. Stires would of ever got over that flu he had three years ago if those two hadn't come and joked with him and laughed him out of it. They had a lot of private jokes."

"What about?"

"Oh, like Mr. Kent used to laugh about the electric, and Mr. James about Mr. Stires's being afraid of women, and all."

"I see. Well, Mrs. Boles, I wish you'd pack those things up an' lock them cases for me. Put 'em in Mr. Stires's room."

"Yes, Mr. Mayo. How are you going to find where he spent Tuesday night, sir?"

"How do you s'ggest?"

"There's a lady, Madame Irene, on Tremont Street," Mrs. Boles offered helpfully, "that found my ring with the two pearls when I lost it. She found a boy that got lost, too. He was the son of a woman I know a friend of and he——"

"Thanks," Asey said hastily, as Mrs. Boles showed some signs of telling us the whole story. "Thanks."

And we departed hastily.

"Asey, how are you going to find where he was?" I asked. "Don't you think it might have some connection with his murder? I mean, a strange disappearance, or delay, or whatever you want to call it, and then his being killed on top of it—it seems to me that if you found out why he went away so suddenly and why he was so mysterious about it, you might get some clue to who killed him."

"True."

"Well," I said impatiently, "what are you going to do?"

"Broadcast. 'Lectrics is scarce enough so that he prob'ly got seen an' remembered. I'm goin' to call up Barnstable an' tell 'em to 'range it for about seven to-night, if they can. Seems," he grinned, "as good an' likely a time as any."

And at seven o'clock, four Boston stations requested information about Stires and his electric. The car was described, the license number given, and the time during which we had no idea of Stires's whereabouts was roughly estimated.

Not five minutes elapsed after the announcement before the first call came in.

CHAPTER FIFTEEN

TWO WHITE BOXES

CALL succeeded call in alarming confusion. Asey sat at the library phone and took notes on a pad until half past eight, when the calls began to drop off.

"What have you found out?" I asked as he rose from the chair. "Where are you going?"

"Goin' to git Phrone an' del'gate her to handle the rest of this mess. She can set out by the hall phone an' save me a lot of trouble."

"But have you found out anything?"

"Learned a lot about human nature," he said, grinning. "You wait till I git Phrone an' I'll tell you everythin'."

He came back in a few minutes and stretched out his lank frame in one of the big chairs before the fire. He leaned back his head and laughed until I thought he would never stop.

"Tell me," I insisted.

"Okay. Here goes for what I got told. Lissen. A man in New Brunswick, New Jersey, he seen an 'lectric on Monday. A woman in Alb'ny seen a black Ford roadster with a s'picious-lookin' man two weeks ago last Sat'dy. A girl in Woonsocket seen a truck with a Missouri license plate that she thinks was the same number as Stires's, somewhere in Rehoboth yesterday.

She ain't sure, as it was dark. There was a 'lectric in Vermont Wednesday, only it was a woman drivin'; there was one in Chicago yesterday. A man with a beard stole a Packard in Wheelin', West V'ginia, an' they want to know if Stires was the same man."

"But, Asey! How perfectly silly! Didn't any one see Stires Tuesday or Wednesday? All that's no help."

"I know it ain't. Honest, Miss Prue, I didn't know there was as many 'lectrics left in the United States. A couple of jokers from New York say that 'lectrics is called street-cars there, an' they don't have number plates. Another feller wants to know how old the 'lectric is. He used to be a dealer an' he wonders if this wasn't one of his ole cars. Sentimental chap, I shouldn't wonder."

"Then all that broadcasting did no good?"

"No, cal'late not. They ain't no one within three hundred miles seen any 'lectric. If they have, that is, they ain't 'dentified it with the one we're after, or with the time we want. In other words, no one saw him. An' he couldn't of been so far away, when you come to think of it, Miss Prue. Say he could make an av'rage twenty miles an hour. That's the very best he could do. Well, give him twenty hours of drivin' out of twenty-four, an' he couldn't of gone over four hundred miles. But his bat'ry wouldn't of lasted all that distance. Either he'd had to of stopped an' got it charged or else of changed bat'ries, an' Tom says he didn't.

Now, all that bein' true, he couldn't of gone outside a radius of a hundred or seventy-five miles in any d'rection. He just couldn't of. Tom don't remember the mileage, but he says he don't think Stires could of gone over two hundred, anyhows. An' he used up over a hundred of that gettin' down here. There you are."

"Then you'd say he went from twenty to forty miles in one direction, came back and drove down here?"

"That's about the size of it. I'd hoped to get some answers from around Boston way, but I didn't. No one around Boston saw any 'lectrics on Tuesday or Wednesday 'cept a cop in Pembroke that saw him Wednesday noon. He had the number an' all, so that's all right. That bears out what I think, that he went some distance north or west of Boston, then come down Wednesday mornin' after spendin' the night wherever he did. They ain't nothin' about Tuesday attall, though."

"What are you going to do now?"

"Well, somethin' more may turn up. Only usually folks would answer a thing like that right away, an' if any one around Boston seen Stires, they'd be sure to let us know right away on account of the broadcast bein' on Boston stations. But they'll ask again later over the whole dum New England network an' maybe that'll bring some results."

"Has Rowena said anything to you about her newest idea?" I asked.

"Nope. She come in here before dinner an' took a couple of big books out. Maybe," he grinned, "maybe she's aimin' to settle it on to you an' me an' Phrone. You can't never tell."

He got up and went to the window. "Car comin'," he announced. "Shouldn't wonder if 't wasn't the lawyer. I sort of expected him sooner."

He went out into the hall and in a few minutes returned with Stephen Crump.

Stephen is not half so well-known as he might be, and I have always felt that if it were not for his firm chin and intelligent face, he might easily be taken for a tap-dancer. He is short and wiry, and he affects suits with stripes.

"I'm glad to see you, Prue," he said as he shook hands. "I'd have been here sooner, but we lost a chain and skidded into a drift somewhere on the Eastham plains. We clogged up the something or other and while it was being unclogged, I took time out and had dinner and warmed myself. I can think of better places to be hung up in than the Eastham plains. But I'm here, anyway. How are things going, Asey?"

"Not so good," Asey returned cheerfully. "Mr. Crump, did you find out about this stray girl we got here?"

Crump nodded as he opened a fat brief-case. "Yes. I called up the real Desire Allerton after I got that telegram from her, but she didn't know a thing about this red-head. So I called up Lesly Crowell—he was a friend of Cass—and got the story from him. The girl's name is Hoffman and she's the friend of a woman named Leah Spengel, who was living with Allerton when he died. The Spengel woman was the cause of her coming as Desire Allerton, from what Crowell said. I don't quite know what her purpose was, but it's pretty certain that she never knew Bert or had anything to do with him."

Asey nodded and told him what the girl had told us.

"Curious," Crump remarked, "but it's probably the truth. Now, what about Stires?"

Briefly Asey told him about the candles and Mary Gross, and of our suspicions regarding Denny, Blake and Hobart.

"You don't think it's the servants?" he asked.

"Nope. It's got a little mite too much brainwork involved for them."

"I think you're right," Crump said thoughtfully. "But do you mean, Asey, that in spite of all this planning of the murderer, you can't get any of the threads?"

"That's it, Mr. Crump. I'd sort of hoped myself that he'd planned too hard, as you might say. But we can't catch up on anything he's left hangin'. Y'see, he planned first that it wouldn't be discovered as a murder. It was. So he planted arsenic for us to find. He tried to get me an' Miss Prue, an' he didn't fail by much. If Mary Gross hadn't made a mistake about usin' her poisoned candles, an' if we hadn't connected her an' Stires an' that closet business, we'd never of known about the candles. But knowin', where's it get us? Lyddy Howes says Mary was goin' to make some special candles for some one last fall. Only Mary didn't keep no letters nor no records. We're pretty much stuck, you see?"

"I see. Yet Hobart had a motive, and that billiard-cue stunt and the ink-bottle cover would seem to indicate that he was the one who slammed the door shut, and the one that planted the arsenic."

"Uh-huh. But Blake's a boy planner." Crump laughed at Asey's choice of words. "An' this pewter-plate business is sort of silly. He could have had Kelley get candles then. He had as much chance for shuttin' us in an' plantin' arsenic as Hobart had. An' Denny James got candles from Mary, an' accordin' to the doc an' Miss Fible, he did his best to keep 'em from huntin' in the cellar."

"What about this fight between John and June?" Crump asked. He had made notes on what Asey had told him, and now he was covering the sheets of paper with tiny rows of triangles. "I don't understand that at all. Of course, John has been known to unleash a nasty and uncertain temper on various and sundry occasions, and I personally bailed June out of jail for being mixed up in some student fights in his college days, but why should the two of 'em brawl?"

"You know as much as we do," I said. "Stephen, what about the will?"

"If you're hunting motives," Crump said, "that will is not going to do a bit of good. Bulk of the estate goes to charity, so do the two houses in Boston and this place here. Harvard and Andover get bequests. Prence, his partner, has an option on Stires's part of the business. The servants get a few thousand apiece, and just for the fun of it, I tried to see if they were in any financial difficulties. The Boleses have a very solid bank-account and Tom saves about half his salary and puts it into postal savings."

"What about the people here?"

"Denny and Blake get some prints and some pewter, John gets some books—most of the library goes to the Museum—and some furniture, and Hobart's given some old guns and a Chippendale secretary. He left none of them any money. All of them have more than they need anyway."

"Nothin' funny about the will? No catches? Nothin' strange?"

"Not a thing, Asey. There is this, however. About a month ago, while I was in London, Stires came into my office with a lot of ideas about a codicil. We—or at least, my son Steve—fixed it up for him. Then the next day, he came in and asked that the codicil be destroyed and that the carbons and memoranda concerning it be destroyed, too."

"What was it about?   D'you know?"

"I thought of it at once when you called me.   But we had no records at all.   Steve had been awfully busy the day Stires came in, and he'd more or less thrust him off on this secretary.   You know her, Prue, that lady with the stiff neck and the shirt-waists.   She's been with us for thirty years and she knows more about the business than I do myself.   Well, here are the notes she gave me.   She won't swear to the accuracy, but this is what she remembered."

He cleared his throat and read.   "As I recall the beneficiaries, they were Victor Blake, Junior, John Kent and Borden James."

"See here," I interrupted, "June and John!   Wouldn't that have some bearing on the fight?"

"It might," Crump said, "except that she can't remember what they were given, or anything definite at all."

"God A'mighty," said Asey disgustedly.   "Mr. Crump, here you go gettin' our hopes all uplifted, an' then you say that.   Didn't she remember nothin' else?"

"Only that Bert's cellar, he still has some pre-war stock, was to be given to one of them.   She rather thinks it was given to Denny James, but she isn't sure. You see, Asey, Stires came in late one afternoon when Steve was up to his ears in work over the Romaine case, and Miss Wheary was just as busy.   She took rough notes of what he wanted, typed out the codicil the next day, but Stires came and got it soon after. If the whole office hadn't been pretty well disorganized, some one would have remembered something more. But that's the way it was."

Asey shook his head despondently. "That's a big pity," he said. "Well, I s'pose it can't be helped. Got 'nything else?"

"These." Out of the brief-case Crump took two small packages. They were sealed with many globs of sealing wax and looked very official indeed.

"What's all that?" Asey asked.

"I don't know. I don't know even for whom they are intended."

"I s'pose," Asey suggested bitterly, "that some one was so busy that they forgot all about them too."

Stephen laughed. "No. I found these in his safe-deposit box. They are to be opened when the will is read."

"See here, Steve," I said suddenly, "what about the Stires emeralds?"

"I don't know, Prue. I've asked Bert about them from time to time, but he never would tell me. He said that he had made his own arrangements, and I took it for granted that he'd given them away or sold them, or something of the sort."

"Couldn't—don't you think that they might be in one of those boxes?"

"Maybe, but I doubt it. That larger one is heavy as lead, and the other seems pretty heavy, too."

"Well," Asey said, "if you've got to read the will to find out what's in 'em, can't you do it? Now we've lost that codicil business, we might get somethin' out of these."

"I suppose," Crump said, "that under the circumstances, it is the best thing. It might be the most important clue in the whole affair, I suppose. Asey, you go and collect every one and I'll read the will and maybe it will make up for the codicil."

"What do you think of it all?" I asked after Asey had gone.

"Frankly, Prue, I think it's frightful. I don't see why any one should kill Bert. He was a good sort, as men go. He had a lot of little eccentricities, but he was kind and decent and all that. I was appalled when I heard about it, and I'm more appalled to find that he was surrounded by a houseful of faithful friends and servants. I don't see how you could have stood it here, Prue, after that closet experience."

"Had to," I said, and told him about Rowena and the tin of biscuit. "She—well, none of us really ate until Phrone came over. She wasn't here when it happened, you know, and somehow it made us feel better. The doctor said when he first told us about Stires that one could be poisoned through clothes, and I give you my word, Stephen, I've kept everything in my bags so that no one could poison me that way. Rowena's never said anything about it, but I notice that she has, too. But after we found out about the candles, I've felt better. I still suspect the sheets though, and Rena's been using a silk nightgown as a bath towel."

Crump threw back his head and laughed. "I suppose I could trust you to see the funny side of it, Prue. But it is frightful. It doesn't seem to me that any one of those men is guilty, yet I agree with Asey that it must be one of them. It couldn't be any one else."

"Asey said you were his lawyer," I remarked.

"Porter left him a tidy sum of money," Crump said, "and I've looked out for things for him from time to time. He's not rich, but he has more than most people give him credit for having. Asey is a great sort. I stopped in to see Burnett at Barnstable on the way down, and he agreed with me. He said that he was being severely criticized for letting Asey handle this, but that as far as he was concerned, if Asey couldn't find out who killed Stires, no one could. His methods, Burnett said, might not be strictly conventional, but he thought that Asey would get results."

Asey came back. "They're all waitin'."

Crump picked up his brief-case and put on a pair of heavy shell-rimmed glasses.

He stood before the fire in the living-room and read through the legal phrases of the will. I have never been able to understand the simplest legal document, and had I not been told the gist of it before, I greatly doubt whether or not I should have understood the small part that I did.

The men, however, seemed to have no difficulty in grasping the essentials from the maze of whereases and wherefores. I noticed that when Crump came to the bequests to the servants, not one of them seemed at all happy at his fortune. They cared, I decided, more about losing Stires than getting his money.

"And now," Stephen said, putting the will back into his brief-case, "now I have two packages here which I have been commissioned to open after Stires's death. I do not know if they are intended for any one in this room, but if such is the case, I hope that the recipient will be good enough to open them at once. I have a particular reason for making that request."

He snapped open a pocket-knife and slowly broke the seals and cords of the two small packages. Every one leaned forward in their seats, much as if Stephen were a magician and they expected him to pull a rabbit and a bowl of goldfish out of the wrappings.

Stephen is something of an actor. But I am inclined to think that he overdid himself that night. Certainly two packages were never opened more slowly, and when he had peeled off the second layer of seals and paper, Asey gave vent to his feelings.

"Many layers as an onion," he whispered in my ear. I watched patiently while Stephen blew his nose, adjusted his glasses and gave a preliminary cough. He picked up the smaller of the two packages, read the name on it, and a look of utter amazement spread across his face. He opened his mouth as though to speak, closed it again, picked up the larger package, read the inscription on that, and cleared his throat again.

"Rowena," he said gravely, "these appear to belong to you."

"To me?" Rowena looked as though she had been struck by lightning.

"Yes. Will you be good enough to open them?"

Dazedly she got to her feet and took the packages. Stephen offered her his pocket-knife ceremoniously and she took it with a little nod of thanks.

She was as quick in opening the little white packages as Crump had been slow.

She opened the bigger box, looked at its contents and flushed a deep crimson. She looked into the smaller one and then did something which I am sure she never did before in her life.

She fainted.

While Phrone rushed to her, I followed the rest to the table to see what was in the boxes.

In the larger one lay half a brick. In the other, the Stires emeralds twinkled and shone.

CHAPTER SIXTEEN

MISS FIBLE

BETWEEN us, Phrone and I got Rowena up-stairs and into bed. She seemed too dazed and bewildered to know where she was or what she was doing—and she spoke not one word. That, I think, worried me more than anything else. For I had known her long enough to be certain that when Rowena did not express herself, the situation was very bad indeed.

"I'll look after her," Phrone said briskly. "You go down an' see that Asey Mayo keeps some one by that telephone. An' here," she passed over a sheet of paper from the pocket of her gray sweater, "here's the rest of his calls. Ain't nothin' about Stires, attall."

I took the list and went down-stairs somewhat reluctantly.

"How is she?" Hobart asked as I passed by the door of the living-room. "Don't you suppose that a bromide pill would do her some good? I've got some up in my room."

Denny James overheard his offer and snorted. He and Hobart had not exchanged two words since Walker had found the arsenic in Hobart's cold pills.

"Pills!" Denny looked at him, went to the phone and called up the doctor.

Asey came out of the library, sensed the situation and

grinned. "Tell you what, Mr. James, after you git through that call, you just stay by the phone. Take down any calls you git about where Stires was, an' just make a note about 'em unless it's pretty certain that it is Stires that they're talkin' about."

"For how long?"

"Till I tell you to stop. Miss Prue, is that Phrone's list? She didn't get anything either? I didn't think so. Come into the lib'ry."

"How's Rena?" Crump asked. "If any one had told me that I should see Rowena Fible faint, I'd have called him an out-and-out liar without any hesitation whatsoever. I don't understand it. Prue, you're a woman and presumably you understand the psychology of your sex. You explain why Rowena fainted."

"Well," I said hesitantly, "I might be able to give an explanation, but whether or not it is the right one, I don't know. You remember about Rowena's knocking out Bert's teeth? That's the beginning, I suppose. Then, when she told John that she'd come here Tuesday, she made him promise that he would have Blake and Bert sit next to her. You know how Bert would have felt at that. That is, she came here for the principal purpose of making Stires squirm. If you remember about the teeth, you recall that Bert said some pretty nasty things about her. She'd always resented them, and I think she came here for revenge. See here, am I being at all clear?"

"We follow," Crump said.

"Well, when Bert came in Wednesday night, so cheerful and pitiful in his dripping clothes, and after he accepted our being here so sportingly,—he just sort of took it in his stride,—Rowena said that she certainly shouldn't think of baiting him at all. And that night when we all came up to bed, she spoke to Stires and told him that she was sorry she'd thrown the brick. He told her that he was sorry for his part, too."

"Gen'ral r'c'nciliation," Asey remarked.

"Yes. That's about all, except that I suppose when she saw the brick and the emeralds, she was overcome with remorse for the way that she had crawled into this party, and for her ideas of revenge, and all that sort of thing. Rowena's a much more sensitive person than most people will admit." Crump raised his eyebrows. "She is, Steve. She felt this murder a great deal more than she pretended to. The rest of us did our best to hide our feelings, so she did too. I suppose this was more or less the last straw. Why do you think Bert left those things to her?"

"The brick, so that she'd know that he never forgot that episode till his dying day; and the emeralds are— er—coals of fire." Crump smiled at his own wit.

"Nonsense! He didn't mean anything of the sort, Steve. He told her the other night that he'd always wanted to apologize for the things he'd said about her, but he'd never known how to go about it. This

is simply his way of apologizing. In fact," I continued, "I always thought that he was rather sweet on
Rena. She'd deny it, of course, but if Bert didn't
leave her those stones as a sort of apology, then it
was sentiment, pure and simple. The more I think it
over, the more certain I am that it *was* just sentiment."

"If you are so sure that it was sentiment," Crump
returned, "why'd you ask me? It's possible, of course,
that you are right, but there's another side to it. You
might even say that Stires suspected that she might
attempt some revenge for the names he called her, and
left her the brick and the jewels just for that reason."

"Steve! Are you crazy? Why, you're practically
accusing her of killing Bert! Asey, you don't believe
that, do you?"

Asey avoided my eyes. "Well," he drawled, "I
dunno's I'd go as far as to say that, but you can't most
always tell. Miss Prue, what did she come down here
for anyway?"

"She'd been modeling a fountain for a gangster and
she wanted to get the household out of her mind. She'd
had to use the gangster's children as models and from
all she's said, I judge that they were pretty nasty. And
she wanted to paint her house."

The two men smiled. For the first time it occurred
to me that it was an awfully weak-sounding reason for
a trip to the Cape.

"Goin' to paint her house in March?" Asey commented. "An' she come here to bother Stires an' changed her mind b'cause he looked so sad when he was drippin' wet?"

"You make me perfectly furious!" I announced.

"Really, Prue," Crump said, "look at this teeth business in another light, and you'll see what we're driving at. Every one remembers about it. Probably no one has ever ceased to remind her of that brick. I used to greet her myself by asking if she'd hurled any bricks lately. Now, if she's as sensitive as you say, can't you see where it would have worn on her nerves to an extent where she'd do anything to stop the cause of it?"

"I do not," I replied firmly. "For one thing, it would only bring the story into circulation again. I can see where she has undoubtedly got tired of hearing about it all, but I can't see a woman like Rowena Fible killing poor Bert Stires for such a reason."

"You must remember, Prue, that the Fibles are an unusual family. They have remarkable brains, and I shouldn't underestimate 'em. The late Governor was one of the most remarkable men I have ever encountered. I was with him at a banquet once when he silenced a dull after-dinner speaker by the simple expedient of ordering a soft boiled egg and tossing it into the electric fan over the man's head. Rowena's mind is every bit as unusual as her father's."

"But, Steve, you certainly can't accuse Rowena of

murdering Bert because her family threw soft-boiled eggs around!"

"Did she ever see much of Stires?" Asey wanted to know.

I shook my head. "She told me she'd never seen him or spoken to him since that day. But she saw a lot of him before then."

"But you don't know," Stephen said, "that she hasn't seen him recently. You couldn't prove it that she hasn't."

"None of us," I answered wearily, "can prove that the moon is or is not made of green cheese, Stephen. But we can be reasonably certain of it. We just happen to feel that it isn't. And I feel that you're just barking up the wrong tree."

"Does Miss Fible like jewelry?" Asey asked. "Did she know about Stires's em'ralds?"

"All Boston does. And Rowena's got her mother's pearls. They're as famous as Bert's stones. Rena's got all of the Fible jewelry. She wears it a lot, and she's fond of it. I—er—I——"

"What?"

"I was just thinking," I said lamely, "of what she said about Betsey's engagement ring." I didn't want to tell them what I was thinking in the least, but with a gimlet-eyed lawyer and a man like Asey Mayo determinedly cross-examining, one has very little choice.

"That ring," Asey mused, "was a square-cut em'rald.

I seen it even before Bill give it to Betsey. What'd
Miss Fible say?"

"She liked it. She, well, she just liked it. That's
all."

"An' she wished," Asey carried on, "that she had
one like it?"

I nodded.

"An'," Asey continued, "she had ev'ry chance to git
candles from Mary Gross. More chances'n any one
else, b'cause she was in town almost all of last summer.
An' when you an' me started out for the cellar, she
knew we was goin' after something. If she'd put that
key in the bowl, she'd of known just where, too. She
was the last one we saw when we started out on that
journey."

"Which reminds me," I interrupted, "that you have
never found out how that key got out of Stires's pos-
session, since William said that not even he or his wife
had one of them. Now, if you're going to say that
a key'd be easy to get, you must admit that it would
be easier for one of the men than for Rowena, since she
never saw him."

"On the other hand," Stephen said gently, "we don't
know that she didn't see him."

I sighed. There was a knock on the door and
Denny came in.

"Any news?" Asey asked.

"No. But the night operator says that we won't get

any more phoned telegrams to-night, and that she'll take any calls that come in an' phone 'em over in the morning."

"Did you ask her to do it," Asey's eyes twinkled, "or did she suggest it?"

"She—er—she suggested it. Very amiable girl. But really, Asey, there's not been a call for hours and hours, and I'm sick of sitting."

Asey pulled out his old-fashioned silver watch.

"Well," he said, "that was to be broadcast again at nine, an' it's near 'leven-thirty. I guess if we ain't got results now, we never will. Okay, Mr. James."

"Thank heaven." He turned to me. "Prue, how about some bridge?"

"She's busy," Asey said quickly before I could answer.

Denny looked at me and raised his eyebrows. "Oh, very well. Getting any forrader?"

"Sort of. Say, do you remember when we was in the closet? Who suggested starting at the top of the house an' workin' down?"

"I don't really remember, Asey. I rather think it was Rena. She'd seen you last and I think she was under the impression that you'd gone up and not down." He chuckled. "Sounds Biblical, doesn't it?"

"You remember if any one sort of held up the hunt?"

"Rowena made us look into every nook and cranny and closet," Denny said. "The rest of us insisted that you couldn't possibly be on the second floor, but she forced us to spend hours there. Or so it seemed. It was a pretty dreary business, that hunt. We were all at our wit's end."

Asey nodded, and Denny went out.

"But Rowena told us that he—that he was the one that did all the delaying," I gasped.

"So," Asey agreed gravely, "so she did. Kind of funny, ain't it? Not funny ha-ha, but plain funny peculiar. Sort of d'vides itself into two schools of thought, this does. You can b'lieve Miss Fible, or you can b'lieve Denny James. Now I come to think of it, Miss Prue, the doc didn't c'mit himself the other day. He told us to ask some one else, b'cause he couldn't remember on account of bein' excited about Mary. So Miss Fible was the only person that told us about Denny. I s'pose that we could ask some one else an' sort of get a line on which was tellin' us the truth."

"Ask them," Crump suggested, "and have them write their answers on a piece of paper with their names underneath. It may not prove anything, but it might."

Asey got up and went out. In a few minutes he returned.

"Mr. Kent," he announced sardonically, "says Miss Fible. So does Mr. Blake. June and Hobart stick out for Denny. The girl doesn't remember which."

"Why don't you try the servants?" I asked.

"B'cause I'd be willin' to wager right now that they'd

be just as muddled up as these folks is. Mr. Crump, you may have been wonderin' why I ain't got no results. Well, here's a good example of what's been happenin' right along. You get a little somethin' on some one, an' whee! It goes an' hitches itself over to some one else. At least, by gorry, we got two people with sort of motives, an' they ain't been no one yet 'cept Miss Prue that ain't had a little s'picion on 'em. I wisht I'd gone to B'muda like Bill wanted me to this winter. I wisht I'd gone to Kal'mazoo." He got up out of his chair and began to pace back and forth across the room. "I wish—what's the matter, Phrone?"

Breathlessly, Phrone told him. "It's Miss Rena. Just after Miss Whitsby went down-stairs, she commenced to cry. She's been cryin' ever since. Her eyes is swelled all up an' her pillow's soakin'. I can't seem to git her quieted down."

"Why for?" Asey asked.

"I can't," Phrone shook her head, "make head nor tail of what it's all about 'cept that she's sorry for somethin' she did to Mr. Stires, an' she keeps mutterin' something about candles."

Asey and Stephen dashed from the room, and Phrone and I followed them up-stairs.

Phrone had not exaggerated when she said that Rowena's eyes were swollen. They fairly bulged from her head. Her face was tear-stained and drawn, and all in all, she seemed to have worked herself into what my modern niece would have called a "crying jag."

Cold cloths and an ice-bag and a drink of whisky seemed to restore her to some semblance of normalcy. Asey fidgeted around, and I knew that he was anxious to ask her why she was "sorry for Stires" and just what the candles had to do with the case, but hesitated for fear of starting her off again.

"I'm sorry to be such a nuisance," she said weakly at last. "Phrone shouldn't have bothered you all. Prue, you'd better get Mrs. Boles to find you another room. I'll probably keep you awake if you stay in here."

I protested.

"Don't be foolish. Really, I don't know what started me off like this. I don't. Except that the combination of that brick and the emeralds was too much for me, after all the goings-on. Really, I've never felt so much a criminal, as when I saw those emeralds, I mean. Do you think that I should keep them, Stephen?"

"They're yours," he told her, "to do as your fancy dictates."

"I've always wanted emeralds," she said, and I tried to catch her eye and signal for her to stop talking about them. "Always. Bert knew how I admired them when his mother used to wear them. But I'm sure that I'll never feel happy about these now. Steve, you don't know how I've disliked Bert all these years. The whole thing makes me feel ashamed of myself."

"Don't be silly," I said, "you and he forgave and forgot that whole tooth affair the other night. That made up for everything."

"But it doesn't, Prue. I didn't tell you about the candles."

I groaned.

"What candles?" Asey asked casually.

"Well, I'd got some candles from Mary Gross last summer, after much fussing around. She wouldn't make candles for every one, and it took considerable persuasion. When I heard that she was dead, I knew I'd never get any others, and I'd been wanting two more to go in some new holders I've just bought. So I—really, this is disgraceful, but I suppose that the sooner I tell some one and get it off my mind, the better I'll feel about it——"

"Are you sure," I asked hurriedly, "that you don't want to go to sleep? I mean, after all this, you must be terribly tired."

"I am. But I've got to tell all of you about this, or I'll never go to sleep in this world. I went up-stairs and actually stole two candles this afternoon, from one of the spare rooms. I didn't think that they'd ever be missed at all, and I did want them terribly. And in the face of my doing a rotten thing like that, Bert goes and leaves me his emeralds."

I drew a sigh of relief. She had, consciously or unconsciously, explained the incriminating statements which Phrone had passed on. But after looking at the expressions on Asey's and Steve's faces, I understood that her explanations meant little, as far as those two were concerned.

"Have you got those candles here?" Asey wanted to know.

"In my dressing-table drawer," she said. "Get them for him, will you, Prue? And do, for mercy's sakes, put them back up-stairs. I shan't feel quite so much like a thief when I know that they're back."

I took the candles as she directed and gave them to Asey.

"I'll be back later," I said, "and do go to sleep."

"Where's the doctor?" Phrone asked. "Didn't some one phone for him?"

"Denny did a long while ago," I said, "but he's probably been delayed on the way."

"I'll look after her all right," Phrone said, "an' I'll get a room fixed up for you an' put your things in it."

Slowly, I went down-stairs behind the two men.

An hour before, I had been convinced that Rowena was as innocent as I was myself. Now, in spite of her explanations, I was beginning to have very great doubts. It is impossible to believe that a life-long friend is a murderess,—yet I couldn't help remembering that another life-long friend had seemed equally as innocent to me on a similar occasion, and had not been.

I nearly bumped into Denny on the bottom step.

"Anything wrong with Rena?" he demanded.

"Oh, Denny," I sighed, "Stephen Crump has some notion that she killed Bert, and now Asey's beginning to believe him, and she's gone and said things that would make any one believe it, and then there are those teeth!"

"Teeth?" Denny repeated blankly. "Oh! Those teeth she knocked out. What do they think, that she missed getting him then, and has finally got him? But that's silly. Of course she didn't kill Stires. Hobart did. It's written all over the man. I don't see why Asey hasn't done something about him before now. Prue, you look tired and forlorn. Why don't you leave those two Sherlocks and go to bed?"

"I can't," I said. "They're going to sit there and convict Rowena, and I've got to stick my oar in and convince them that they're all wrong."

"Prue. Will you promise me something?"

"I've promised you that I won't open a bomb or play with a loaded gun or anything like that."

"Yes, but, Prue, when all this mess is over, providing that Hobart doesn't feed me any more pills, and you don't go wandering into any more closets, and we're both alive, won't you promise that you'll——"

The knocker on the front door sounded, and without

waiting for the door to be opened, Doctor Walker strode in. He was followed by Lyddy Howes. Both were breathless, and in the manner of all people who have something important to say, they began at once, stopped for the other to go on, began again at the same time, until at last Asey came to the rescue.

"Heave away, Doc," he commanded.

"It's Mrs. Howes," he said. She's——"

"In the cook-book," Mrs. Howes interrupted. " 'Twas in that cook-book. The *Universalist Ladies' Cook-Book* that I borrowed from her about two months ago to see if it had Tamsin Cole's recipe for makin' watermelon pickle. She made about the best pickle——"

"Borrowed from who?" Asey asked.

"From Mary Gross, of course. Who else? I couldn't remember just how much sugar she used in her sirup—not that I was makin' any watermelon pickle this time of year, but I wanted it for that Mrs. Hopkins, the Brown's Neck one——"

"An' what?"

"Land's sakes, Asey Mayo, won't you give a body a chance? I'm gittin' there just's quick's I know how. I couldn't find my own book, an' then I remembered I'd lost it an' borrowed Mary's. An' that was how I found the letter, b'cause I just thought I'd hunt it up b'fore I went to bed. It was on my mind like——"

"You found a letter? To who? From who?"

"To Mary, of course. Who'd you think? It was right next to Effie Follette's recipe for makin' soap. She always made the best soap of any one I ever knew. Better than the kind you buy now——"

"Who was it from?" Asey used his quarterdeck voice, but it did not startle Mrs. Howes.

"It's signed by that butler person. William——"

CHAPTER SEVENTEEN

A LETTER AND A SCRAP-BOOK

Asey dragged Mrs. Howes and the doctor into the library, and somewhat bewildered, I followed.

"Let's see the letter," Asey demanded. "Where is it?"

"I got it right here with me. Found it just as the doctor was startin' out, an' if I didn't have a time tryin' to get him back!" She reached into the pocket of her tweed coat. "It's right here. No, 'tain't neither. Doctor, you don't s'pose I left it at home, do you?"

"I hope not. Try the other pocket."

She brought out a driving license and a small-change purse, a key, a package of soap dye, and finally she produced the letter.

"Here 'tis," she said with a sigh of satisfaction. "I certainly almost thought for a second that I'd gone an' forgot it. I was so excited about findin' it that I was liable to of done most anything."

Asey took the letter and read it aloud.

" 'My dear Miss Gross:
" 'I am sending you to-day material for the special candles about which I spoke to you last summer. There is one extra wick, in case you should meet with any difficulties. I will let you know later as to where they may be sent.

" 'You have been very kind to do this for me and I assure you that I am most grateful.

"Faithfully yours,
" 'WM. BOLES.' "

"Well!" I exclaimed, "and you were so certain that the servants had nothing to do with this, Asey!"

"I'm still," he scanned the letter, "I'm still not so sure. This is written on a typewriter, for one thing, an'," he licked his forefinger and rubbed the signature, "this name's been put on with a rubber stamp. An' for another thing, Miss Prue, William may talk kind of formal like, but this 'about which I spoke' business would of been too much for him. He'd of said 'that I spoke about.' An' he'd of used 'got into trouble' instead of all this 'meetin' with dif'culties.' An' 'Yours truly,' not 'Faithf'ly yours.' Nope, William's name may be at the bottom of this, but I'm bettin' that it ain't William that wrote it."

Crump had been hunting around in his brief-case, and now he produced a check and gave it to Asey.

"One of William's endorsed pay checks," he said. "See if the signature is anything like it."

"It's just like it," Asey said, " 'cept for the *e*. The *e's* dif'rent. See, Miss Prue."

"It's a Greek *e*," I said. "I use it myself."

"Funny," Asey said, "that the feller should make that break. Darn funny. I guess we'll get William down an' see what he has to say about it."

William read the letter and gasped. "I never wrote that," he said. "Honest, Mr. Mayo. It looks like just the way I write my name, but it's different, somehow."

"How dif'rent?"

"I can't tell." He picked up the letter and examined the signature closely. "Yes. It's the *e*. I don't make that kind of an *e*. Mr. Stires always used to, though."

"What?"

"Yes, sir. There were three *e*'s in his name, and I often noticed how he made them. I"—William coughed—"I tried to make 'em that way myself once, long ago, but it was too hard. I gave it up. I don't think I ever signed my name with one, anyway. I just practised, as you might say."

Asey nodded wearily. "Okay, William. That's all."

"I wonder," Stephen said, "about this 'extra' piece of material. How many poisoned candles have you found?"

Asey laughed. "One, really. Only one we're sure about. But there was six at Mary's house an' five in Stires's room. That would mean that he ordered a dozen."

"A dozen plus the extra one," Crump corrected. "But why aren't you sure about the eleven?"

Asey explained the method by which the wicks had been left unpoisoned for the first and last inch or so.

"I see," Crump said, "but, Asey, how was it that six candles were left at Mary's anyway?"

"Slip-up of some sort, I reckon. Certainly the feller didn't leave 'em there on purpose. Wouldn't be no reason why he should spoil the show when it was a hundred-to-one chance no one'd ever find out about the candles, an' it's sure as shootin' that he wouldn't of killed Mary on purpose. 'Course, he might of, but I don't think so."

"What are those two candles on the table?" the doctor asked.

"Some Miss Fible says she swiped from an up-stairs room. I clear forgot about her. You go up an' see her, Doc, an' then when you come back, you look at them wicks."

The doctor picked up his bag, then put it down and looked at the candles again.

"Say, Asey, one of those is marked."

"Where?" We crowded around.

"Here. See, on the sides. There are three single little bayberries stuck in a row in the wax. The other whole ones that I looked at weren't like this."

"Let Miss Fible wait," Asey directed, "an' see about this now." He turned to Mrs. Howes, who had picked up the letter and was reading it again. "Anything strike you about that?"

"Yup. Look here, Asey. This feller talks about special candles. Well, you remember when I told you about that James man gettin' the candles on Tuesday, then the Hobart feller comin' in after? Well, he asked if they wasn't Stires's special candles. D'you s'pose that means anything?"

"Lord," Asey said gravely, "knows an' no one else. Asked for special candles, did he? 'Member how many Mary gave 'em?"

"I'd say there was three 'n' a half or four dozen."

"Hm. How you comin', Doc?"

"Hold your horses, Asey."

We held our horses, so to speak, for fifteen minutes, at the end of which time Walker straightened up from his work.

"Marked one's arsenic," he said. "Other's all right."

"Six," Asey said, "an' five an' one in the closet an' then this. A dozen, plus one. Well. An' Miss Fible had it!"

He yawned abruptly.

"What are you going to do?" Crump asked.

"I'm goin' to bed," Asey said. " 'Nough's 'nough. An' this p'tic'lar camel refuses to carry any more straws for one night. Mrs. Howes, I thank you kindly. Doc, you see Miss Fible an' tell Phrone what to do."

"What about Greta Garbo on Monday?" I asked slyly.

"Mebbe," Asey informed me as he opened the door, "mebbe I'll git to see her grandchildren, but I got my doubts even of that."

And mentally, I agreed with him.

I slept that night in a bedroom where Phrone had

thoughtfully placed my clothes. I was too tired even
to remember the precaution of locked doors and bar-
ricades; I was too exhausted to care particularly
whether or not some one murdered me in my sleep.

The strain of the last four days suddenly began
to tell. I felt like an air cushion that has been sat
upon once too many times.

It was after nine Sunday morning when Phrone woke
me up.

"Nothin's the matter," she said in response to my
question. "Only Miss Rena wanted to see you. I sort
of hated to bother you, but I banged an' yelled like a
wild Indian outside of your door, an' I kind of thought
'twould be a good thing to come in an' make sure that
no one done away with you durin' the night."

"No one has," I assured her with a yawn. "I don't
want to rise and shine, Phrone. If I had my way I'd
never plan to see daylight before ten-thirty. What
does Rena want?"

"I dunno what she wants. Seems kind of wrought
up, she does. Say, Asey told me about them candles
an' Mary. Wasn't nothin' wrong with them candles
you took last night, was there?"

I nodded, and Phrone clucked her tongue. "Well,
I'm pos'tive Miss Rena didn't have nothin' to do with
all this, even if they prove it. Miss Prue, I'm dependin'
on you to see that them men don't get her mixed up
with Stires's death."

"I'll do my best," I said, "but I have my doubts."

I went down to the yellow room to find Rowena still in bed.

"I wanted to get up," she explained, "but that doctor's a determined sort and Phrone simply won't co-operate. Prue, there was arsenic in those candles, wasn't there?"

"How'd you know about the candles?"

"Oh, Phrone told me. But in those you took, I mean. Something was wrong with 'em, wasn't there?"

I nodded.

"And Asey and that shrimp of a Stephen Crump are beginning to suspect that I killed Bert, aren't they?"

"Well," I began lamely.

"Prue, you couldn't prevaricate if you wanted to. They do suspect me. Well," she sighed as she wriggled around in the bed, "I suppose they have every reason to think so. But they're wrong."

It occurred to me that Blake had said exactly the same thing.

"I know that they're wrong," I said, "but how can you explain away that candle?"

"Mrs. Boles," she said calmly.

"Mrs. Boles? How could she have had anything to do with it?"

"Just before dinner yesterday I came up-stairs, and I saw some one slipping into the room. I switched out the light in the hall and pretended that I was a part of the wall. Pretty soon she came out. She had some dirty towels under her arm, and I s'pose she came to bring clean ones. But—she could have hidden the candles she substituted for mine under 'em when she came, and taken mine away, all covered up. See?"

"Did you look at the candles after she left?" I asked.

"Nope, as Asey would say. The only reason I watched her so closely was that I've become wary of people slipping into rooms. But when Asey snatched those candles last night and you began to make faces, I decided that something undoubtedly would prove wrong. It seems to have."

"Rowena," I said sadly, "why didn't you leave me alone and——"

"And let you buy your orange silk? Pish-tush, Prue. And two pshaws. Things would have happened here whether we'd come or not. And you'd never met up again with Denny, and I'd never have had the chance to do Blake's head. Are you going to marry Denny, by the way? He's so jealous of Asey that he can't see straight, and he's so furious with Hobart that what he does see is bright crimson. You really should put him out of his agony. Prue, be a lamb and fetch Asey, and then I won't tease you for blushing."

"I'm not blushing," I told her coldly. "And what d'you want with Asey?"

"You'll see. Look here, Prue, before you go. Are

they convinced that I killed Bert, or are they only suspicious?"

"I couldn't say. Hobart and Blake and Denny,—oh, every one's all muddled up. I don't think Asey's made up his mind on anything. Why?"

"I just wondered if they'd believe my new idea, or if they'd think I was trying to push the blame off on some one else."

"I see. Is it awfully important, or may I get my breakfast first?"

"Eat first, by all means."

And I did a lot of thinking as I breakfasted. Tom and Lewis were the only ones left who really hadn't been involved in the case. I reflected that the whole situation was somewhat like watching my favorite stocks go down the previous fall. At first they had all seemed of sterling worth and above suspicion—but they proved to be otherwise. So here, every one of whose innocence you were absolutely convinced seemed to droop, point by point, toward new lows of guilt.

Asey wandered in.

"Look like you'd lost your last friend," he remarked. "What's the matter?"

I told him all that Rowena had said about Mrs. Boles and the candles. "Don't you think," I concluded, "that it's possible that that letter is genuine, and that she and William are in back of all this?"

"Seems that way, an' yet it don't."

"When are you going to do something?" I wanted to know.

" 'Round t'morrow. Cheer up, Miss Prue. The Lord will provide. An' He helps them as can't help themselves, or He's s'posed to. An' if that's all true, we should ought to be provided an' helped pretty soon now."

"Rowena's got another idea," I said. "She wants to tell it to you."

"We'll go up when you finished that toast."

Rowena greeted us cheerfully. If she felt at all worried about her position as temporary suspect, she gave no indication of it whatsoever.

Instead she held up a large book. Asey grinned.

"One of them you wouldn't tell me about? What've you discovered? Ink spots?"

"Don't gibe, Asey. I still think that the ink-bottle-cover idea is good. But look here. This is a scrapbook of goings-on during Bert's Harvard days. There are a lot of amusing items, like the Chandler Ball,— remember that, Prue?"

I nodded. "I wore pink satin——"

"No, you didn't. It was blue silk with pink rosebuds and you wore a very daring scarf of pink tulle, that is, if you can believe these clippings. I——"

"Did you find anything in them clippings?" Asey asked patiently.

"Yes. You see, I'd run through it Tuesday after

dinner, and I thought it might unearth something important. Well, there are three clippings here from the *Transcript* that tell of Denny James and Stires coming to blows."

Asey and I reached for the book simultaneously.

"Mm," Asey said, "looks from these stories like they had a good fight, don't it? But it don't say why. Just says resumey of battle. Where you goin', Miss Prue?"

"I'm going to get Denny and have him explain."

And when I told him about the clippings, Denny laughed. "Of course I'll explain to Asey," he said. "I haven't thought about that in years."

"What was it all about?" I wanted to know.

"Carrying on a family fight. Father—good lord, Prue, you must remember. My father and Bert's were both running for Congress. That was when we lived in Boston, you know. Stires was a Democrat and father was a Republican, and Bert and I thought it would be rather a good idea to get a little publicity for 'em. That's all there is to that. Don't tell me Asey's been digging out things like those cut-and-dried battles?"

"Rowena did it. It's one of her ideas," I said.

Up-stairs he told the story to Asey, who chuckled appreciatively.

"I guess, Miss Fible," he said at last, "that this wasn't as good an idea as the——"

He stopped short as Denny casually crossed to the table next Rowena's bed and replaced the cover on the much mooted ink bottle.

"—other," Asey finished quickly. "You're a great one for neatness, ain't you, Mr. James?"

"Not usually," Denny returned, quite unconscious of all the excitement he was causing. "Only that ink bottle looked a bit precarious. Why? You all look so grim."

I drew a deep breath.

"Mr. James," Asey said, "you told us last night that Miss Fible was the one that hung up the search party for us on Thursday when we got stuck into that closet. Now, would you——"

"He said that!" Rowena cried. "He said that I was the one? How perfectly—why, Denny! That's a lie and you know it is! You held things up yourself!"

"I!" Denny's voice was incredulous. "I held them up? I did nothing of the sort, and you know it. It was you that did all the delaying around."

"See here," Rowena sat up in bed and her face was bright pink, "see here, Denny James. For Prue's sake I've not mentioned the fact that I found your handkerchief on top of my dressing-table the day that arsenic was planted around——"

"My handkerchief? *My* handkerchief?"

"You sound like a poll parrot. Yes, your handkerchief, with your initials on it. But this is just a little too much. I didn't think that those clippings were worth a hoot, and I'll admit that I thought you were too worried about Prue to know what you were doing when we hunted for her and Asey, but when you begin to accuse me of——"

"I'm not accusing you of anything."

"You are. And you know it——"

Denny looked at her, surveyed Asey and me and cleared his throat. "Asey, I've kept my temper and not made any fuss about Hobart's lies because I thought that it wasn't necessary. But this is the end of all that."

"Where are you going?" I cried as he started out of the room.

"Going to phone my lawyer, and until he comes, I'm going to take a page out of that red-head's book and keep quiet. I can't keep people from trying to involve me, I suppose, but I can at least refrain from saying anything that will be used against me." He looked at me reproachfully.

"Now," Asey said soothingly, "now don't go an' get excited about this, Mr. James. The doc told you the other day that I didn't want to go around pryin' into folks' business, but I got to. What Miss Fible thinks an' what I think is two dif'rent things. An' prob'ly Miss Prue here thinks even dif'renter. Now, Mr. James, won't you just cool off an' forget all about this silence-is-golden idea? I ain't accused you of anythin', an' after all, I'm sort of the one who would."

Denny hesitated.

"Please," I said.

"Oh,—oh, all right." And he turned on his heel and left.

"What about me?" Rowena asked indignantly. "He was trying to make me——"

"No," Asey said firmly, reaching over and picking up the scrap-book, "he wasn't. Where's that hand-kerchief?"

She produced it from under her pillow.

"Here. But I think——"

Asey's eyes glittered dangerously, but Rowena paid no attention.

"I think, Asey, that that ink-bottle top clinches the matter for him."

"You," Asey said with a certain restrained gentle-ness, "you just rest. Come along, Miss Prue."

"Asey," I said as we got out into the hallway, "she never told me about that handkerchief. I think she's making it up. And that ink bottle was sort of rock-ing. I nearly put the cover on myself. Really, I did. I don't think it proves a thing."

Asey looked down at me and smiled. "Cheer up, Miss Prue. Cheer up. What's the matter, William?"

"Gentleman to see you, sir."

"Who? If it's them reporters, I'm dummed if I don't skin them fellers alive. I told them motorcycle cops that if they let one through I'd report 'em f'r gross negl'gence."

"It's not a reporter, sir. It's a doctor."

Asey and I hurried down to the library.

A chubby, apologetic-looking little man with a pug nose jumped as we entered.

"Mr. Mayo?" he asked indecisively, looking first at me, then at Asey. I wondered if he thought that *I* was Asey Mayo.

"Yessir. Right here."

The little man extended a hand as though he were feeding lions in a cage.

"I—er—my wife, she thought—that is," he made a mammoth effort. "I'm Doctor Jerome. Doctor Joseph Jerome." Then, as Asey and I still looked blank. "I'm a dentist. That is, I'm Mr. Stires's dentist."

Asey looked at me and grinned from ear to ear.

"J. J. Five hundred dollars," he said.

"That's it," Doctor Jerome said, apparently overjoyed that we had finally placed him. "That's it. I told my wife it was a lot. That's why I came when I—that is, when my wife heard that broadcast."

CHAPTER EIGHTEEN

J. J.

ASEY waved him to a chair.

"Set," he said briefly. "An' tell us the whole story, if you'll be so kind."

Doctor Jerome backed into a chair and sat very suddenly.

"My brother died a year ago," he began abruptly. "He left me quite a lot of money. So I—that is, my wife—decided that we'd give up our practise. She was my assistant, you see. We left Boston and took a little house outside of Lexington."

He wet his lips nervously. "Mr. Stires had been one of my patients for a number of years and he still continued to call on me every once in a while. My wife and I did all his plates for him. Even after we left Boston, he still came to me. He seemed to prefer our work. Er—people used to call me old-fashioned," he added parenthetically, "because I wouldn't send my plate work to a laboratory. But we preferred to do it ourselves, and, as I said before, Mr. Stires liked my work."

Asey nodded with grave understanding. "I see."

"Tuesday afternoon," the doctor continued, "Mr. Stires drove up in front of our house just as we were leaving. He was most excited, most upset. He had

broken his plate and he wanted us to make him a new
one at once."

"But he had spares," Asey protested. " 'Cause William told us he'd packed 'em."

"That's what I asked him, where was his spare set?
But he said that he'd taken them out of his bag to put
them in after he had broken the others—he was at his
Club, he said—and some person had stolen them."

Asey leaned back and roared. "Some joker took 'em,
huh? An' he had only the busted ones?"

"That's it. That's it. And he wanted new ones
made at once. Now, my wife and I had kept some
of our equipment, but we were hardly prepared to make
him a new plate right——"

"Right off the bat?" Asey asked, still chuckling.

"Yes. And besides all that, we were starting off on
a trip. But Mr. Stires said he was giving a party and
that he couldn't possibly attend it without any teeth."

"Vanity," Asey intoned piously. "Vanity. Nothin'
but vanity. Whyn't you mend the busted ones?"

"That's just what I suggested to him. 'Mr. Stires,'
I said, 'we can mend that broken set in a jiffy. In a
jiffy.' But he wouldn't hear anything of the sort."

"Why not?"

"He said that it might break again and that he'd
be in a more embarrassing position than he was then,
what with being so far away. I told him that we
couldn't possibly do it, so he said he was going to stay

right there until we did. Very determined, he was.
My wife and I were starting off for a few days at our
camp in Maine, and we—well, we didn't want to leave
him there, on our door-step, as you might say, so
finally we said we would. He made out that big check
and—and sort of waved it at us, and when my wife saw
it, she decided that we could delay our trip just as well
as not."

I began to have a fairly adequate picture of Mrs.
Joseph Jerome.

"So we got one of the local men to help us, and
Mr. Stires spent Tuesday night at our house while we
worked."

"I wonder," Asey said thoughtfully, "why there
wasn't any one in Lex'n'ton that saw the 'lectric an'
answered that broadcast."

"We live out of the town," the doctor explained,
"and there are two old ladies in the vicinity who still
use an electric. I suppose that Mr. Stires's didn't
cause as much attention as it might have. Anyway,
we finished the plate as quickly as we could—the other
dentist had a lot of material we could use—and then
we left Wednesday morning for Maine, and Mr. Stires
came on his way down here."

"An' in all that time," Asey said, "Stires didn't make
no 'tempt to get in touch with his house-party?"

"I suggested that he call, that is, my wife suggested
it, but he wouldn't. He said he wasn't going to let

them know just why he'd been delayed, and that his teeth were his own affair and none of their business. He said that they'd think that his car had broken down, and that they could go right on thinking that way."

"Why didn't you tell us before?" I asked.

"We left for Maine Wednesday morning, and we didn't hear about Mr. Stires's death until last night. Our radio was out of order and we hadn't bothered with papers. It was my wife's brother that finally called up and told us about the broadcast, and I was going to phone you right away, but my wife said that in view of that check for all that money, I'd better come down and explain. She seemed to think," he added regretfully, "that the money would seem suspicious and that it was all my fault that we took it."

"I wonder why Stires was so touchy about those teeth," Asey said. "I mean, there was only his friends here, an' I shouldn't think that they'd mind if he had teeth or not."

"That's what I told him. But he said that he had a niece here, and that there'd be a lady to chaperon her, and he didn't want to meet them without any teeth. He was very sensitive about his teeth. He'd joke with my wife and me about them, but once in a while I guess his friends made comments and he didn't like it. Once in a while he's said that he couldn't see why they wouldn't let him alone, because they were nothing—well, nothing to brag about themselves. That was his idea."

Asey laughed. "Was he all right when he was with you? Cheerful an' all?"

"Oh, yes, indeed. He seemed eager to see his new house. He told my wife all about it and she said that a woman couldn't have taken more interest in a house than he did. Seems too bad that after all his planning, he couldn't ever live to enjoy it. My wife and I felt very badly. She always felt sorry for Mr. Stires, though I couldn't ever see why. He had all the money he needed to do anything he wanted with. But she said he was wistful."

I mentally wondered how Mrs. Jerome catalogued her own husband. Sat upon, I thought, would have been a good description of him.

"Then he spent Tuesday with you, all well enough an' happy 'cept for the teeth. I see. I'm much 'bliged, Doctor, for your comin' all the way down here."

"It—er—it wasn't bad," Doctor Jerome said quickly, "I mean, Christina planned it all out. I took the train to Boston last night, then I started from there in my cousin's car early this morning. She—Christina—rather expects me back to-night. Do you think you'll want me any more?"

Asey shook his head. "I guess you can start right along. If you're tired of drivin', Doc, I'll send one of my men up's far's Barnstable with you."

But the doctor demurred. "I can manage very well."

And after knocking over two ash-trays and bumping into the table, he finally left.

"Well," Asey said, after he had escorted the doctor to the door, "we know where Stires was, I s'pose, but it don't seem to be an awful lot of help. I was sort of hopin' that we'd find out somethin' excitin', but this kind of killed it."

"See here, Asey," I said, "what about that other check to cash? Why didn't you ask Doctor Jerome about that? Don't you think he might have had something to do with it? Mightn't he have been keeping that back?"

"You think he was holdin' out on us?" He smiled. "Nope, I don't think he was. No, sireebob. Christina'd never let him get himself involved in anything bad 'n' wrong. If he'd had anything to do with the other check, he'd of told us."

He picked up the scrap-book and fiddled through its pages.

"Some dinners, the ones these fellers give," he said. "Hey—look." He showed me a post-card picture labeled "Revere Beach—1900," in which Stires, Kent, Blake, Hobart and Denny were grouped stiffly around a mammoth beer mug. Denny held a teddy bear, and Stires had a large balloon tied in his coat lapel. "The old sports," he commented. "Runnin' around the Beach."

The card was not pasted into the book, but thrust into slits on the page. I took it out and held it up to the light. But before I could examine it, Asey took it from me.

"The back," he said suddenly. "They've written their names on the back. Look. Every last one of 'em but Kent uses that funny-shaped *e* like was on that letter. Hobart uses it in his middle name. Huh. Didn't I see one of them books around that you write your name in?"

"Guest-books? Yes. There's one on the table in the hall."

He got it and brought it back. "Blake still uses it," he said after he'd flipped through the pages. "An' so does Denny James."

"But, Asey, what does it all amount to?"

"Miss Prue, you're a card player, ain't you?"

"Yes."

"Well, Bill Porter made me learn bridge a long while ago b'cause lots of times he'd have two fellers down an' they'd need another hand. Don't care much for the game,—you c'n give me good honest poker any day,—but they's one thing. You know how sometimes you'll have three-four trumps left, an' one lone little card, like a jack, that some one's got the queen of?"

"Yes," I said, not understanding in the least what he was driving at.

"An' you know how you'll lead out them trumps,

pretendin' you got nothin' but 'em, all the time hopin' like fury that folks'll throw away that queen?"

I nodded.

"An'," Asey continued, "if you do it determined enough, it's dollars to doughnuts that they will throw the queen away an' hold on to something that don't matter."

"Yes, yes," I said impatiently, "I know what you mean, but I don't see what it's got to do with all this."

"The feller behind this is a planner. We know that. Well, it's sort of been flashin' through my mind that the little jack in his hand is still there. They's always a weak spot somewheres, even if folks plan dif'rent. Now, that little weak spot in this case is the motive. You don't c'mit any sort of crime that you don't have some reason for c'mittin' it. You don't rob a bank less'n you expect to get money; you don't burn a house down less'n you want to destroy it. With murder it's kind of a harder prop'sition, on account of the reason bein' harder to find out. But it's still there."

"That's all very true," I argued, "but he might not have any reason. He might be a maniac. It might never come to light just what his motive was, anyway. And on the other hand, there might be a score of people with good motives for killing some one, and they might not be connected with it at all."

"Yup. I grant you all that. But this feller ain't no maniac. They kill whoever's closest to hand. This

feller killed a partic'lar person an' went to a whole lot
of trouble doin' it. Now, if you work hard, you can
say that Hobart an' Denny an' Miss Fible got motives
in this. Only you got to do a lot of philos'phizin'.
You can say maybe that the girl's a tool of this woman
friend of Allerton's, or maybe the Allerton girl. But
it's all come out. What I'm gettin' at is that this feller's took all the tricks up till now. But he's been discardin' trumps for us to play on. An' that little Greek
e, that was sort of a trey. He's gettin' low. An' he's
got that little jack sittin' in his hand, an' he ain't awful
sure that we got rid of the topper."

"I'm way behind," I said.

"Well, point is that he's got a motive. He's been
leadin' us on, hopin' that we'd get so excited followin'
up all the false clues he stuck around, that by the time
we get to his jack, that is to say, his motive, we won't
give it a thought. Just like at bridge sometimes you
don't think you been led astray. You don't realize
you been doin' what the other feller wanted you to.
You think the reason he got the last trick on his ole
jack is that he was clever. But I'm goin' to hold on
to my queen now, an', by gorry, he ain't goin' to get
it away from me."

He tightened up his belt buckle, gave a hitch to his
trousers and howled for William.

"Want the girl," he said, and when she came, he
wasted no time in preambles.

"Tuesday mornin'," he said, "you was at the house in Boston with Stires. Tom was there. Kent an' Hobart come to call. That right?"

She nodded.

"Did you hear what they said? Did you see 'em? What'd they talk about?"

"I saw them, and Mr. Stires introduced me to them. I went up-stairs then to get cleaned up. I'd come over on the midnight. I don't know what they talked about. Mr. Kent wasn't there long. I heard him and Mr. Stires laughing—I think that they were wondering who to get as a chaperon for me. Mr. Stires had been upset, but Mr. Kent tried to make him see the funny side of it, I think."

"An' Hobart?"

"I looked out of the window in time to see him leave. He kicked an alley cat as he went down the steps," she added reminiscently, "and he slammed the door of his cab so hard that I thought the door would break."

"Okay. Tell William to send Tom in, will you?"

Tom appeared, fastening the top button of his tunic.

"What'd Kent say to Stires Tuesday mornin'?"

Tom looked blank.

"You got Stires's breakfast, didn't you? Didn't you see Kent or Hobart? Didn't you hear what they talked about?"

"Why, er, yes. Yes. Mr. Kent and Mr. Stires

talked about the girl and who they could get as a chaperon. Mr. Kent said it was a pity that Mr. Stires hadn't married or that he didn't have any available lady friends, an' Mr. Stires quoted the Bible. Something about the mote an' the beam."

Asey grinned. "What about Hobart?"

"Oh, I didn't hear much what he said. Just talked about business, I guess. But Mr. Hobart was sort of excited when I let him out."

"That all you remember? Yes? That'll do. Send Kent in here."

"Mr. Kent?"

"Kent," Asey repeated firmly. "Send him here."

I was too bewildered to know what was going on.

John strolled in. "What can I do for you, Asey?"

"What was that piece of the Bible Stires quoted to you Tuesday mornin'?"

"What! Bible? Tuesday? Good heaven, Asey, I'm sure I don't know. We were talking about chaperons—I told him he should have married or had some woman friend who could help, but he didn't quote the Bible. Really. Bert wasn't the sort to make Biblical quotations."

"Sure?"

"Wait. Let me think. Oh, he said something about never quite achieving the golden mean—yes. That's it. But that's not the Bible, Asey. That's Horace. That was it. He admitted that he'd never reached the

golden mean as far as women were concerned. That
was it."

Asey nodded briefly. "Okay. Thanks."

"What," I asked piteously, "what is this all about?"

" 'Cordin' to Hoyle," he announced with a grin.
"When in doubt, take the trick."

"Where are you going?"

"Got to see Phrone. S'pose you stay with Miss Fible
while she does things for me."

I met Stephen Crump in the hallway. "Going to see
Rena? May I come along?"

"Do," I told him. "We've been having scenes with
her and I'd be delighted to have you with me. Will you
do just one thing, Steve? Will you please talk about
anything but this murder?"

He laughed. "Fed up?"

"No. Confused."

Up in the yellow room he sat down and proceeded
to tell funny stories about cases he had had. At the
end of five minutes I felt better; at the end of fifteen,
I was nearly normal. Stephen can be very amusing
when he chooses.

But Rowena did not seem to enjoy our presence.
And it got rather annoying to be the only one to laugh
at Stephen's sallies.

I was about to suggest that we go when a tremendous
din arose somewhere down-stairs.

Stephen stopped in the middle of a story, jumped

to the doorway and I followed him as fast as I could.

Just as we stepped into the hall, we saw John reach the top of the stairs and dive into his room.

But that was not all.

At the foot of the stairs, Hobart ranted and raged. His head and shoulders were dripping wet. Little rivulets of water trickled down his face, and he literally spluttered as he talked.

In front of him stood Phrone, stiff and defiant. Beside her was a pail of water.

And against the wall leaned Denny and Asey and the rest, fairly shrieking with laughter.

CHAPTER NINETEEN

ASEY TAKES A TRIP

"WHAT in the world," I demanded, "is all this muddle?"

Denny pointed to Hobart, tried to speak and could not get the words out.

"It was Phrone," June bubbled. "She was going up-stairs with a pail of water. She slipped or something and the water went over Cary."

I wondered just why Phrone had been taking a pail of water up-stairs, but Hobart's anger stopped me from asking.

"Slipped? She did not slip. That woman picked up that water, deliberately picked it up and threw it at me, I tell you." He brushed his sleeve across his dripping face. "She picked up that pail and hurled that water at me, and I want an explanation. I will not have every creature in this place throwing things at me. I won't stand for it. I tell you, Mayo, this has got to stop."

"I say I slipped," Phrone announced firmly, "and I mean that I slipped. I'm sorry if you got wet, Mr. Hobart"—I caught the little flicker in her eyes and knew that she wasn't sorry one bit—"but if you'd take my advice, you'll go git some dry clothes on an' forget about it."

"That's right," Asey agreed. "You go git some dry clothes on, Mr. Hobart. You ain't no wetter than Mr. Kent was, an' he didn't stand there like a nincompoop talkin' about it. He went up-stairs an' got himself dry things."

"Did John get wet too?" I asked June.

He nodded. "He and Cary were coming out of the living-room and I guess that they scared Phrone as she was going up, or something. Anyway, she slipped and the bucket of water went over on 'em. It must have held ten gallons, I guess."

"Twenty," John said, as he descended the stairs. Either his toupee had escaped a soaking, or else he had put on a dry wig, for I noticed that his hair was perfectly dry. A light pull-over sweater replaced his tweed coat. "At least twenty. Why didn't you side-step, Cary? I howled at you as I ducked."

"I didn't hear you," Hobart grumbled. "You might have yanked me out of the way."

"I tried to, but you wouldn't be yanked. Hustle off, Cary."

And with very bad grace, Cary left.

I looked inquiringly at Asey. He glanced at Hobart's retreating figure, surveyed John a moment, then turned to me and grinned.

Phrone picked up her empty pail and started off to the kitchen.

"I'm goin' up again in about five minutes," she threw

out over her shoulder as she left, "an' you'd better all of you look out."

"We will," Denny said. "Lord, I'd pay her to do it again. I really would. I wouldn't have missed the sight of that man gasping like a fish for worlds."

Asey winked at me, jerked his head toward the library, and Stephen and I followed him into the room.

"Why?" Crump asked simply.

Asey stuck his thumbs in his belt. "Why what, Mr. Crump?"

"Why did you have Phrone throw water over Hobart? What did you expect to gain by it?"

"Don't expect," Asey informed him cheerfully. "Am sure. Am dum sure. Yessir."

There was a knock on the door and one of his men came in, bearing a large English kitbag.

"Got everything all right?" Asey asked.

"Yes, sir. Everything. I put in both pairs of cuff-links and I couldn't find only one blue shirt, so I put in one white an' one blue."

"Got the key?"

He passed over a key.

"An' will you see that the Monster gets filled with gas an' oil an' has her tires pumped?"

"One of them chauffeurs looked it over yesterday, but I'll give it the once-over."

"Thank you kindly. I'll want it in about half an hour."

"What are you going to do?" Crump and I asked the question in perfect unison.

He picked up the bag.

"Goin' to make sure I git the last trick, Miss Prue. I'm goin' huntin', but I can't wear my duck-huntin' clothes. These is the ones Bill made me git last fall, an' I just had 'em brought over. I hate like fury to have to git dressed up, but it 'pears like I'll have to."

"Where are you going?"

"Orleans, Brewster, Dennis, Ya'mouth——"

"You're going to Boston!"

"Uh-huh. Shouldn't wonder."

"You're going to leave us here alone? Why are you going to Boston?"

"You ain't exactly alone, Miss Prue. I'm leavin' plenty of men around, an' the doc'll stay up here. No need to worry none. I'll be back t'-morrow. Right now I got to hurry."

And before we could ask him another thing, he had picked up his bag and left.

"Stephen, what's he after? And what's he getting what he calls dressed up for?"

"I don't know, Prue. But if he looks half as well as he did the last time I saw him in town, he'll be doing well. Bill sent him to Forbes and Vail. Didn't you see him at the wedding?"

"No, I didn't see any one. Bill lost the steamer tickets and Betsey mislaid her traveling clothes."

He laughed. "The reason why you didn't see Asey was because he personally ironed out the ticket situation. In a cutaway, too."

"Cutaway or no cutaway," I said, "I wish he'd tell us what he's after. Has he told you what this is all about?"

"Not a word. But he won't get out of this house," Stephen asserted, "until he *has* told us."

In less than half an hour, Asey appeared. He was clad in a beautifully fitting blue suit, a blue shirt, and a tie that even Denny James would have been proud to own. His black oxfords were polished to just the proper degree, and as he caught my glance at them, he chuckled.

"Silk stockin's, too. I'm c'mplete, all but the way I talk, an' I mimicked Jimmy Porter's accent so much that I can do it pretty well. I mean to say," he clipped his words, "I'm able to speak as I should." He laughed. "That's the whole dum trouble about dressin' up. You got to be so careful about grammar an' all, an' it's an awful sort of strain. Mr. Crump, I want some letters. The to-whom-it-may-concern kind. Sayin' that I'm A. A. Mayo an' a worthy soul. An' that I want things done in a hurry an' a good cause."

"Certainly." Crump sat down at the desk and pulled out his fountain-pen. "I'll give you a letter to Steve, too."

"What's the A. A.?" I asked.

"Asa Alden," he confessed. "I don't s'pose I ever used it all more'n three times in my life. But it kind of goes more with these clothes than just Asey. Thank you very kindly, Mr. Crump. I'll be seein' you to-morrow. Keep your weather eye peeled, an' remember the *Maine*. An'," he grinned at me, "you can have these to play with."

"These" consisted of the letter Phrone had brought over, the false teeth he had taken from Stires's pocket, and finally, the scrap-book.

"Asey Mayo," I began disgustedly.

"Yup. I'm a mean sort. But you knew it—puzzle it out, you two. Keep it to yourself, an' don't burn no candles."

"Asey," Crump exploded, "tell us more. You can't go off like this."

"Okay. Miss Prue, whyn't you tell me Kent was bald?"

"Why didn't I tell you? What's it got to do with all of this? Asey, what did you throw water over Hobart for?"

"What do all these—these exhibits mean?" Crump demanded. "Do you mean to tell me you know who did this,—from these things?"

"I'm discardin' everything but my queen," he announced. "It may be a wrong guess, an' Lord knows it's crazy, but there you are. Yup, I think I'm pretty sure, but I'll be surer b'fore I tell you. I got everything but a leetle sounder basis'n what I need. G'-by."

Crump and I stood at the window and watched him get into the Monster; he waved the neat felt hat which had replaced the rakish Stetson, sounded the musical horn and the Monster roared off.

We went back to the table and surveyed the "exhibits."

"He," Crump said, "is a better man than I am. I admit it. What do you think?"

"I agree," I told him, "but if he can find a murderer out of that motley mess, so can we. Steve, I challenge you."

Without a word he went over to the desk, took two small blocks of paper, an assortment of blotters and pens and pencils, and laid them on the table.

"I write better than I think," he said. "And we'll have to write this mess out. Go ahead, Prue."

And we set to work.

We took time out for dinner, and went back again to our game.

It was evening before Stephen threw down his pencil.

"This," he said, "is worse than making out an income tax. You always feel that there's no reason why you should understand an income tax blank, anyway, but it seems that we should be able to get this. Are you done?"

"Done?" I echoed disgustedly. "Done? I was done before I started. I've been spending the last few hours trying to find an impregnable defense for Betsey's method of playing tit-tat-toe."

He laughed and passed me over his paper.

"This," he said, "is the revised version. It's my final idea."

I looked at the first name. "Steve! You think it's Rowena?"

"Don't see how it could be any one else, Prue. Listen: her reason for coming down to the Cape is absurd, and you know it. It seems to me that she must definitely have known about Bert's party and made up her mind to come. You were a good foil, so she got hold of you. You admit that she was the one who actually made the bargain of coming over here. And her motive was to get revenge for things that Stires had said about her. You say she apologized, but that was undoubtedly a bluff. She had every chance of getting those candles. She has one, in fact, now. That is, she did have until Asey took it away. Remember, Prue, it's the only actual poisoned candle that's been found in its entirety. Now, she had every chance of shutting you up in the closet. It's not been actually settled that she wasn't the one who delayed the hunt for you. Then, there are those emeralds. She likes the stones; it's possible that she may have seen more of Bert than any one realizes, possible that she knew Bert was going to give them to her, particularly if, as you seem to think, Bert was sweet on her long ago.

Look at her present state; she's only bluffing. I'm sure of it. And she's tried desperately hard to put the blame on Hobart——"

"And Denny——"

"Yes."

"Maybe that accounts for the teeth," I said, "but what about the letter and the scrap-book?"

"That Greek *e*. Underneath that picture post-card is a dance program. When Bert was in college and used to go to an occasional dance. She's written her name on it. She uses a Greek *e*."

"But what's that all got to do with the pail of water, and all that?"

Crump shrugged. "That may have been an accident after all. I don't know. What d'you think of that?"

"You've made a case," I admitted. "But——"

"But she's a friend of yours? Remember Emma, Prue. She was a friend of yours, and she murdered a man."

"I know it."

"Well, who's your number one?"

"Hobart. He was mad when he left Stires Tuesday morning. He fussed when Bert didn't come. He saw him last Wednesday night. He deliberately gave Denny those pills. Then there's that business of the ink-bottle top. And Asey doused him for some reason. He makes Greek *e*'s—or used to, once. He got the candles, went in after Denny, and took 'em, Tuesday at Mary's.

He could have substituted the marked ones. He's behaved like a fool—getting mad and losing his temper, but there's been something theatrical about it. He's planned to act that way. He had a perfectly good motive, when you come right down to it. He could have locked us up—he could have planted the arsenic, and that candle on Rowena."

"What about the teeth?"

"Can't fit them in," I said. "I simply can't."

"What about Denny?" Crump said thoughtfully.

"He's not guilty," I said with some intensity. "Rowena's tried to implicate him—that delay and the ink-bottle top——"

"I haven't heard about that."

I told him the story. "And a handkerchief, too, of his. She says she found it the day the arsenic was planted and that she didn't show Asey on account of me!"

"Boomerang. It all goes back to Rowena, Prue."

"There's that *e*," I said, "but I don't see how Denny's connected with the teeth. He hasn't any real motive except Rowena thought that those college fights between him and Bert constituted one. I'm sure that he's just been—been——"

"A victim of circumstance. Well, I rather agree. What about John?"

"That fight," I said, "that's sort of against him, though I'm sure I can't reason out why. And I'm sure I don't know what his false hair's got to do with this, if it *has* anything to do with it at all. He gave a different reason for starting the fight than June did. And he was mentioned in that codicil, too."

"So was June," Crump added.

"Really, Steve," I said, "I'm convinced that it must be June. He's got absolutely nothing against him."

Crump laughed. "I'm just as convinced, really, that it's William and his wife. After all, we're not sure that that letter's not genuine."

"And Rowena said she thought it was Mrs. Boles that planted the candle."

"And Blake—we haven't touched on Blake. There's all that candle business."

"And then there's Kelley. And Tom."

"And the girl. And the cook." Stephen got up and made a little ball of all his papers and tossed them into the fire. "There. I'm darned if I know or see any one's who connected with the teeth and that scrapbook—I've looked it all through, even though you say that Asey didn't look at anything but that picture—and the letter. I don't see what Asey had Phrone hurl water around for. I'm sure I don't understand about that fight, or what he's after."

Slowly I tore up my own papers and tossed them into the waste-paper basket. "We may be dullards," I said, "but it's beyond my feeble brain."

The doctor came in, looked at us and smiled.

"Asey bet me that I'd find you here working over this," he said. "He dropped in just before he left. Got any warmer?"

I shook my head. "Did he tell you? His clues, I mean?"

"Yes. I'm pretty well convinced, Miss Prue, that you and I did it. Or Phrone and Lyddy Howes. Have you seen the finished figure of Ginger and the black kitten, by the way? You ought to look at it. I've just been down in the game-room, and Miss Fible's started to work on that Peke of the girl's, now."

"I'm going to bed," I said, and quite unconsciously I went, not to the yellow room, but to the one I'd used the night before. Not that I agreed with Steve about Rowena, but somehow, well, I just didn't want to be with her.

I've never really figured out how we worried along on Monday. Noon came and went and still Asey did not arrive. We went through some pretense of eating lunch, but it was a very weak pretense. Crump had put the teeth and the letter away in his pocket, and he told me that they were burning him like so many hot coals.

At one o'clock a car drove up before the house, but it was only reporters who had somehow got by the motorcycle cop. A roadster was sighted at three, but it was only some one who had lost his way. He was promptly sent back.

Denny finally decided that something had to be done.

"We might name the kitten," I said in desperation.

"Call it Penrod," Denny said. "I had a nice Scottie once named Penrod. He got pois——" he stopped. "Maybe Penrod's not such a fine idea."

And we argued and made labored witticisms over the kitten's name until tea-time.

At last we drew lots, and it was found that "Toxin" had won. It was the doctor's choice, and he was very pleased.

"Call him 'Tox' for short and 'Sin' when he's bad. I think it's neat."

"What time is it?" I whispered to Stephen.

"Four fifty-eight," he replied instantly without looking at his watch. "He ought to be here."

And he had no sooner got the words out of his mouth than the arrogant notes of the Monster's horn floated out.

Asey walked in, cheerful and grinning. The circles under his eyes were deeper than they had been the day previous, otherwise he seemed as nonchalant and as amiable as ever.

"Tea?" I asked brightly.

"Nope," he said with a twinkle, "glass of milk, if William'll bring it. Been all right?"

"Fine," Denny said without enthusiasm. "Good trip?"

"Real good. Made the trip down in somethin' under

three hours, not countin' the half-hour I stopped off to see Burnett at Barnstable."

William brought in a glass of milk and placed it on the little table by the side of Asey's chair just as Ginger, for reasons best known to himself, jumped at the Peke.

After much running hither and yon, the Peke was removed, quite intact save for a scratched nose. We resumed our respective seats.

"Er—as you were saying, er—Asey," Crump prompted him diffidently.

"Uh-huh." Asey played with the black kitten. "Give this a name yet? Toxin, huh? Like anti-toxin or the sort of thing that rings an 'larm? Can I give it some of my milk?"

Blake was stirred at last from his calm. "Feed the whole animal kingdom, Asey, but get to the point!"

Deliberately, Asey poured some of the milk from his glass into a plate.

"Have a drink on me," he informed the kitten. "Well, some of you know it an' some of you don't. Maybe it's got noised 'round, as you might say, that Stires died from inhalin' pois'nous vapor from a candle that had Paris green in its wick. Mary Gross that made the candles, she died the same way."

He stopped and reached for his milk, then changed his mind and bit into a sandwich. As he took a bite, his eyes strayed down to the kitten. Quickly, almost too quickly, he looked up again.

Curiously, I looked down. Ginger had slapped the kitten with his paw, pushed him away from the plate. Now he stood before it, his back arched, his yellow tail swelled double its size. He was hissing noiselessly with all his might and main at the plate of milk.

I looked at Asey and started to speak, but I caught the quick shake of his head. Leaning over, I picked up both cats and put them together on my lap.

"What with one thing 'n' another," Asey continued calmly, "I had a couple of funny ideas, an' they sort of turned out to be right."

He picked up the glass of milk, fingered it, turned it around and around in his hand. I wondered why he didn't drink it, and I wondered, too, what had got into Ginger.

"I was right," Asey repeated.

He set down the glass and got up from his chair. I watched him as he walked over to the windows and looked out. Every eye in the room was following him, but if he intended his announcement to cause any alarm, he was disappointed. No one, not even Rowena, looked particularly frightened or guilty.

Asey turned around.

"I think," he said, "that we'll end this here an' now. That milk was the endin'. This p'tic'lar camel's had 'nough. I don't know what's in the milk, but cats is awful canny. If they won't eat somethin', it ain't fit to be et. An' if they hiss at it, it's bad. I'm right glad that cat was around. Now, June——"

I gasped.

"June," Asey continued, "you just call in my strikers, will you?"

"Stop, June. You're wrong, Asey. It's just beginning."

I thought at first, as did Stephen, that this was all part of some prearranged plan. Then we saw the nasty-looking gun that Kent was pointing at Asey.

CHAPTER TWENTY

THE LAST TRICK

NONE of us spoke. We couldn't. June seemed frozen on his way to the door.

"What," Asey lifted up the flaps of his vest and hooked his thumbs casually in the straps of his suspenders, "what are you aimin' to begin?"

"You fool! Did you think that I'd planned all this—to have you smash it at the last minute? Do you think you've got me? My dear little Asey Mayo, you'd far better have drunk your glass of milk and let it go at that! This isn't going to be the end. You've not got me! If any one of you moves, I'll put an end to him. That goes for you, Prue, and Rena. Try to help your precious hayseed and you'll get it as soon as the men."

Asey stood with his back to the windows, facing the rest of us. Kent was directly in front of him, the rest of us behind John and to Asey's right.

"What," the latter asked again, "are you aimin' to do? You can't do much, you know. My fellers are outside."

John laughed. It was not a pleasant laugh to hear.

"Third time, Asey. I set the candle for you and you ducked out of that. Why? Because you and Prue together were more than I'd bargained for. You

ducked out of that. The cat saved you from the milk.
But there won't be any more slipping out of trouble
for you. Not with this gun. You call your men and
I'll get you—and some of the rest, too, before any
one gets in."

"You admit all this?" Asey's voice was calm and
composed.

"Of course I admit it."

Asey sighed contentedly. "I'm glad you told me.
I was goin' to have a stiff job provin' it to a jury.
You won't be able to git us all b'fore my men get here,
an' some of the s'vivors'll be witnesses. Y'know," he
added speculatively, "if I'd of been you I'd of sat tight
an' sawed wood. You'd maybe of lied your way out."

John's face was black with rage. I expected him to
shoot Asey down, but he was too infuriated to act. He
had to talk.

"Maybe." He started to back to the door. "Move
over there, June. Your car is outside, Asey. So is
mine. I've been having Tom put it in shape. Either
will do me. And there's nothing left that will catch
me. I've attended to that. I've cut the telephone
wires. I'll take one of those cars and fix the other
and be out of the country before you know what's
happened. Only you won't be here to know. And I
shouldn't count on your men. When I helped William
take that dog out, I told him you wanted all your men
sent over to Rowena's. They've all gone."

Asey nodded. "You think of everything. I handed it to you once, an' I hand it to you again. But now you're so certain to git off, you do me one last favor, an' tell me why you killed Stires. If I got to go to m'grave, I might's well have one question answered."

"You know why," John said. "You found out about the money. You had it written on your face when you came into the room. I never intended to pay him back. I'd been planning to get rid of him—and besides, I'd got sick of his damned gibes about my hair."

"An'," Asey interrupted tantalizingly, "you was wrong about them gibes. He never thought he was teasin' you. He didn't care a rap about your hair. He just did it to stop your talk about his teeth. You know, false hair an' false teeth *is* funny——"

I saw John's fingers curve around the trigger of his gun. I looked at Asey, still grinning. His right hand slid out from under his vest and in it was a long six-shooter. He fired twice across his hip. John's gun tumbled out of his hand before he could shoot, and his hand fell limply to his side. I watched, half fascinated, as a spot appeared on the gray of his sleeve.

Asey moved forward as Denny and June and the doctor jumped from their seats to grab John.

"It was an awful nice plan," Asey said. "Awful nice, but it didn't work. Take him out, Doc. You'd better see if he's got 'ny more guns on him an' I know he's got some sort of poison. He put it in my milk while we was separatin' the cat an' the dog. Take this whistle, an' blow for my men, please."

"Wait." John spoke as he was leaving. "Asey, do you always carry a gun? I didn't see that you had one, and I looked. If I'd known that you had a gun I'd have let you have it."

"Ain't packed a gun," Asey said reminiscently, "since I was in China durin' the Boxer kick-up. Not till to-day. This is the same gun, a forty-five single-action Colt. You know, even a big gun stuck in the belt of your pants an' held up by a s'spender-strap don't 'tract any attention. It's the only way a gun don't show. You had yours in your hip pocket an' I spotted it right off. Remember this trick," he added with irony, "in case you ever get a chance. You was on my left, an' you couldn't see what I was doin'. I just stuck my thumb in my belt an' eased it out."

John looked at him and managed a grim smile.

"Cat an' a Cape Codder," Asey observed, "is a hard comb'nation to beat. Walker, you look after his arm. That's the trouble with civ'lization. Plug a man, an' then you have to sew him up."

The door closed behind them.

"Now," Stephen said, "explain. What about the teeth and the scrap-book and the letter?"

"And how," Hobart asked in relieved tones, "about dousing me?"

"What money?" Rowena demanded.

"What about the fight?" I asked. "And what's his hair got to do with this?"

Asey smiled. "You knew that Kent wore a wig, Miss Prue."

"A wig? But what of it?"

"Well, I was sort of chucklin' to myself about them false teeth, then I thought of the false hair. Now, I used to cook on a boat an' the cap'n of it had false teeth an' the mate had false hair. The two of 'em first of all just kidded each other about it. Then they got so every time one or the other of 'em mentioned teeth or hair, they had a reg'lar knock-down-drag-out fight. Y'see, the first couple of times you joke about a thing like that, it's funny. Then it's an insult. Then it's a fightin' matter."

"But I never knew he had false hair," Denny said blankly.

"Well, I didn't either. That is, I sort of s'spected it, but I wasn't real sure. They ain't many wigs about that's as natural-lookin' as Kent's an' that looks so real. But after that fight he had with June, when his hair was so dum dry an' June's was all wet an' they'd both taken a dousin', I begun t'wonder, kind of in earnest like. That's why I had Phrone throw water over him, so's I'd be sure. Kent ducked an' beat it, but not before I knew. Then when he come down with his new wig all dry an' said casual-like that Hobart got the worst of it, I was pos'tive. False hair, when it's

wet, is false hair pure 'n' simple. June, 'member when
you told me about that fight, you said you'd spoke
about Mr. Hobart's baldish spot? An' he went for
you? Y'see, he thought you'd found out about him,
an' was twittin' him, an' he got mad. N'en there was
what Tom told me. He said Kent an' Stires had been
talkin' an' Stires said something about a mote an' a
beam. It was while they were talkin' about gettin' a
chaperon. What mote an' what beam? I asks myself. Somehow it sort of grew into the teeth an' the
hair. He evaded the question real graceful, an' said
they was talkin' about the golden mean, but he'd already changed around what June had said. So I figgered he'd done it again.

"Y'see, Stires knew about Kent's hair. Kent knew
about Stires's teeth. Stires was tired enough of bein'
kidded so's he spent Tuesday night at his dentist's
gettin' new teeth to come here with. Kent was sens'-
tive 'nough to lay into June. Together they must of
had some swell times. But Stires didn't talk about
the hair, prob'ly, 'cept in self-defense when Kent
started in on the teeth. See what I mean?"

"Still," Stephen began, "that wasn't——"

"Still that wasn't reason enough for one feller to
kill another. Yup, Mr. Crump. It wasn't. Now that
will of Stires was awful simple. It didn't say anything about cancellin' loans, not even private loans.
Now I'd found two checks in Stires's check-book that'd

been used. Both was to cash. One of 'em was to cash
for five hundred, an' we found out that that went to
Stires's dentist. The other was for two thousand. That
kind of roused my cur'osity, p'ticularly as Kent asked
us right off the bat if we'd found anything in Stires's
clothes or things that might be a clue."

"I remember," I said. "I told him we'd found two
checks to cash, too."

"Yup. An' he blinked. An' there was that other
check. An' then, you told me he had something to do
with the *Clarion*. I read that paper, an' I noticed that
it begun to get pretty slimmish last summer, an' then
it sort of picked up. So first thing when I got to Boston, I hunted up a friend of mine that works on the
paper; an' he told me all about how it had got into a
hole an' then it had begun to pick up. In other words,
Kent'd been out of money, an' then he had begun to
git it."

"But John had plenty of money," Blake began.

"You sort of took it for granted, Mr. Blake. Anyways, I got hold of your son an' he an' I mesm'rized
people at Stires's bank after gettin' hold of Burnett
an' havin' him pull wires. We found that from last
July on, Stires'd been makin' out big checks to cash
an' cashin' 'em himself. 'Course, they might have been
for his new house, but we found where he'd paid for
them bills by check. Stires cashed them checks for
cash all himself, an' then the money sort of melted into

thin air. Then we pried around a little more an' found out that every time Stires drew out a big check to cash, Kent's account got bigger by the same amount. We even tallied some of the numbers on big bills. An' then the last bit was findin' that two thousand dollars had gone into Kent's 'count Tuesday mornin'. That sort of clinched the matter, b'cause Stires had cashed his own check for two thousand an' d'posited it to Kent's 'count. I s'pose that Kent's been borrowin' all along, never intendin' to pay Stires back. He said as much. Mebbe Stires begun to ask for it an' along last fall, Kent decided to get rid of Stires, 'cause that's when he wrote that letter to Mary about the candles, usin' a rubber stamp with William's name."

"How do you know he wrote it?"

"Well, it sounded like him, for one thing. N'en remember the picture in that scrap-book? Well, all the names on it had those funny *e*'s, all 'cept Kent. An' in the guest-book, Mr. James an' Mr. Blake still used 'em. All but Kent. Now, you think this thing over an' you'll see that all the way through, like plantin' that arsenic, Kent never meant for any one, that is, any one in p'ticular, to be s'spected. He put in that *e* on purpose so's to make it stick out like a sore thumb if any one ever found the letter. He didn't even want William to be s'spected, see? But that was sort of spreadin' it too thin. If he hadn't done that, if he'd used just a reg'lar *e*, we'd just of said it was a plant, that letter, and that

it'd fit any one. As 'twas, it fitted any one but Kent.
He cut it a little mite too fine."

"Why," I demanded, "did he want to do away with
me as well as you?"

"Both of us knew about them checks to cash, an' you
knew he was bald, even though it didn't 'cur to you that
it had anything to do with the affair."

"How did Mary get those candles? Did he intend to
kill her?" Rowena asked.

"Nope. That's somethin' I still don't und'stand. I
sort of think he only had six sent to him. Y'see, he
prob'ly read about them candles in a book or heard
about 'em. You can't very well tell just how ac'rate
things like poisoned candles is going to be. They ain't
like a knife or a gun or a rope. I sort of figger that he
left six with her, so's if anything went wrong, she'd be
the one that had 'em, an' so, I s'pose he'd have more if
he needed 'em. But Mary ran out of ker'sene oil. An'
she prob'ly took out Kent's candles by mistake, instead
of her own. That's about how I figger it."

"But why didn't Mary ever tell?"

"Mary didn't git no chance to tell. Even if she'd
heard Stires was killed, it wouldn't mean anything to
her. She didn't know what was in them wicks. She
may of known who William Boles was, but prob'ly in
some letter that we'll never see, he told her that it was
somethin' secret an' not to talk about 'em. Must of,
or she'd of said more to Lyddy Howes about 'em. She

never knew what she was makin'. He picked a good maker, b'cause Mary was just off enough so's she'd never suspect anything anyhow."

"Asey," Stephen said, "you're a trump. I take my hat off to you. Piecing that together——"

"No piecin' attall. I was just holdin' on to my queen. Miss Prue'll explain about that. You see, Kent's last card was that he was bankin' on us runnin' astray, or gettin' too plumb confused, like over those *e's*, to see him. His money business was all set. Wasn't much chance of any one findin' out that. Not unless somethin' else started people off. Kent killed Stires for his money. Prob'ly on Tuesday mornin' he told Kent that that two thousand was the last an' he expected t'be paid back pronto that an' all the rest. But this crazy hair situation probably was the spark that set the whole dum thing off. He had planned an' planned the murder, but his silly old vanity had to git his dander up before he got in motion. Now, if we hadn't found out about the spark, as you might say, it'd of been all right. He knew Miss Prue an' Miss Rena an' Phrone knew about his hair an' that he was bald. He didn't know but what he was right in thinkin' that June knew—an' June might well of told me, for all he knew. He must have been sure when I had Phrone throw the water over him that I knew about the hair, an' what would I be wantin' to know about that for if I hadn't c'nected it with the teeth? He must of known Stires carried extra teeth with him, an' that I'd notice 'em an' ask about 'em. He must of known that I'd find out, one way or another, about how sens'tive Stires was about his teeth. The servants could of told me about how they got peeved after joking at each other's append'ges, as you might say. Even if he hadn't guessed I knew, he still wa'n't takin' any chances. He cut the wires an' got his car brought 'round anyway, but I'm bankin' that a guilty conscience made him s'spect I knew as much as anythin'. He was hopin' I'd go astray, an' I dum near did."

"Well, you're a trump all the same," Denny said. "We've been too stunned to be appreciative——"

"Yes—yes." Asey said hastily. "Yes—yes."

"Where are you going?"

"Goin'? Goin' home. Home an' git on the clothes I b'long in. I'm goin' to see that Benny Rogers ain't starved my hens to death, an' then I'm goin' to fry me a few flounders. I kind of hate to say it, but I've had ind'gestion ever since I begun to eat here. Rich food. Then," he added as the doctor came into the room, "then after supper I'm goin' up to the movies."

The doctor looked at me and grinned.

"It's Greeter Garbo," Asey continued calmly, "an' I ain't seen her this winter. 'By." And with a cheerful wave of his hand, he started off.

"Wait," Denny said. "Wait. Prue, twenty-seven years ago, I asked you to marry me. I——"

"Denny!" I protested, very much aware of the amused looks. "Please——"

"No, I won't wait. I've asked her to marry me every year for the last twenty-seven years. I've suggested it daily for the last four days. Now——"

"Denny," I said firmly, "please——"

"No. Now I'm asking you for the last time. You haven't got your niece to look after. You haven't got any one to look after. Will you, or won't you?"

"Oh, dear——"

"Yes or no."

"Yes," I said with a sigh. "Yes. I've always meant to, sooner or later, but really, Denny, you might as well have hired a hall."

Crump chuckled. "I hope," he said, "that Denny won't mislay the steamer tickets."

"It won't make the slightest bit of difference if I do," Denny returned serenely. "Asey's going to be my best man—you will, won't you?"

"In a Prince Albert?" Asey demanded. " 'Cause if——"

"No. You can wear your corduroys, if you want. Will you? Yes? Then I can lose the tickets with a clear conscience. Asey'll find 'em."

And, of course, Asey did.

THE END